CELIA'S JOURNEY

a novel
by

Heather Muzik

To learn more about Heather Muzik, visit heathermuzik.com

Celia's Journey
© 2010 by Heather Muzik
www.heathermuzik.com

Cover Design © 2012 by J.Muzik

ISBN-13: 978-1475209761
ISBN-10: 1475209762

To Thelma and Richard

Acknowledgments

A huge thank you to my fearless readers who took time out of their own lives to help me with mine: Deidre Pickering, Jeff Picken, Sam Kirchmann, and Mindy Waters. To Kristie Worrell, for her friendship and support from the initial release through the rerelease and beyond (http://needcoffeeplease.blogspot.com).To my parents, Margaret and J.S. Moyle, for their example (in everything) and for bending as needed. To Jack—once reluctant reader, turned staunch critic—I love you. To Jaxon and Dustin for showing me the way.

How long does it take to upend and then transform a family? To lose yourself and those you most cherish, then redefine yourself—your purpose—your unit?

In our case it was a journey of 39 weeks. A journey that began before we even knew it had begun. It started with a tiny spark of life and grew through death, grief, guilt, despair, frustration, fear, hope, healing and intense love; until we learned to laugh and rejoice and trust that life was worth living again....

~Lindsey Strane

-1 Week-

"You do realize that you are going to kill that man someday," he said with a smirk that crinkled the skin around his soft blue eyes into deeper folds than usual.

"Just so long as I get everything I need out of him first."

"That's cold, Lindsey."

"But, Ed, that's the plan. Then we can be free to run away together. I should hope that you know by now that I come in here for more than paint and spackle," she said, winking at him before turning her attention back to the display of paint samples. "Now, what do you think about these?" She fanned out the paint chips she had been plucking from the rack like a woman possessed.

"You know, I can hardly keep up with the stock of samples the way you hoard them. I think you really might need some professional help." He made a move to take the cards out of her hand.

"Oh, don't start sounding like my husband," she complained, closing the fan and pulling the stack out of reach. "He says the walls are going to fall down from the weight of so many layers of paint." She waved her hand dismissively at the thought.

"Could happen," Ed chortled. "I mean, if there is a risk of such a thing it would be at your house."

"Does my husband pay you to give me a hard time?"

"I put it on his tab… you know, the one that keeps you stocked full of all your home improvement needs."

"Figures. He just can't let a girl have unsupervised fun," she grumbled. "It's not like I do this all for my own enjoyment; it's for the good of the house—the whole family."

"But if—"

"Whose side are you on? If he cuts me off, then you'll be cut off too. Remember, I help keep you in business."

She stopped in at least once a week for tools, advice and opinions, and they both enjoyed the good-natured sparring that had developed between them over the years. Ed had never actually met her husband, but the bond between men and against their wives was strong enough that he often showed pity for Jerry's plight. Like any good dealer, though, he sold her the items she sought anyway.

Ed pretended to zip his lips. He was a spry seventy; average in height, but he appeared taller due to a straight posture that spoke of military experience. As far as she could tell, he had no deficiency in mind or body. His vision was clear. His movements were not feebled by the abuses of time or injury. He was the picture of health, and Lindsey hoped that she and Jerry would age as well through the years.

"So, are you going to help me choose a color for my dining room?" she asked, getting back to the business at hand.

"I'll help you narrow it down, if only to make sure my other customers still have a fighting chance to find their perfect paint." He pointed at her one-inch stack of chips. "But I won't let you *buy* any paint today."

"Now what kind of salesman are you?" she pouted.

"I am just trying to make sure harmony reigns in your house. You'll be throwing money away if you buy the wrong paint today because you didn't bother to take the samples home and look at them in the right light—"

"Blah, blah, blah... I know already. Fine. But you do know that sometimes I pick perfectly well on the first try."

"Even a blind squirrel finds a nut once in a while."

But she wasn't listening anymore, her attention drawn to the garden center that had materialized since her last visit.

"You like it?" he asked, following her gaze. "I figure that if I'm going to compete with the big boys, I need to set up more like them." He gestured in the general direction of the highway outside, where within five miles in either direction there was a Home Depot and a Lowe's. "If you can't beat 'em, join 'em."

Ed's Hardware had survived in spite of the crunch from the big corporations. His store was a blast from the past on its face, but over the years he had added a sizeable warehouse to the back end that housed a respectable selection of lumber. The secret to his success had been his ability to diversify from the standard stock of the big chains, carrying more unusual cuts and types of lumber and furniture-grade woods. By offering hard to find items, he managed a respectable profit. Smart business practices and local charm kept people like Lindsey coming back to him.

"It looks great! Ooh, Ed, what about—"

"Oh no. I can't let you do it, Lindsey," he warned. "That will certainly make your husband come unglued."

"Of course I'm not going to buy this one. Heck, it's only the size of a phone booth," she laughed, looking over the white gazebo display with interest. "But a full-size one—are these the plans?" She reached for a pamphlet.

"Yes, but Lindsey, he'll have my head," Ed pleaded, rubbing at the only hair he had left, a fine white peach fuzz that had evaded the razor.

"You're right. If we are going to have a gazebo, Jerry would want to design and build it himself. I just need to take the pamphlet to light the fire under him. A picture is worth...."

*****

3

"I'm kind of busy right now, Shelley. I've got to get this thing inside before the Gestapo comes home and finds it," she said, struggling with the large box that had been deposited on the porch while she was out.

"What's in the box, Lindsey?" she asked, coming down the driveway to help heave it over the threshold into the house.

"Oh, nothing much."

"Another unauthorized acquisition?"

"Can you just help me with it?" she begged, lifting her end.

"I'm not Jerry, so spill it, Lin," Shelley chided, picking up her side.

They carried it into the foyer and set it down, where the brown box quickly became the elephant in the room. She tried to avoid her friend's eyes and the sea of cardboard between them, but there was nowhere else to turn.

"It's just an ottoman," she blurted out. "I couldn't pass it up. It will be perfect in the living room. You don't know how long I've been looking for something just this size and shape. It was a steal, and the color is to die for!" By the end, she was gushing with pride. She felt the same familiar tingle of excitement—like it was Christmas morning—whenever she got a package, even if it was something she had bought for herself.

"And how, pray tell, do you think you are going to keep a new piece of furniture a secret from Jerry? I know you've gotten away with pictures, vases, and even a rug here or there that he didn't even notice until weeks later, but a new piece of furniture? He isn't that oblivious, is he?"

"You just wait. I have my ways." Lindsey's eyes were glazed over, imagining the finished living room and basking in the glow of her new possession.

"Why can't you have a normal fetish... like shoes? We gals are always shopping, buying and hiding new shoes from our men. We're supposed to; it's in the constitution or our wedding vows or something. Why make it hard on yourself? You might as well be trying to hoard elephants!" Shelley chuckled.

"I don't do this to make it hard on myself," she said plainly. "I do this because I love my home and I want to make it into my picture of perfection. I'm working toward a goal here. Sometimes the steps to that goal don't follow Jerry's perfect picture of our financial steps, but I have to follow my passion."

"Cripes! Your passion? Did you seriously just say that?"

"Yes, I said that. It's just what I'm driven to do."

"Well, I'm sure that Jerry wouldn't mind so much if you did it for a living."

"Jerry's quite happy with the way things are right now," Lindsey reminded her.

"Yes, but he could be happy-*er* if this thing you do was shared with others—for a paycheck. Between your shopping, reorganizing and redecorating the place all the time, I don't know how he takes it. Hell, when the man makes a move to sit down in his own home, he never knows if his ass is actually going to connect with a seat or land on the floor."

"That only happened once," she said defensively. "And if we'd had this ottoman at the time—"

"You are incorrigible and you know it. You're like the Lucille Ball of home improvement."

"Now what's that supposed to mean?"

"Remember Lucy and the hats, or Lucy and the meat freezer, or Lucy and the brick barbeque pit, or Lucy and *every single show* Ricky ever tried to do at the Tropicana."

"Come on! I'm nothing like—"

"And I seem to remember there being a home decorating episode."

"So, what's your point?"

"All I'm saying is, when Jerry comes home, you got some spla—"

"Thanks for all of your *ass*-istance," Lindsey said, cutting her friend's impersonation short and pushing her toward the door. "Don't you have somewhere you need to be?"

Shelley glanced at her watch. "I do have to jet. Listen, I actually stopped by for a reason. Rob wanted to know if you guys have a floor nailer that he could borrow… and possibly a person who knows how to install hardwood, too," she snorted. "Gotta love the guy; he is absolutely useless on the home repair front, but great in bed!!"

"And yet, he doesn't know how to use a nailer?"

"You have a sick little mind, Lindsey Strane."

"But I have a man who is good with a screw, nail, or anyway you want to get it together—I'm just saying."

Shelley disregarded her with a roll of the eyes. "So, I'll tell Rob that someone will be coming over to put in the floors on Saturday then." She turned to leave, giving a one-fingered salute overhead as she walked up the driveway to her idling car and took off like a bat out of hell.

Lindsey watched after her from the mouth of the doorway, silently praying that no little children or old ladies would be trying to cross the street up ahead. She drove like life was one large obstacle course and she had no brakes in the car; like her only option to get from point A to point B unscathed was to dodge and weave around slower moving vehicles and stationary objects. The only reason Shelley had her license at all was because even at sixteen she had a phenomenal set of breasts. Her driving instructor had been too busy ogling them to care about her lead foot, rolling stops and wanton disregard for proper blinker usage.

Retreating inside, Lindsey turned her attention back to the problem at hand. She had to get her latest acquisition out of sight before the boys came home from school and started asking questions that she couldn't answer without incriminating herself. If the kids found out what was in the box, it would only be a matter of time before they would spill the beans to their dad.

Unfortunately, now that her accomplice had left the scene, she was seriously limited in where she could move it. There was no way she could get it upstairs to the attic where it could wait entirely out of sight and mind until she was ready to come clean. Instead, she would have to leave it in the box and put it in the corner of the dining room, where it would hopefully blend in with its surroundings, considering the current motif was "storage room" anyway. It would only be a temporary diversion, since she was already gearing up on plans to work in that space, but by this point her life had boiled down to a great migration of stuff from one room to another, while floors were laid, molding installed, windows replaced, and painting was completed.

She reached down to grab hold of the box and was taken by the pure size of it. *There better be a lot of packing material in there.... Please, don't let this be the hamper all over again.*

Five years had not been able to ease the pain of the hamper incident. It still haunted her. She had ordered the hamper in good faith, to replace the one that was leaving splintered wicker shards in their clothes. The transaction was entirely aboveboard; Jerry knew all about it before it even came. But then it arrived in a box the size of a refrigerator. And inside that box was a hamper that, as he put it, was large enough to hide her body in when he strangled her for excessive shopping and decorating. And her only defense was that it looked so much smaller in the picture. No, he didn't let her return it. It was a perfectly sufficient hamper, and as far as he was concerned it was a mistake she should have to live with. To this day the beast stood sentry against the wall in their bathroom, mocking her, daring her to defy Jerry and replace it.

She shook her head at the possibility of screwing up on that scale again. Then she reminded herself that she had checked and rechecked the dimensions this time. Grabbing hold of the box, she lifted one side of it and pivoted on the other, alternating back and forth to walk it slowly through the foyer, into the living room, and through the archway to the dining room. She pushed it into place up against the far wall next to several stacks of boxes. Then she took a few boxes from the other stacks to place on top and stepped back to admire her work.... Perfectly camouflaged.

*****

It had been a day of aggravations, now all he really wanted to do was get to the end of his tiresome commute, drop everything, and enjoy the comforts of being home with his family. As he drove the familiar streets of the neighborhood, Jerry hoped that he would find peace awaiting him. He loved his wife, but he really prayed that today would not be one of those days he would walk into some crazy mess Lindsey couldn't help but get into.

He knew that she did her best to have her projects cleaned up before he got home. She tried to have dinner in the works and the kids under some kind of control, or at the very least out of the house playing. She tried to make his homecoming as calm and inviting as possible. It was how she had been raised. But while her mother was apt to have to rush to put away the ironing board or sewing machine before her father came in the door each night, Lindsey might have scaffolding and lumber and power tools to squirrel away.

He loved the fact that she was so creatively stimulated and self-driven. She always had a plan or a project up her sleeve, and she never put any stock in the feminist line that being a homemaker was akin to being put in bondage. Actually, she took her title quite literally, and if given the proper tools and time, could probably make a house from scratch. That being said, she was also known to get deep into some sticky situations that inevitably required his assistance. Then she would turn into a damsel in distress, standing in the middle of her destruction, batting her eyelashes coyly in hopes of getting him to come to her rescue.

It never ceased to amaze him that she had never lost herself in the transition from girl to woman, or wife to mother. Lindsey had always been exactly who she was—opinionated, headstrong, practical, artistic, loving and totally sexy. She was more beautiful now than ever before, juggling the many hats that brought their family domestic tranquility.

Just thinking about his wife, Jerry could feel the big goofy grin that spread across his face. He felt his heart beating a little faster and his palms were tingling and slightly slick.

I'm in love.

Sixteen years into this thing called wedded bliss, and he still felt the excitement of seeing her—a light flutter in his stomach; the stirring of desire. He felt lucky. He really had it all. He never looked beyond his life because everything he wanted was right there in front of him.

To think that this all started on a whim, a hankering for a plate of pancakes from the diner. Looking back, he was thankful for the two dollars in his pocket that night; any more and he might never have met her. With pancakes on the brain and frozen waffles in the budget, he ended up in the grocery store next door and met the girl with the dancing green eyes and thick ponytail of chestnut hair who would change his life forever.

*****

Lindsey knew that Jerry had pulled into the driveway, not from the sound of his car but the sound of the dog's claws on the slate floor in the foyer. Sadie was the welcome wagon for the house, dancing at the door for that first bit of attention as members of her pack came home. It was pointless to compete with the frolicking furry mess, so she busied herself in the kitchen with dinner until their reunion was over.

"Hey there, girl! How are you today? Did anybody pay attention to you? Anybody?" Jerry asked, in tones reserved for pets and babies who can't speak back. "Oh, you want me to pet your belly? Of course, I'll pet the belly! Who's got a cute pig belly?"

He loved the mutt, even though he had tried hard not to, unwilling to let her take the place of his childhood dog. She had broken him, though, with her calm and independent streak that she occasionally let down to expose a playful and fun-loving side. She was a mix of Samoyed and Chow—all white but for the cinnamon colored tufts of fur between her toes and a small patch on her chest. And when she yawned, she exposed a black smudge in the shape of Alaska on her pink tongue. Sadie had an affinity for chicken, cheese and ice cream—all foods that at some point had fallen onto the floor as she waited nearby with baited breath. Now, in the wisdom of her keen dog mind, she had learned that a certain sad and hopeful face, played at just the right times, would mean scraps of this sort would magically fall out of the air onto the floor in front of her.

As he came down the hallway toward the kitchen, Jerry called out, "Where is everybody?"

"I'm in here. The kids are outside somewhere. They hardly got a foot in the door from school before they were clamoring to get back outside. I had to wrestle them into play clothes, and I still don't know if I got Max changed out of his school shirt. There was too much interference." Lindsey shuddered at the memory. She could only hope that he wouldn't come back with any holes or tears, or grime that wouldn't come out, but considering last week he had come home from playing with a gob of sap on his pants, she wasn't holding her breath.

"They're a couple of squirmy suckers," Jerry chuckled, coming over and kissing her on the temple.

"At some point, I might just have to give in to nature and let them go around with dirty hands and feet, and ripped clothes, but I am fighting it with every ounce of my being. It drives me crazy," she muttered, turning back to the green peppers that were still and silent on the cutting board, waiting to go under the knife. "This is why I like cooking—no wrangling required."

"So, how was your day otherwise?" he asked, placing his travel mug on the counter to be washed.

"Oh, fine." She realized that she didn't have much to say about the day after subtracting out the new ottoman and paint samples— things that would just make him start questioning why she wasn't tied up with other things during the day, like a paying job.

"Just fine?"

"Yeah, fine. What do you have to say about yours?"

"I got through it."

"Likewise." She turned to face him, staring him down, challenging him to dig deeper.

"Okay, well, now what? Do we just slip into awkward and stony silence for the rest of the evening?" His eyes twinkled mischievously.

God he was handsome. His brown hair was still thick and wavy, with a small salting of gray hairs that gave him a distinguished look. His eyes were the color of melted chocolate. Light stubble shadowed his strong chin and his clothes were slightly rumpled from a long day. A part of her wanted to jump his bones right then and there— the part that wasn't concerned about the water about to boil on the stove, or the peppers lying prone on the counter, or that fly in the house just waiting to dive-bomb any bit of food left unprotected in the room.

"What is it?" he asked. "It's like you're looking right through me."

"Oh, nothing. Just spaced out there for a minute." She grabbed the knife and turned back to the vegetables.

Jerry came up behind her and ran his hands along her sides and down her hips, leaning in and kissing her low on the nape of her neck, just off to the left. He knew the spot well—how it made her toes curl.

"I have a knife, Jerry," she whispered.

"I'm not afraid."

"You know how I am with cutlery. I need to focus. Aren't you the one who threatened to take the knives away from me while I still have fingers left?"

"Then put it down." His breath was hot against her skin.

"The kids will be in any minute, and I have to get the pasta in the pot."

"I thought I smelled meatloaf," he mumbled, nuzzling her neck.

"Fried meatloaf and buttered pasta."

"You know I love your fried meatloaf. You feed me well."

The sound of footsteps galumphing up the porch steps stopped his wandering lips and hands.

"Saved by the boys," he said, letting go and pinching her butt for good measure.

He went down the hall to unlock the front door, calling back from the foyer, "Now what did you get from UPS this time?"

Shit, if only we had been busy doing other things. She wondered why UPS would come a second time in one day. *And what the hell else am I expecting?*

"Wow, now there's a guilty look if I ever saw one," he taunted, coming back through the doorway into the kitchen.

"No, I was just—"

"Just trying to figure out what you might have purchased this time?"

She stood with her hand on her hip, defiantly. "Actually, I was thinking that I don't remember buying anything. Maybe I'm a victim of identity theft."

"And the criminals purchased things in your name and sent them to your house?" he asked incredulously.

"Stranger things have happened."

"No, dear, I don't think they have."

Jerry looked at his wife, knowing that he had gotten her this time. "I'm just kidding. It's the kids. They're out on the porch taking their muddy shoes off."

Lindsey let out a breath she didn't know she had been holding.

"You really thought there was a package out there. Now I *know* you've been shopping… as usual."

"Maybe the look you saw on my face was *concern* that it was a package of unknown origin that could have been a bomb of some sort." She tried to hold a straight face.

"Drop the knife, lady," he said, as if she were brandishing a weapon.

She released the knife onto the pile of peppers, and he swept her into his arms as she burst out giggling.

"Why are you so cute?" he whispered in her ear.

"Eeew, what are you guys doing?" Adam asked. He wondered if something was wrong with his parents. He had been at his friends' houses and never caught their parents laughing and hugging and being goofy like this.

"Yeah, wha'choo doin'?" Max demanded, standing firm next to his big brother.

Adam was a perfect, half-sized copy of Jerry. It was like he was a clone, rather than the result of a random combination of their gene pool. Max had a head full of thick, golden blond hair that didn't seem to fit in the family portrait, and he still held on to childlike features of a button nose and a mouth full of gaps and baby teeth. But his smile and his knees were undoubtedly Jerry's, and his eyes were the same shocking shade of green as Lindsey's.

"I'm interrogating your mother."

"What's that?" Max asked Adam.

"He's questioning her about something."

"Like what? Is it about the mark on the wall in the hallway?" Max whispered back.

13

"Shut up!" Adam growled under his breath, pinching his brother's arm.

Max shut his mouth and rubbed his arm.

"What are you two going on about?" Lindsey asked, pulling herself from Jerry's grasp.

"Nothing," they said in unison.

"Really?"

"It's nothing, Mom," Adam said, hoping she would leave it alone before Max cracked.

"You two go and wash up for dinner," she said, eyeing them carefully.

They both scurried to get out from under Mom's stare.

"Way to go, Max. You weren't supposed to mention anything about the wall... ever," Adam said, as they left the room.

"But—"

"But nothing. We need to have a united front. It's just a scuff on the wall. Mom will probably be repainting anyway. There's no reason for us to get in trouble for it."

"Okay." His voice was small and shaky.

"Max, I wouldn't steer you wrong."

"I know, Adam," he said, looking up at his brother with certainty.

-3 Weeks-

"So, what's the prognosis?"

"Prognosis?" Lindsey asked, staring at him blankly.

"Diagnosis?"

"Now you make it sound like you're checking me for a disease."

"Don't play dumb. You know what I mean. The thing... with the thing," Jerry said, moving his hands comically in an effort to pantomime what he didn't want to say out loud.

"Do you have trouble discussing lady parts?"

"Aw, come on."

"If this is difficult for you—"

"Just tell me already," he said impatiently.

"I'm going to tell you the same thing I told you last week and the week before. I'm done, Jerry. I'm no longer checking just for the sake of checking. It sucks. I don't want to *try* anymore. Let's just *not* try to prevent it."

"It's the same thing, Lindsey. Who do you think you're fooling?"

"I just feel like it is too much pressure to put on my uterus," she said, touching her stomach.

"But we *like* trying," he moaned.

"I am not putting a kibosh on the sex, Jerry. I'm just saying that we can take it less seriously."

"Since when have I ever been too serious about sex?"

15

"You know what I mean. I just want to do what feels good when I want to do it. No schedules. Why can't we just fly blind?"

"I thought that was basically what we have been doing."

"But we do it, like, every day," Lindsey pointed out.

"I have news for you; that isn't because of any schedule. *That* is just because I want you every day. And, to be quite honest, you're a bit of a whore."

"Jerry!"

"Seriously, you're too easy," he said, shrugging his shoulders.

"Well, I just want to put the other stuff out of mind. Let's enjoy ourselves, and if I don't get my period and it seems like I might be— I'll check."

"Are we not even saying the word anymore?"

"It's not that. Come on, Jerry. Don't give me a hard time. Listen, I'll keep a test on standby." She kissed his cheek as punctuation to her point.

"But you aren't regular enough to know if you even missed it," he pointed out weakly.

"I'll know, Jerry. I know my body."

"But you haven't had your… ummm… *friend* in months." His face was scarlet.

"It's so cute the way this flusters you. For some reason singing out loud in a crowded parking lot—badly—doesn't embarrass you, but feminine issues on the other hand—"

"Come on… for me?" he begged, ignoring her.

"Jerry, you get as down about this as I do each week. Let's just chill and enjoy the means without worrying about the ends." She fluttered her eyelashes flirtatiously.

"So, you mean you want me right now?"

"Jerry!"

"I just thought that was what you meant," he said innocently.

"Go to work." She shooed him out of the bedroom.

She wanted another baby, and Lindsey knew that she wasn't really going to be able to put pregnancy out of her mind. It wasn't like she was going to stop taking the prenatal vitamins her doctor had prescribed when they started trying. Little would actually change. And she knew that each time they had sex, a part of her was still going to wonder if that would be the time they created another life between them. But hoping and wondering was very different from trying and failing.

*****

Jerry understood her aggravation. It did seem to be taking a long time to get pregnant, and it was difficult to see the stick of their future showing a bleak fortune each week. This was new territory for them. It hadn't been hard for them to conceive Adam or Max. Actually, it was too easy with Adam—an unexpected and unplanned addition. But Max was planned, and it still hadn't been this much time and effort. Not that he minded the effort. He still ran incredibly hot around his wife, even while other men he knew were fizzling out in their marriages—due to their own waning interest or resigned to their wives' lack of interest. As far as he was concerned, he would have kept up this "trying" thing on infinitum if Lindsey were game.

Parenthood was the most important thing to both of them, and it was Adam who showed them the way. In the beginning they wasted their time preparing to have kids, not realizing there was no foolproof formula for having them. When Adam came along, giving them no choice but to take the parenting step, they were suddenly part of a world that was so much better than where they had come from. Now here they were, over a decade later, nestled in a house filled to bursting with love and family, still wanting more, and trying… and failing.

He could understand how Lindsey wanted to cool it with the constant pregnancy tests, but he just didn't want it to turn into a lack of interest in having a baby entirely. He knew that she felt her biological clock ticking away, and he suddenly feared that at any moment she might pronounce it "shut down."

It would be just like her to blame herself for this; to think she waited too long to complete their family. She would point out that men don't have a cutoff for baby-making. But Jerry, on the other hand, chose to look at this as a "we" problem. If they couldn't get pregnant again, it was something they would deal with together. Just as if they did have another baby, they would raise it together. There was no "he" or "she" as far as he was concerned.

*****

"Let me guess, you've picked the paint color."

"I did what you insisted I should do from now on. I taped the samples to the wall. I've been looking at them for the past two weeks and I finally figured it out."

"Don't tell me…. You don't like any of them," he cringed.

"No. Actually, I picked this one—porcelain bisque," Lindsey said proudly, pulling the sample out of her back pocket. It was just the faintest whisper of color. "I thought it wasn't going to be enough, but you were right. It looked much darker in the dining room. And it will be the perfect subtle backdrop to make the white moldings stand out."

"Excellent! So this is a simple paint purchase today… no angst about new projects? Don't tell me you're staying on task!" Ed chortled, his laugh lines deepening.

"Well, not exactly," she admitted, biting lightly at her lower lip. "Jerry—"

"Did he give you that not so subtle hint to get a job again?" He winked.

She played along, shaking her head slowly. "You'd think he would have learned by now."

"I guess he just doesn't know who he's dealing with, huh?"

"Nope. He constantly underestimates my ability to avoid going to work."

"So what's the excuse this time? What project are you starting?"

"I'm thinking about trying to smooth my stippled ceilings," she said, wincing in expectation of his response.

"In the dining room?"

"Think bigger."

"The whole house?" Ed chucked himself in the forehead lightly with the palm of his hand, like the news was too much for him to take.

"Yup, eventually, but I'm going to start with the dining room. I might be a bit rash in my home improvements but I'm still realistic."

"You know, if you ever run out of things to do and want to make an honest living, I could always give you a job. You're here all the time anyway."

"I might just take you up on that offer someday, Ed. For now, though, this wicked little dance we do is too fun to put an end to. Besides, I have fourteen ceilings to do."

"Don't fool yourself. You'll have another eight projects started in the middle of doing those ceilings."

"That's all part of the plan. Always keeping myself useful."

"How are the kids doing? They must be getting really big now."

"They're growing like weeds. Adam's in fifth grade and Max is in kindergarten, so I'm able to do most of my running without them. It's nice not to have to ply them with bribes to keep their mouths shut to their dad about what I've been up to," she said mischievously.

*****

Lindsey watched the bus from a safe distance, staying out of sight in the house because Adam would be mortified if his friends saw him being babied. He was certain he didn't need his mom to watch for him anymore, so she did her best to give him his space, but she didn't give him his way.

The bus was stopped for an inordinately long time, making her wonder what might be the problem. She hadn't seen either of the boys exit yet. Just as she made a move to go to the front door to check, she saw Max and then Adam descend the steps. They raced down the driveway and up onto the porch, bursting through the front door at top speed.

"Well, hello," she said, a note of surprise carefully nestled in her words.

"Hi, Mom," Max said, coming over to hug her.

"Hey," Adam grumbled.

"What's up?" she asked.

"He fell asleep on the bus," Adam said, jerking his thumb toward his brother. "I had to wake him up to get off."

"Really?" She looked down at Max, who stared back at her with sad eyes.

"Yeah, really," Adam said.

"Well, I'm glad you didn't just leave him there."

"Thanks, Adam," Max said softly, tears welling up in his eyes.

"Whatever." Adam stomped down the hall to the bathroom.

"He's cranky," Lindsey whispered to Max, who giggled.

*****

"So, what's the news tonight?" Jerry asked, as he sat down at the dinner table. It was his standard dinner conversation starter.

"I saved Max's life today," Adam said with pride.

"What?" Jerry asked theatrically.

"Dork fell asleep on the bus," he answered, around a mouthful of bread.

"So?" Max challenged.

20

"If I hadn't been there to wake you up, the bus driver would have finished the route and then parked the bus in the lot and locked it up for the weekend, where you would have starved unless you ate the ABC gum off the bottom of the seats."

Max stared across the table in horror.

"That's enough, Adam," Lindsey interjected forcefully. "You are taking this ornery preteen thing too far. There's no call for that."

"I'm just saying—"

"You're *just saying* enough to go to your room without dinner," she cautioned.

Jerry sat at the end of the table, lost in the conversation. "Wait a second, what happened?"

Lindsey answered, "Max fell asleep on the bus and Adam had to wake him up to get off. It's just that simple." She looked at Adam. "Thank you for taking care of your brother and making sure he got home. Now drop it."

"What's ABC gum?" Max piped up.

"Oh, it's great! I have some you can try later."

Lindsey gave him a warning look.

"It's just a joke, Max," Adam said. "It's Already Been Chewed gum."

"Yuck!" Max laughed. "That's funny!"

Jerry looked at the faces around the table, surprised at how often he felt like he was thrust into the middle of their private joke. There was no question in his mind that they were a close-knit family, but this part of their lives was simply out of his reach. He felt that familiar jealousy that simmered low inside of him when he realized all of the things that he had missed through the years. Lindsey was neck deep in everything that happened around here. She was there for every milestone and moment. She was the point person for all things regarding the kids. He had missed both of the boys' first words and first steps. He had missed the first tooth they each lost and missed watching them go off to their first days of school. Sure, he got to play the Tooth Fairy and Santa, but there was no glory in that. The kids didn't know that he had a hand in those treasured moments.

They *knew* who fixed all their peanut butter and jelly sandwiches. They *knew* who made their cuts and bruises feel all better. They *knew* who bought them their favorite snacks at the store, and who always made sure their favorite pajamas were washed and back in their drawer for a good night's sleep. They *knew* who they could count on being there for them when they came home each day. Jerry could understand this because Lindsey was these same things for him.

He wondered whether the boys could truly understand what it was that *he* contributed to their lives and the household. Even when he was home, he was like a satellite orbiting them as they orbited Lindsey, the center of their universe. That relationship was something he would never have, and it saddened him but also filled him with a fierce, protective pride. These were the most important people in his life, to see them prospering because he was able to support and provide for them was truly powerful.

"How about we have Mom make some buffalo chips for a snack?" Adam asked, continuing with the elementary school food jokes.

"What are those?" Max asked, his eyes wide with interest.

"Don't you need a buffalo to make those?" Jerry asked, finding space in the conversation.

"Buffalos can't cook!" Max laughed.

"But they can poop!" Adam yelled.

Max looked at his dad, confused.

"Buffalo chips are what they call buffalo poop, Bud."

"Wow, now we have really digressed," Lindsey said, putting her hands out in surrender.

"Is that all the drama for the day?" Jerry asked, laughing along with his sons.

"Pretty much," she said.

"Really? There's nothing going on in your world?" he asked pointedly.

"Absolutely nothing," she said, keeping her voice flat, knowing he was intimating their morning conversation. Then, to get his mind off of thoughts about pregnancy, she unleashed the bombshell of her latest project plans, "Although, I was planning to flatten the ceilings."

Jerry choked on his milk. "What?" he sputtered, noticing the defiant gleam in her eye.

"I was thinking of removing the stipple from the ceilings. You know, go room by room until the whole house has smooth, white ceilings. It shouldn't be that hard."

He stared at her incredulously.

"It's messy and time consuming, but not hard," she said simply, as if the difficulty concerned him, rather than her rabid need to delve into something new.

"But the dining room—" he started to complain.

"That would be the first room to do since we're working in there anyway."

"Did I hear *we*?"

"Yes. Of course I might need some help with the molding and whatnot, but the ceiling is my job *completely*. You don't have to worry about a thing."

He rolled his eyes. He had to worry about everything she did, since it usually escalated into massive upheaval and *always* ended up with, "Jerry, could you…?"

*****

He slipped into bed and hooked his arm around her waist, pulling her tightly to his chest and wrapping himself around her warm body.

"This is less of a spoon and more of a ladle, Jerry," she said, squirming sleepily.

"Yeah, it's my own personal move," he whispered in her ear.

"Do you try it on all the ladies?"

"Only the most important ones," he said, as a matter of fact, allowing his hands to wander with the comfort of possession.

"And how's it workin' for ya?" she asked, noticeably more awake now.

"You tell me."

Lindsey turned to face him and kissed him deeply, then pulled away, holding his face in her hands and looking deep in his eyes.

"I love you, Jerry Strane."

"Are we being formal now? Is this some kind of role-playing game?" he joked.

"Come on. I am trying to say something important," she protested.

"Fine. Go ahead." He pretended that it was hard to put on a serious face.

"I'll turn back over if you keep this up," she warned, like a teacher talking to a naughty student.

"Oh, I'm keeping it up," he snickered.

She made a move to turn and he grabbed her, holding her fast.

"I'm sorry. I'll be good."

She propped herself up on her elbow. "What I said about the whole pregnancy thing this morning, I meant it. But I don't want you to think that I don't want another baby, Jerry. I *do*. I was watching the boys tonight and thinking about how much I adore the life we have—even all the commotion, when you guys are driving me nuts. We do this well, you know." She hid her face in an attempt to hide the intense emotion that flickered across it.

"The sex is just marvelous darling; you know I've always thought that."

"I meant the parenting thing, actually."

"But?"

"Yes, Jerry, the sex is marvelous."

"So, is this a green light?"

"Day-glo green."

"Your wish," he said, pouncing.

-4 Weeks-

"You never cease to amaze me. We haven't finished half the projects you've started around here and you want to start another one? Just last week you were talking about the ceilings," he pointed out.

"First of all, remember, the ceilings have nothing to do with you. They're *my* project, done by *me*."

"As opposed to all of *your* projects done by *me*?"

"That's about right."

"Do you know how many projects you start that end up needing me?"

"Most of them."

"But you assure me that the ceilings aren't—"

"Exactly."

Jerry just looked at his wife for a moment. He found her certainty, mixed with her unabashed acceptance of her shortcomings, absolutely adorable. She had no shame at all, like she was entitled to his assistance and support no matter what she asked.

"And second of all," Lindsey continued her original argument, "the ceilings are the *reason* I am mentioning this right now. I mean, this change would affect the ceiling in the kitchen, so it would need to be done before I work in there. I'm just trying to be efficient."

"But you aren't even done with the dining room yet! You haven't actually even *started* the ceilings for that matter. You need to

26

stop thinking up more things that get in the way of finishing the other stuff on the list."

"That's not what I'm doing," she protested.

"If it's not that, then what do you call this proposal of a project right now, while we're in the middle of something else?"

"I am just *preparing* you." Her eyes were wide with surprise that he might possibly consider her unreasonable enough to demand something more be done right now.

"Preparing me?" he huffed.

"May I be totally honest?"

"Certainly."

"You always freak out about my new strikes of pure brilliance, so I have to prepare you well in advance when I need you to do something."

"Brilliance?"

"Well, isn't it obvious? Look around you," she said, pulling a Vanna White, with a sweeping arm gesture at the room around her.

"I see a holy hell of a mess."

"But what it is going to become…" she said wistfully.

"You are one piece of work, Lindsey." He shook his head in defeat.

"I just want to know if it *can* be done. I'm not asking you to do it."

"Well, of course it can be done," he relented. "But it isn't going to be easy."

"Will you think about it? You know, sometime in the future it might be something to consider." She shrugged her shoulders, like she didn't care that much about it either way.

Jerry knew exactly what she was up to. This was how she got him to do the majority of things that he did around the house. It was manipulative, for sure, but since he wasn't blind to it, he let her have her fun. And when she left the room, he couldn't help himself; he started mentally calculating what it would take.

*****

"Seriously, Lin, he didn't have a problem with you asking him to take a wall out of the kitchen?"

"I didn't say that he didn't have a problem with it. But I did get him to consider it, which means he'll be challenged to do it, even though he thinks that I'm crazy to ask. It's all part of my wicked little plan."

"Lucy…. What plan?" Shelley asked, in a bad Cuban accent.

"My ultimate plan?"

"Yeah."

"To get the entire house renovated."

"Well, duh, isn't that his plan too?"

"Basically…. But my design ideas have sort of burst through the box of our original intentions, so I need to tweak things as we go. If I only ask for a little bit at a time—move the cable line, reroute some plumbing, bump out a wall—"

"So what can't you say? And where do I get me one of those?" Shelley interrupted.

"Oh, you've got it good."

"Not like you do. Your man lives for you. You guys truly are of one common interest—each other. Rob is… well, he's Rob."

"And what's that supposed to mean?"

"It means just what I said."

"Is something wrong?" Lindsey asked, worried.

"No. I'm just saying that Rob still holds a piece of himself away from me. And there are things about me he doesn't care—let's just say that I wouldn't dare pull your shenanigans for fear that he would walk right out the door without a backward glance. Sometimes I wonder if he is in this thing all the way."

"But you have kids! You guys have been married longer than we have! How do you not know his heart inside and out by now?"

28

"We aren't all like you and Jerry," she said with a smirk, like she just bit into something bitter.

"What's wrong with me and Jerry?"

"Nothing. It's... nothing. You two have some sickening bond that most of us schleps out in the world don't have."

"But you seem... I don't know.... I get that all relationships are different, but what you have seems to really work."

"What Rob and I have does work. But it isn't what you have."

"So?"

"God, you don't even know, do you?"

"What the hell are you talking about?"

"It can be hard to be your friend," Shelley grumbled.

Lindsey felt like she had been stabbed in the gut. "Why would you say something like that?"

"Wake up, Lin. I see your life here—you've got it all."

"But you guys have that beautiful, new, huge house. And all the trips you take! You get to have *fun*!"

"No, you're having all the fun," she corrected, seriously.

"We hardly ever do anything or go anywhere."

"Do you know how jealous I am that you guys don't have to go anywhere? You're happy and in love... and enjoying life. The rest of us out there are just scrambling to find what you guys have."

Lindsey's eyes widened as she began to comprehend what she was taking in. "Please tell me that you and Rob are—"

"Oh, we're fine. We're not heading toward divorce or anything. But I do wonder about people who split after twenty-plus years of marriage, and I have to think that maybe those people were in marriages like mine. Yeah, we get along fine and we still have a great sex life. But we don't live for each other."

"But I—"

"You guys—you and Jerry—are two halves of a whole. You respect each other. You support each other. And you dream and scheme together. God, I should have put money on you guys from

29

the beginning. Instead, I thought you were crazy when you announced you were getting married after, what... a month of dating? Hell, everyone thought you were crazy, or knocked up! You hardly knew each other! But we were all wrong."

Tears started to well in Lindsey's eyes, and she felt a tingling sensation deep in her nose that meant turning back the tide was going to be difficult.

"Oh stop blubbering, you sap," Shelley snapped.

"But that was so sweet, and you're usually not swee—"

"And now we see why. Shit like this happens and now I'm gonna have to kill you just to shut you up," she griped.

"What's wrong with sharing a tear between friends?"

"It's what I like to call pansy-ass weakness. That's what's wrong with it."

"You wouldn't cry if someone kicked a puppy in front of you."

"Probably not, but I'd kick that someone's ass."

"Well, as long as your priorities are in order," Lindsey said wryly, her eyes shining with the tears that she still tried to hold back.

"Yeah, I got my shit in order. I'm the queen of ethics and morals," she said, standing up straight and righteous.

"Morals? Seriously? After what you and Tony Gatinelli did in the shop car junior year?"

"We call that a teaching moment. By the time I got him, he was already misguided—sexually speaking—and I couldn't have people thinking he learned the crap he was doing, and how he was doing it, from me." Shelley shuddered at the memory. "I had to make sure he knew how to do things right, to protect my rep."

"To protect your rep? You dumped him two days later and everyone called you a slut."

"But who made the man? .... I did. He knows it and I know it."

"Shit, Shell, everyone knows it!"

"Exactly."

"Again, as long as you have your priorities in order."

30

"That's all I'm saying," she said smugly.

"I don't know how we ever became friends."

"It was that damn sandwich you shared with me when I forgot my lunch in first grade. I knew I should never have taken it."

"Aw, you remember."

"Don't let it go to your head. I have to ask myself why we're friends every single day, so that fateful moment is always close at hand."

"You love me," Lindsey taunted, poking her in the shoulder.

"Whatever."

*****

"What did *you* do today?" Jerry asked, sizing Lindsey up. He noticed a slight sheen of sweat on her forehead, and she was sporting an adorably disheveled look. Her hair had escaped her ponytail in unruly waves of burnished chestnut that fell haphazardly around her face. She was wearing one of his old dress shirts that she had commandeered for work clothes, and a pair of ripped and permanently paint-splattered jeans. He could see white powder residue on her clothes and face that he was certain wasn't flour. She was definitely up to something.

"I asked you first."

She was purposely blocking his way out of the foyer, where she had come running to meet him. Sadie had probably acted as her alarm, tapping out Morse code for "the hawk flies at midnight" with her dancing claws on the slate floor, and then distracting him with playful frolicking until Lindsey could intervene.

"No, you didn't," he said, using the inches he had on her to look over and around her. He couldn't see any destruction in the kitchen. She was obviously working deeper in the house.

"It was implied."

"Implied?"

"Yeah. When I asked how your day was, that was meant to be an open-ended question."

"Is this some kind of test?" He brushed past her into the kitchen.

"No, I'm just setting you straight that 'fine' isn't really what I was looking for," she said, fighting to keep herself in the way of the path toward the family room.

"This is some kind of woman thing, right?"

"I guess you can call it that if you want to make it sexist," Lindsey chided.

He purposely gave her a wide berth as he went to the counter to put down his travel mug from the morning. "Let me guess, have you been hanging with Shelley today?"

"Yes, I saw Shelley today," she said mockingly. "But that has nothing to do with my desire for more from you when we have a conversation."

"So next time, just ask me what I did and I'll tell you," he laughed. "You girls make it so hard. Just come out with it."

"Well? What did you do today?" she asked pointedly.

He answered like he was giving a status report, "First, I returned some emails. Then I made a few phone calls. I finished creating my presentation, wrote a memo for the—"

"Stop! I give up! You really don't know what I mean, do you? Tell me about the aggravations, the conversations you had, what you—"

"Don't try to turn me into a girl," Jerry warned with a laugh.

"Forget it." She waved him off as a lost cause. "Why are you home so early, anyway?"

"My radar went off and I knew you were up to something at home that I needed to put a stop to."

Lindsey just stared at him, unable to formulate a comeback considering he was absolutely right. She was up to no good.

"Seriously, my last meeting ran short so I figured I'd get home and spend time with you. What about you?" Jerry prodded. "What did Ethel have to say about your latest scheme?"

"Another Lucy crack? Do you and Shelley share a brain?" she asked in disbelief. "And, by the way, *Ethel* just rolls her eyes and says that you're a saint."

"Well, it's about time someone noticed the qualities beyond my studly exterior."

"Did you really just say that?" she snorted.

"Yeah, I said it. And I'm not ashamed to admit it."

"You should be."

"No, you should be the one who's ashamed. You've been using me for my body for too much of this relationship and it's about time I got respect for my other fine attributes."

She rolled her eyes.

"You've got nothing you want to say to that? Perhaps an apology or an endearing sentiment?"

"I got nothin'."

"Well I never," he said, in mock disbelief.

"Don't let the compliment go to your head. Shelley also said that Kim Jong-il may just be misunderstood—you know, on account of the language barrier. We aren't talking about the sharpest tool in the shed or the best judge of character. You do remember her first, extremely short and absolutely disastrous marriage, right?"

"Let's not revisit that place. She had you so spun up in her drama..." He shook his head as if to clear the offensive memory from it like an Etch A Sketch.

"Well, the point is, Shelley is not the person the Catholic Church consults on elements of sainthood. So take a chill pill and let the swelling in your head go down a bit."

"Oooh, aren't we feisty today? Is this foreplay for now or later?" he asked, sidling up to her.

"Later... if you're lucky. Right now, I need you to help me tear out the sheetrock on this wall," she said, realizing that she wasn't going to be able to hide what was going on in the family room and deciding to enlist instead.

"And just why would I be doing this?" He came around the corner into the family room to find a stack of tools and no less than a dozen investigative holes in the sheetrock. As he suspected, he had caught her in the act and her feistiness was a case of the best defense being a good offense.

"I told you that I wanted to take out this wall here, and our neighbor just got a new roof. You know what that means? He has a dumpster, Jerry." Her eyes were aglow with the news.

"So now we're going to be dumping trash under the cover of night?"

"No," she said, exasperated. "I asked him if we could put some stuff in it. I thought it would be a good way to get rid of that old carpet we tore out a while back. And it only makes sense to do this while we can get rid of the carnage, too." She pointed at the partially dismantled wall. "You know I hate storing construction trash."

"Call me confused, but why are we doing it at all? You mentioned wanting to take out *that* wall," he said, pointing toward the kitchen. "And, by the way, I did *not* agree to do it. Is this your way to get back at me... deciding to do this one instead?"

"First of all, this is not *instead*; this is *in addition*. And secondly, do you ever listen to me?" she asked, in awe.

"Did you ever mention this to me before?"

"Once. A while back," she mumbled.

"If it was during sex, it doesn't count. You know damn well that I have a one-track mind."

"It wasn't during sex," she said, exasperated. "At least I don't think so," she added under her breath.

He leveled a speculative stare, until she cracked.

"What does it matter, Jerry? Seriously, shouldn't you just be happy that I'm asking for your help?"

"I believe that I actually caught you in the act, so now you've decided to include me.... Would that be more accurate?"

"Whatever. Can't we just agree that it's better that you're here, so I'm not just taking a sledgehammer to the wall and doing some real damage to it and everything else nearby... including myself?"

"Aw shucks, when you put it that way." His voice dripped with sarcasm.

"Shut up and help me," Lindsey whined.

"This is all part of your plan to put me in a home, or better yet, in the ground before my time."

"Well, I gotta get rid of you somehow, while I can still kick it. I wouldn't want to be all dried up when I'm looking for husband number two. These kids do need a father figure, you know."

"Ouch! Right through my heart, Lin."

He grabbed the sledgehammer from her grasp. "You don't even have the proper tools for the job. There is a much better way to go about this. Just wait right here and *don't touch anything.*" He enunciated very slowly to remind her that he saw right through her ways.

Jerry came back from the garage with his arms loaded down: drill, reciprocating saw and pry bars. As he approached, he warned her, "I see you mentally cataloguing what a project like this requires. Swear to me that you will never just start taking another wall out without me. If you got it in your head, I have no doubt that you could do it, but if it happened to be load-bearing—" He shuddered.

"I'll never take out a wall without your express consent and instruction," she mouthed, in a monotone reserved for reciting exceptionally bland oaths.

"Good, now that we got that out of the way, let's get this wall out of here." He gave her a wink that said, you're getting your way for now, but you'll pay for it later.

35

*****

The new openness of the space washed over her. Even amidst the carnage of sheetrock and two-by-fours, the room felt like a fresh canvas. Standing back, appraising the view, she could finally see her latest imaginings coming to fruition. She just had to figure out how to get the rest of it realized without driving Jerry crazy with more projects.

"What are you thinking?" he asked warily. "It better not be something like, 'Gee, honey, I *thought* that this was going to open things up, but now that I see it, I think it was better with the wall there.'"

"No," she said absently, ignoring his ribbing. She was still thinking of the additional changes she wanted to make, trying to picture them in the new space.

Jerry came up behind her and whispered into that perfect spot on the side of her neck, "So why are you a million miles away?"

She felt heat flush through her body in reaction to his lips, moist against her skin.

"I'm right here," she said breathily, giving in to his mouth and hands.

"Good, because I'm here too."

Her shirt was unbuttoned to her navel, and her hands were on the zipper of his pants, when they heard the sound of the front door handle. Sneaking through the kitchen, they peeked down the hall to the foyer. They could see two heads outside, trying to peer back at them through the beveled glass in the door.

She heaved a sigh of relief. "Thank God they don't have a key."

"You didn't tell me they would be home any minute."

"I didn't have time to look at the clock, Jerry."

"Shit!" he groaned in frustration.

"You just go back in there and think yourself down. I'll get the door." She clipped her bra and buttoned her shirt as quickly as she could.

"Yeah, you make it sound easier than it is," he grumbled after her.

She swung the door open like a butler. "Good afternoon, Master Max. Good afternoon, Master Adam. How are we this fine day?"

"Hey, Mom. Why was the door locked?" Adam demanded, ignoring her.

"Just habit, I guess," she said, smoothing her hair nervously, afraid that she looked as red as she felt.

"Why's Dad's car in the driveway?" Max asked.

"Because he's home, dork," Adam answered, rolling his eyes.

"Oh, yeah," Max mumbled, looking defeated.

"So, where is Dad anyway?" Adam asked.

"He's just cleaning up from a little project in the family room," she said, hoping Jerry had cooled down by now. "Walk this way, and I will serve you a snack in the belfry."

"Isn't a belfry where the bell goes... like on a church or something?" Adam asked.

"Actually, yes, but I thought it sounded cool." She ruffled his hair. Adam never ceased to surprise her when it came to the pure amount of stuff he already had stored in his young brain.

"It does sound cool. Can we have a belfry?" Max asked. "Can we?"

"Well, I don't know about a belfry, but we might be able to talk Dad into a cupola," she conspired.

"Can we eat snacks in a cupola?" Max asked.

"No, you can't really do anything in a cupola," she admitted.

"So why would we want one?"

"Yeah, Mom, why would we want one?" Jerry parroted, coming around the corner into the kitchen and giving her a knowing look.

"Because they look cool… and you can have a weathervane on top," she said, quickly grasping the best argument she had for the unnecessary but aesthetically pleasing addition of a cupola.

"A weathervane?" Max asked, blinking his confusion.

"That *would* be cool," Adam chimed in.

"Yeah, I like that." Max added, still not knowing what it meant but ready to champion any cause for his big brother.

"So this is how you do it? You get everyone on your side and then I'm on the roof building a cupola," Jerry said, shaking his head. "We already talked about this. I have other things to do and maybe sometime—far in the distant future—I can add a cupola."

"That's all I needed to know," she said innocently.

"Using young children to get what you want. That's sick, Lin. Really sick," he snickered, retreating back into the family room.

"Like you don't hold your good deeds over my head to get—" she paused, clearing her throat, "—stuff you want."

"But did I actually get that stuff?" he called over his shoulder.

"Oh, you're gonna get it all right." She took the dishtowel she was drying her hands with and whipped it in his direction.

"Promise?"

"Boys, wash up and I'll get you a snack," she sang out, ignoring his degrading banter.

"Just a minute, Mom," Adam said, following his dad out of the kitchen. He loved it when Dad came home early. Usually he would get home at dinner and there was no time to hang out and be "guys". Days like this meant there was a chance he would get to help with a project or, even better, maybe get him to go outside and play football.

"Holy cow!" Adam exclaimed, when he saw the unexpected and unobstructed view of the family room. "You took the wall out! It looks so much bigger in here now!"

"That's all I'm saying," Lindsey called out from the kitchen.

Jerry turned and looked at Adam, rolling his eyes and circling his finger next to his head like Mom was crazy.

"Mr. Strane, did I just see what I think I saw?" she prompted, having snuck up behind them.

"Nah, you're imagining things. Kind of like you're *imagining* what else you want me to do in here."

"Touché." She retreated to the kitchen. "Adam, I said to wash up for a snack," she called over her shoulder.

"But I can help Dad with clean up, first," Adam offered, hopefully, thinking that the faster they cleaned up the more likely he could get his dad to play with him.

"Me too," Max said, bounding into the room, not wanting to be left out.

"Come on. You don't ever like to do work around here," Adam whispered under his breath.

"I do!" Max protested.

"You don't and you know it. You'll pick up one thing and say you helped."

"So? That's helping."

"Hardly," Adam scoffed. "I'm the one who really helps out."

"You're bigger and older," Max pointed out, wisely.

"I was doing this stuff when you were still in diapers," Adam said importantly, as he poked Max in the shoulder.

"Stop it!"

"Stop what?" Adam egged him on.

"Stop touching me or I'll tell Mom," Max threatened, pushing back.

"If you can find her."

"She's right there," Max said, pointing toward the kitchen.

"I mean your *real* mom," Adam said mischievously.

Tears filled Max's eyes. "I'm not adopted," he whimpered, shoving Adam.

"That's what you think," Adam taunted, shoving him back.

"Both of you stop, right now," Lindsey demanded, coming into the room. "Nobody is helping anyone with anything if this is what it's going to amount to." She gave Jerry a look that questioned why he had let it go this far already.

"But—" Adam protested.

"But nothing. It stops right now," Jerry said, giving both boys a stern look. Then he turned to Lindsey and shrugged his shoulders lightly, admitting he had tuned out the scuffle.

"I'm sorry," Adam mumbled.

"I'm sorry too," Max said, always happy to let it go and get on with being friends again.

*****

"Am I adopted?" Max asked, as he carefully pushed mashed potatoes, peas, and pot roast without gravy to the far reaches of his plate. A strict separatist, he didn't want any food tainting any other food without his express consent—casseroles were an out-and-out abomination.

"Now what would make you ask a question like that?" Lindsey asked, directing her attention toward Adam.

"I was just wondering," Max mumbled, putting a few peas on the end of his fork in an effort to look like he was eating them; then carefully allowing them to roll back off before they reached his lips.

Adam could feel both sets of parental eyes on him. "I was just joking," he grumbled. Egging his brother on was one of his favorite hobbies, but he knew that he was dangerously close to big trouble for the adoption comment.

"I was thinking about being a tomato for Halloween," Max said randomly, unwittingly taking the heat entirely off of his brother.

Adam burst out laughing. Lindsey and Jerry tried to squelch the same response, but quickly lost it too.

"You think a tomato would be that funny? Cool," Max said, nodding his head to congratulate himself for a good choice.

"You do know that Halloween is a long way away, Bud," Jerry reminded him, gently.

"Yeah, I know…. But I can't stop the good ideas when they come. Besides, I like to be prepared."

"Where does he get this stuff?" Adam asked, looking at the adults as if he were one of them.

"I don't know." Lindsey shook her head in wonder.

"See, he must be adopt—"

"Don't push it, Sport," Jerry warned.

*****

Lindsey stopped outside the door, her hand poised above the knob, not wanting to break the spell. The sounds of giggles and crashes and roll-around laughter meant an awful mess in the works, but a disaster of brotherly love was at the center of it. She marveled at how Max and Adam could be sparring one moment and best friends the next. This was what family was about, though, and she wouldn't trade a moment like this for anything—not even for the peace of getting them to bed on time.

Jerry brushed up next to her. "Hey, slowpoke, I thought you'd be halfway through Max's story time by now."

"Shhhh!" she whispered, putting a finger to his lips and batting his hand away as he reached for the knob. "Listen to them. Let's give them a few more minutes."

"And what are we going to do in the meantime?" he asked, raising his eyebrows.

"Is your mind always in the gutter?"

"No, it's just that you look so sexy."

"I look like a walking mess," she complained, pointing at the old sweatpants she had changed into before dinner.

"Like *my* walking mess," he corrected. "And besides, I know how easy those are to take off, almost like—oops—they could fall off on their own." He gave them a light tug. "Now that's sexy."

"Just cool your jets a little longer and we'll have the all clear, 'kay?"

"Oh, all right," he groused.

Suddenly the noise reached a discordant crescendo, changing the mood and peaking curiosity. They both grabbed the knob and opened the door, more like a SWAT team at a flophouse than a mom and dad into their kids' room. Inside there was a tangled mess of blocks and cars spread across the rug, and two young boys moving like Godzilla through Tokyo.

"I blame you," she said, poking Jerry in the ribs.

"Moi? What did I do?" he asked in shock.

"Everything," she sighed.

"I never showed them Godzilla!"

"Yeah, but you know it's got something to do with that darn Y chromosome you gave them."

-7 Weeks-

"Guys, this is the last stop and then we can go home. We have to get some groceries, but as long as we stick to the stuff that is actually on my list, we can do this quickly."

"Got it!" Adam said, always happy to serve.

It was one of those hot, sticky days—a harbinger of the summer to come and a fitting start for Memorial Day weekend. The air conditioning blasted through the vents, but the short drive time between each stop didn't allow for the car to cool down before they were getting out again. She really wished she hadn't pushed off the weekly errands until today. Normally she did them on Thursday mornings, but she had spent yesterday cleaning out the boys' closet in an attempt to get rid of some unneeded junk without their consent or knowledge. And this is how she repaid her kids for her subterfuge, dragging them around town in the insufferable heat to start off their four-day weekend with a bang.

"Max?" she prodded. "Max, did you hear me? We need to stick to the list."

"Yup," he called from the back seat, then turned to his brother and said, "I hope candy is on the list."

"And why would candy be on the list, Maxwell?" Lindsey asked.

"Because I want candy, and you said we can only get stuff on the list," he answered plainly.

"Good point," Adam agreed.

43

She parked the car and turned to eye the two imps in the backseat. "We'll see, boys...."

They got out of the car and went into the store, where they immediately started to fuss over who would push the cart.

"Not a good start, if you're hoping for candy," she warned. "Max, you start as pusher. Adam, you get it when we're getting full."

Both quickly fell in line, hoping to ensure their treasure at the other end of the store.

They went through the aisles with little incident—Max only knocked into one cardboard display and it didn't actually fall down. When a few items dropped onto the floor, he picked up the mess himself. Adam had no problems getting the things on their list, and even remembered a couple necessities that Lindsey had forgotten to write down. She made them switch jobs in frozen foods, and when they finally reached the checkout she rewarded them with their choice of candy.

Adam picked a Hershey bar and Max decided on Skittles.

"You will not eat those until we get in the car," she warned.

Adam allowed his candy bar to be bagged with the rest of the groceries, but Max wanted to hold his precious red package of Skittles.

As they walked out of the store, she glanced at her watch—1:17—it had only taken about an hour longer than usual to do all of her errands. She grabbed the side of the cart, pulling Adam up short, poised at the top of the ramp to the parking lot. She looked left and right; the path was clear. As they descended the ramp, she kept one steadying hand on the cart in case the weight of the milk and dog food proved too much for Adam to handle on the uneven surface. Her other arm was out to the side to guide Max to stay with her while they made their way across the main thoroughfare of the lot.

She heard tiny hail stones hitting the pavement in a rush, and it took a moment for her brain to understand the sound in the middle of this beautiful, sunny day. Then her eyes took in the bright rainbow colors bouncing on the asphalt. Even though she didn't consciously know what had happened, she heard herself yell, "Max!" as if from far away. Her cart hand gripped hard and stopped Adam at the bottom of the ramp. And then she felt Max's shoulder brush past her hand, which closed in a death grip on the air behind him.

A split second—

Max was chasing the little rainbow candies along the pavement. He caught the first of those treasures in his fists and stood up to chase the rest, and then his little body was up in the air. It was impossible to understand what was unfolding before her. She watched as his head hit the windshield of a dark green Honda Accord—glass suddenly turning into a web of cracks. She wanted to look away—if it had been anyone else, she would have looked away—but her eyes remained focused on Max, his small body rolling and sliding down the sloped hood of the car, and finally landing on the ground with a sickening thud.

That thud was followed by many more, as the only sound she could hear was her own heartbeat in her ears—that muscle, a relentless machine that was suddenly impervious to emotion because otherwise it would have already stopped by now.

She let go of the cart and grabbed Adam by the hand, dragging him with her toward Max. Unmanned, their cart rolled away across the lot and into a curbed island—food left forgotten to melt, spoil and wilt in the heat. Closing the few steps to where her son's body had finally come to rest seemed interminable, like running in a dream. She felt her stomach lurch and her throat begin to swell and ache as she approached.

Her eyes involuntarily took in the scene around her—an elderly woman, pushing her cart into the back end of an SUV—a mother, shielding her young daughter's view of the car and the little boy on the pavement—a man in uniform with a cell phone to his ear, running toward Max—a toddler, his hands over his eyes and his mouth open in a silent scream—teenagers huddled by the ATM machine, joking with each other, oblivious to anything outside themselves.

As she reached Max's side, she felt someone's hands touching her and she shook them off. Insistently, the hands grabbed for her again, tugging on her sleeve. It was Adam. She must have let go of him, and now he was trying to find a way to hold on.

His voice cut through the thumping sounds of her heart. "Is he okay? Is Max okay? Tell me he's okay," he pleaded softly.

Lindsey felt her insides turn to jelly.

She heard someone saying Oh my God over and over again and wanted the sound to stop, not realizing that she was the one making it. She was the one who couldn't stop.

She collapsed onto the warm asphalt, not feeling the hard, loose pebbles that insistently dug into her knees through the thin fabric of her pants. Max lay on his left side, and it struck her that in another place and time it would have looked like he was napping. She could see only mild abrasions on his exposed skin—cuts that could have just as easily happened as a result of a spill off his bike rather than a collision with a car.

Somewhere in the deep recesses of her brain she thought, *don't touch him… don't move him… you could hurt him worse.* That voice battled with her need to comfort him and hold him—mother him and make everything all better for him.

She put her head to his chest, wanting to hear his heart beating… to feel it moving. And that was when she heard the gasps of the people who had gathered around her. She looked at her son's face, hoping their shock was that Max had moved or responded in some way. What she saw instead was that her movements had shifted his body, and his head had turned to expose the left side that was caved in…. And she couldn't understand how his brain could still fit inside his skull. Then she noticed his eyes—glazed over and unseeing—and she knew…. What she saw before her was bad. It was very bad.

Max is already gone.

She looked up at the faces of strangers who had collected to share in the spectacle of her tragedy, as if imploring them to tell her that what she believed was actually wrong. She had been right there with him, and yet she hadn't been able to stop him—not from stepping into the path of the car and not from leaving her alone on this earth. She hadn't been able to say anything to him. She hadn't been able to comfort him.

She laid herself gently across his small form, wanting to feel the warmth of his body, to assure her of the life that had coursed through it just moments before. She wanted to hide him and protect him. She didn't want him to go from being an adorable, cherished boy to a horrific spectacle.

Lindsey noticed that her heart had quieted now that Max's no longer beat. There was silence beneath her and a barrage of sounds from above—background street noise, sirens, voices of people trying to make sense of what they had just seen, carts rattling on asphalt, the swoosh of the automatic doors to the store.

She could feel Adam's hand on her back, and she began to weep for both of her boys.

*****

"Hey, Shelley, what are you doing calling me? Where's Lucy?" he joked.

"There's been an accident," she said grimly.

He felt himself turn inside out. "Where is she, Shelley? What happened to Lindsey?"

"It's not Lindsey. It-It's Max."

"Where is he? Is Lindsey with him?" His concern quickly building toward panic.

"Jerry... he didn't make it," she sobbed.

"What the hell?" It just didn't make sense. He shook his head like he needed to jumpstart it into working. "What happened?"

"There was an accident at the grocery store. Max was hit by a car in the parking lot."

Again, he just couldn't compute what he was being told. They went to the grocery store all the time. How could this happen?

"Where is Lindsey? Where's Adam?"

"We're all here at NorthLite Hospital. I'm with them, Jerry."

"Why didn't she call me?" he demanded angrily.

"She didn't call me either. I just happened upon the scene after they cleared it."

"When?"

"About an hour ago. Listen, Jerry… she isn't doing well."

"What do you mean? Of course she isn't doing well."

"Really, I'm worried."

"Is Adam with her?"

"He won't leave her side. They're just clinging to each other," Shelley said, her voice raspy with emotion.

"Don't leave them. I'll be right there. I'm already walking out the door."

"Hurry."

He hung up the phone. He didn't have to be reminded to hurry. He could think of nothing else. He didn't lock his office, or grab his laptop, or tell anyone where he was going. He was oblivious to the office commotion around him. All he could see before him were imagined visions of what might have happened. His mind was desperately trying to piece together some version of events that would make sense, but of course nothing like this could possibly make any sense.

His body was on autopilot, maneuvering past offices and through hallways to the parking lot and his car. His heart was pumping too fast with adrenaline. His body was cold with dread. His fingers felt too stiff and awkward to manipulate the keys on the ring.

He sat in the car and fumbled for what seemed like an interminable amount of time until he was finally able to get the right key and fit it into the slot.

Everything seemed unreal. The steering wheel in his hands was a solid object, yet even it seemed like a tenuous hold on reality. As he drove, the sounds of street noise were muffled by the sound of anguish in his own mind. *How? How can Max be dead?*

*****

He had never liked going to the doctor. Waiting rooms were totally boring, and doctors always made you wait forever, even when you had an appointment. But this was the worst. He didn't know what they were waiting for. He didn't understand what was going on. He knew that Max was dead. He had known it as soon as he saw him lying on the ground. He knew it from all the whispering adults were doing around him. He knew it as sure as he knew that he could have stopped it.... But it had happened—he had let it happen. He couldn't take it back and nobody could make it better. Now he wondered if they would ever be able to leave this place.

He hated the smell. And he hated the old magazines everywhere that were written for even older people to read. He hated that his mom wasn't whispering jokes in his ear and challenging him to a thumb war like she usually did when they were stuck in a waiting room. She had taken him to every checkup he'd ever had, and every sick visit too. She had always been there to help keep his mind off of waiting and make the time go quicker. But this time she ignored him.

She hadn't even looked at him, let alone spoken to him, since they took Max away in the ambulance. He wondered if she knew....

*****

"Shelley, where are they?" Jerry asked, coming through the emergency room doors.

"They're both in the chapel. I thought Adam might like it in there." She stopped him with her hand before he could leave. "Jerry, it's like she's catatonic or something. There's no connection there. I just took her by the hand and walked them over, and she never said anything."

"And Adam?"

"He seems okay. He will look at you when you talk to him, but he won't say much—my God, Jerry, he saw it happen. He saw everything." Shelley stifled a cry.

Hearing her say those words made him feel ill. Adam's innocence and his little brother—*my son*—stolen away in a single moment, while he was pushing paper at his desk.

"Where is Max?" he asked. He didn't know what horror in his world to address first—where to go—who to see—who to talk to— what to do with the rest of his life, or even just the rest of this day or hour or minute.

"When they got him here, they put him on machines to preserve his body in case you were willing to consider organ donation—can you handle this, Jerry?"

"What?" he asked, not realizing that his gaze had left her face and was wandering the hall as if hoping to find answers there. "Tell me."

"By the time I got here, it was already done."

"What was done?"

"I guess Lindsey signed off on the donation. She agreed to let them do it."

"But you said—"

"I know what I said. Nothing seems to be getting through to her."

He chewed on the information coming at him. *Organ donation? How would she know what to do? How bad could she be if she had the presence of mind to agree to donation? I wouldn't be able to make that decision right now,* he thought. He didn't even know if he should be bothered by the fact that she *did* make that decision— without him. They had never discussed such a thing.... *About our own child?* It seemed morbid to even think about it. Max had been a living, playing six-year-old. *And now—what do you do when he's gone and you haven't even thought about it?* But it was done. She had made the decision. Just like they each had decided to put "donor" on their driver's license. *Maybe it was really that simple. But how could she answer that question when she couldn't, or wouldn't, even speak to her best friend?*

"Jerry?" Shelley asked, worry in her voice.

Snapping out of his thoughts, he asked, "So where is Max?"

"I don't know, Jerry. They won't tell me."

"Take me to Lindsey. I need to see her. I need to see the boys."

The hospital corridors seemed an impossible maze to his bewildered mind and broken heart. He felt a sense of foreboding that he would never find his way back out of here again. It was like he was being led to Hell, where he would spend every moment of eternity trying to rush to the aid and comfort of his family and never be able to reach them.

Shelley stopped at the intersection of yet another beige cinderblock hallway. As they turned the corner, Jerry could see Lindsey hunched over on a bench up ahead, underneath a dangling sign that read "Chapel." She looked like a lost waif—stringy hair hanging unrestrained and hiding her face. Adam was next to her, clinging to her arm as if trying to keep her in his world.

Adam turned his attention down the hall when he heard their footsteps. As recognition came over him, he slid off the bench and ran toward Jerry, throwing himself into his dad's welcoming arms and melting into the embrace with relief.

"Hey Sport, I got here as fast as I could." Tears streamed down his face.

He picked up his son and held fast to the hug, continuing down the hall toward his wife. In normal circumstances, Adam was too old to be carried around anymore. But right now even Jerry would have welcomed a stronger, more certain presence to hold and carry him along.

"Lin? Lindsey, I'm here," he said gently.

There was no response—not even a twitch to let him know she heard his voice.

Shelley stepped closer and spoke firmly. "Lindsey? How did you get out here?"

Again, there was no response from the hunched form before them.

Adam lifted his head off of Jerry's shoulder and looked from him to Shelley. "They made us leave the chapel because Mom was making too much noise."

"What do you mean, Sport?"

"She was moaning and stuff. It was dis-disruptive," Adam said carefully.

"Who moved you out?" he asked, concerned.

"Two big guys in blue hospital clothes. They kind of took Mom by the arms and steered her out of the room. She hasn't made a sound since. Dad... I'm scared." His whole body was shivering.

"It's going to be all right, Adam. Mom's going to be all right. We're all going to be all right," he soothed, hugging him closer while at the same time fear was squeezing his broken heart.

He put Adam down and sat on the bench next to Lindsey. "Honey, I'm here. Please, look at me. Say something," he prodded. He took her hands in his; they were smooth and soft, but so cold and stiff. It felt like death was with her.

How can she feel so lifeless?

He made a move to fold her into his arms, trying to hug her, but she was all awkward angles. Again, he got no response.

He looked up at Shelley, who was standing near the bench and holding Adam tight against her. "Has a doctor checked her out?" he asked.

"No one formally admitted her. She wasn't part of the accident, so I guess she would have had to admit herself. But when she first got here, she must have been functioning reasonably normally. Then somehow, she just shut down."

"I can't do this right now—I need to see Max," he said suddenly, panic edging into his voice.

Adam perked up and asked hopefully, "You mean he's here?"

Jerry's heart fell even further into despair. He reached for Adam's arm to pull him closer, fighting to find the right words. "Max is in heaven. His body is here, but he is with God now." His throat was quickly drying up and the words were choking him. Even as he said them, he couldn't help but wonder how God could let this be. It didn't make sense that He would want such a vibrant soul to leave the earth before he was done lighting up the lives of those around him. Jerry felt anger flicker like a fire inside him, but he knew that he couldn't let Adam see it. He had to give his son comfort even if he was having a hell of a time finding it himself.

"Can I see Max too?" Adam pleaded.

"Like I said, it isn't really Max."

"I know, Dad. I just—I just wanted to tell him something," he said, his voice falling off to practically nothing.

Jerry looked up at Shelley, questioningly, but she didn't have an answer ready either. He didn't want to traumatize his son anymore. Adam had seen something horrible today—something even adults would find impossible to cope with. He looked at Lindsey for a moment as if to punctuate his thoughts. He understood that his son was asking for the same closure that he was searching for himself— but viewing his brother's body?

"Look, let me go talk to the doctors. Why don't you stay here with Shelley and watch your mom for a few minutes? Okay?"

"Yeah, Dad. Maybe we can get Mom to talk to us," he said somberly.

"Good idea."

Jerry hugged his son once more, and then gave Shelley's arm a squeeze of gratitude as he went off down the hall in search of answers.

*****

It was so bright everywhere that it made her eyes hurt. Like glaring sun, the lights reflected off of the shiny institutional floors and glossy painted walls. She could feel Adam beside her, stroking her arm—being there. She was supposed to be that person for him, but it was easier to retreat into the darkness that was waiting for her deep in her mind.

She remembered being in the truck—someone telling her that Adam couldn't ride along—getting out—standing on the pavement just feet from where Max stopped—a yellow candy just inches from her foot—watching the doors close on his small form—wanting to throw herself on the back of the ambulance, even if it meant being dragged behind it to the hospital. It was only her thoughts of Adam that prevented her. He couldn't be left behind, alone.

And now she was here, where everything was an assault on her senses—the brightness and noise and constant movement and the smell of antiseptic that mingled with the odors of sickness and death. What happened in between was completely gone. She hadn't driven them, but who actually brought them here was not important enough to sear through the pain of what she had witnessed and the emptiness she already felt.

Before, she had answered questions, signed forms and made decisions—the clarity in her mind a stark contrast to the mangled emotions in her heart. Then the darkness closed in upon her, and she welcomed it.

54

*****

"Hello, I wondered if you could help me?" he asked the woman at the emergency room admittance desk, who looked like she had countless other things she would rather be doing than helping him. "I don't know if I am in the right place."

"Probably not," she said under her breath, but just loud enough for him to hear.

"Listen, my son was brought here. He was hit by a car... and... uh... my wife agreed to organ donation." Each word came harder than the last and the tears couldn't be stopped. "Where can I find him? And who can I talk to about—"

The woman's breath caught as he spoke. "I'm sorry. Please... let me find the admitting physician. He should be able to explain the status of your son's body." She shuffled quickly through some paperwork on the desk. "I spoke to your son's mother—"

"My wife."

"She provided the insurance information and filled out the form, but I need a signature in order to process it."

"Yes, of course." He took the form and looked it over. He didn't know what he was expecting—swirls and dashes and dots instead of letters that formed real words? But everything looked completely normal. Even the patient history was complete, as ridiculous as that history seemed considering no treatment was required. It certainly didn't look like it was filled out by a crazy person. He signed the bottom of the form and handed the clipboard back to her, stressing, "*She* filled out the form?"

"Yes."

"Did she speak to you?"

"Briefly."

He stared at her, willing her to continue.

"She asked where they were taking her son and what she would need to sign for organ donation, if they considered him a prime donor."

"Really?" he asked in disbelief.

"It takes a lot of strength to do what she did, sir. Donation is life giving and in the wake of a tragedy—"

He shook his head quickly. "That's not it. It's just that… she isn't responding to anything now. I can't get her to talk to me or look at me. I don't even know what happened to my son." He started to break down. He had been running on pure adrenaline up to this point; now he felt his knees buckle and his body slacken. He grasped the counter to steady himself. *God, don't let me faint right here.*

"Sir, I have seen a lot around here," she said, touching his hand gently. "We all handle things differently. People come in here weeping and sobbing, or absolutely silent, or steady and sure. We can admit your wife if you think she is a threat to herself or someone else, but ultimately this may just be her way to cope."

Jerry looked into the eyes of the woman behind the counter. They had softened since he first approached. She probably wasn't even thirty yet, but she had much more wisdom in this regard. Her words helped to steady him.

"Is there any way that I can see my son? Speak to a doctor? Find out what happened?"

"Certainly. I will call Dr. Badarri. If you would please just sit tight, I'll look into it."

"Thank you." He was resigned to the fact that he was on their time.

Taking a seat well away from the few other patrons in the waiting room, he finally allowed his mind to wander. He tried to remember the last words he had exchanged with Max. He wanted so badly to be able to reclaim that moment now, after having sloughed it off like it was any random moment in their lives. If he had only known it would be his last moment with his precious child, he would have made it something more—*no, I never would have left his side at all.*

He hadn't even seen Max today. An early meeting had him out of the house before the boys were up. His final words were, "'Night, Bud," when he tucked Max in last night after performing his usual round of jokes that always got a lot of giggles. And Max had challenged him to a video game. They were supposed to play tonight after dinner. It was all part of their normal nightly ritual, nothing had given him any pause or any feeling that it would be their last goodnight.

Jerry had always wondered about death. Could you feel it approaching? Could you feel it when it was close—something wrong or different in the air, ready to steal you or someone you love away? Obviously not. The life he loved—the routine he expected and lived for—was over. Suddenly, unexpectedly, without any warning... it was all over.

He bent his head down and wept for the man his son would never become and the experiences he would never have... for the hole he would leave in their family forever. Everything was unraveling in his heart, and he truly understood what it felt like to be broken.

"Sir? Excuse me, Mr. Strane?"

He looked up into the kindly face of a short older man with thick glasses, a hooked nose and a pale complexion. The white coat signified his profession, and his demeanor belied that he specialized in children. Not attractive by any stretch of the imagination, his features were peculiarly kind and giving. He felt a fragile sense of relief that his son's case had been given to this gentleman.

"Yes," Jerry responded, making a move to stand.

"No, please, stay where you are. I'm Dr. Badarri. I was called in to oversee the organ donation." He sat down in the chair attached at ninety degrees to the line of chairs Jerry was in. "Your son exhibited no signs of life at the scene," he began in a gentle monotone. "The

EMTs arrived on scene very quickly and began CPR. They were able to keep his organs functioning, so when he arrived at the hospital and was determined to be brain dead, he was put on machines to maintain his state. Your wife agreed to organ donation."

Jerry was silent, desperately trying to take it all in.

"The choice has to be made quickly, and I know it is hard. But because of that decision, there are children who will be getting a second chance today."

"I—I understand that. I'm—was there really no hope for my son?"

"No, I'm sorry. There was no brain activity. The damage was severe."

"How could this happen?" he asked, under his breath, imploring the unseen forces of the universe.

"Is there anything more—"

"Is the surgery done? Can I see him?"

*****

"Shelley?" he asked, lifting his head from the crook of her arm where he had been resting.

"What is it, little man?"

Adam noticed immediately that she asked in her usual cool way, as if nothing awful had happened. She hadn't used the tone of syrupy sweet concern that usually dripped from adult voices when they were worried about protecting young ears, and it made him feel stronger and more certain of himself.

"Max asked me to open his candy," he said, trying to match her cool tone the best he could.

"What do you mean?" she prompted lightly.

"He asked me to open the Skittles when we were leaving the store."

"Oh, Adam…"

"I said no. I said that Mom told us to wait until we got in the car. He just wanted to try one little piece, but I wouldn't help him."

"Oh, sweetie." She gathered him up in a hug.

"I didn't mean for him to do it himself. I would have helped him in the car…. I would have helped him." He sobbed softly against her chest.

"Adam, you didn't do anything wrong," she soothed, rocking him. "Nothing that happened today is your fault. It was an accident. Just a—an accident."

He pulled away, suddenly wizened to the unfairness of death. Horror-stricken grief perverted his young face. "But if I hadn't been so worried about following all the rules. If I had just opened the bag."

She held onto him, forcing him to look at her. "You didn't do this. Do you hear me?" she demanded.

He nodded. Tears were dripping down his cheeks and his nose was starting to run.

"Don't you *ever* forget. No matter how hard this gets. You didn't do this."

He threw his arms around her, hugging her tightly, wishing that he could believe that as strongly as she did.

*****

When he finally found his way back along the proper corridors to the chapel, he discovered Lindsey alone on the bench outside. Adam and Shelley were no longer there, probably off for a walk or to the cafeteria. He sat down next to her and touched her hands, lying lifeless in her lap. She had been in the same position when he left her.

"I saw Max," he said softly. "He looks so peaceful. It doesn't seem possible, Lin. What happened? How did this happen?" he asked; his grief grabbing hold and shaking him, making his voice tremble and the tears fall from his eyes.

He felt almost imperceptible movement beneath the cradle of his hands, and he lifted his head hoping to find her looking back at him. Instead, he found himself staring into haunted and faraway eyes.

My God, have I lost you too?

He heard footsteps approaching quickly. Then he felt Adam's arms around his neck, hugging him fiercely.

"We went to check out the vending machines and stretch our legs," Shelley said.

"They only had healthy food in the machines," Adam complained, remembering the candy bar he hadn't gotten a chance to eat. He wondered if it was still in their cart, melting in the sun with the rest of the groceries. His stomach felt queasy; maybe he didn't want another candy bar.

"Sorry, Sport." Jerry wiped at his face and tried to keep his voice light. He mouthed "thank you" to Shelley, certain that the distraction was good for Adam.

"Did you handle what you needed to do?" she asked.

"Yes. I talked to the doctor."

"And Lindsey?" She gestured toward his hands, which still covered hers.

He shook his head grimly. "Was there any difference while I was gone?"

"No."

"I'm going to give her a little time," he said, trying to shed some of the darkness from his tone. "I want to take her home. I'll keep an eye on her."

"But Jerry—"

"She'll be fine, Shelley. I just need to take her home." This place was giving him the creeps. Suddenly, he couldn't stand the thought of being here for another minute. Maybe Lindsey felt the same way, and unable to leave, she had just tuned her surroundings out.

"Do you need me to do anything? Can I help?" Shelley was almost pleading.

"I'll call you. I think that we just need some time. We need to let this...." His words drifted into oblivion, following him there. He didn't have the energy to hold himself together much longer, and he really wanted to make it at least as far as the car—preferably all the way home—before his body split open and his insides gushed out in a violent mess.

He didn't know if he needed to sign anything else or discuss the care of his son's body or handle any other matters that were of importance only in an earthly sense. He just wanted to make a break for it, without getting caught up in a net of administrative hospital issues. They had all of his contact information; anything they deemed important could be handled later, sometime in the future when there was more oxygen to breathe in this world.

Getting Lindsey up off the bench was easier than he had feared. She was highly suggestible in her current state, like someone deep in a hypnotist's trance—eyes wide open in a blank gaze of blindness. All he had to say was, "Lindsey, we have to go home now," and he felt her body shift next to him. He took her gently by the forearm and elbow, much like one would help guide an elderly person across the street. She stood easily and walked.

Shelley whispered to him, "Take her out the main entrance. I'll go back through emergency. We will handle everything later."

"Thank you," he said earnestly. He squeezed her hand to reassure her and himself that they would be okay.

"Jerry, talk to Adam. Help him understand. He needs to be reassured," she said quietly.

*****

As they walked through the automatic sliding doors, out into the warm sun and fresh air that didn't fit this day at all, Adam almost said it. *"Wait, where's Max?"* It was on the tip of his tongue before he realized what he was doing, and he bit down hard to stop the dreaded words from slipping out. Even the copper taste of blood was better than letting that question hang in the air between them.

He couldn't count the number of times they had gone somewhere and one of them had asked that question—at the store, movies, bowling alley, arcade, park or anywhere else they had ever gone together. Max was prone to wandering outside the family perimeter and known to do it quietly. They would be going about their business and suddenly, either he or one of his parents would stop and say, "Wait, where's Max?" Then they would all spread out and look for him.

The thought struck and hit Adam hard. He knew where Max was. He was lying somewhere in the building behind him; probably behind one of those little metal doors with the roll out tray that he had seen on TV. He swallowed those words, hating the bitterness they left in his mouth, the lump they created in his throat, the ache they caused in his chest and the queasiness in his stomach.

*****

Funerals were for old people… or sick people who had fought hard and welcomed the release of death. They were the aftermath of a life lived long and well. They were the inevitable end to a story that had run its course. *They aren't proper for the young.* Lindsey was indignant, like denying it would make this day—this event—go away.

When Jerry slipped out of bed, she clutched at the covers and tried to grasp hold of him before the day did. She wanted to bring him back against her so she could breathe again. As he fumbled around in the dim light of a tired morning, throwing on enough clothes to be able to walk through the house without giving her parents a heart attack, she peered through her puffy lids at him.

He was the picture of strength. Since the accident, he had been an almost constant presence for her, asking nothing in return. She hadn't even spoken to him. He had done what needed to be done to prepare for the funeral and notify people of Max's death. He had done all of it, and afterward, he still fed her life through his touch. He held her, sat with her and laid with her, whether she was silent or sobbing, as if he knew that he could do no more and refused to do any less.

As he reached for the doorknob, attempting to sneak out while she was still asleep, she wanted to cry out to stop him. She felt an ache welling within her, a certainty that when he walked out of this room and the day began, everything between them was going to change. She bolted upright, hoping to stop whatever was about to happen to them, hoping to catch him before he broke the seal on the morning.

"Jerry," she said, through a voice thick with sleep and sorrow, and tight with lack of use.

"Oh, I didn't mean to wake you," he whispered, a tinge of relief mixed with surprise in his voice. He turned back toward her.

"You didn't." She rubbed her eyes.

"I was going to make coffee for your parents so they aren't banging around downstairs, trying to find everything, when they get up." He leaned over the bed and kissed the top of her head, right where her hair was naturally parted—so she could feel the kiss, he always used to say.

"Thank you," she said, peering at him through eyes that had not fully adjusted to being open after so many hours at rest. She made a move to get up.

"You don't have to be up yet. We have a couple hours."

She didn't speak, just poured herself out of bed and shuffled to the bathroom.

*****

"Lindsey?" he called through the bathroom door. He could hear her rustling on the other side, but no response. He leaned his head against the wood and put his hand up flat against the paneled surface, as if he hoped to feed her what little strength he had through the partition between them.

There was the sound of something rattling around in the porcelain sink, and her choked voice, "Damn it!"

"Is everything okay?" His unease was growing; she had been in there for two hours. "Can I help?" he asked.

"No," she said, resigned, like she was beyond help... or hope.

"Are you sure?" Jerry asked, concern dripping from soggy words.

"I'll be there in a minute." She listened until she heard his retreating footsteps.

She had spent the first hour sitting in the bathtub, hugging her knees to her chest, terrified about what lay ahead for her today, next week, next month... for the rest of her life. She couldn't imagine how she was going to get through this day, paraded around as an object of people's pity. She didn't want pity. She didn't want to be on display for others to sympathize with. She wanted only one thing....

When she finally got up to start getting ready, she was totally inept—makeup brushes slipped out of her hands, the mascara wand poked her in the eye, clasps and buttons seemed impossible. It was like someone else was pulling the strings. Her fingers felt huge, and the earrings were so tiny. She hated the pretense of even putting on earrings. What the hell did they matter at this point, except to prove that she was capable enough and strong enough, in spite of her loss, to accessorize properly. Lindsey struggled to pick up the back of the earring that lay in a tiny puddle in the sink. It had been trapped by a water droplet left by the faucet, or perhaps by one of her teardrops—they looked the same. Fighting to slide it onto the post, she felt nausea sweeping through her again.

She had just enough time to seat the earring and spin around to throw her head over the toilet bowl. She quickly flushed her weakness away and grabbed a handful of toilet paper to dab at her mouth as she sat on the lid. Doubled over, she wondered how she was going to make it through the next several hours when she hadn't made it more than ten minutes in the last hour without throwing up again.

The past few days, she had only been able to bring herself to nibble at food here or there; the same queasy nausea had been coming and going in waves like the tide. It felt like her body was revolting from the truth, refusing to accept that Max was gone. She was physically ill and scared—scared to tell anyone—scared to be found out—scared that if she kept throwing up she would turn inside out. She had nothing left in her.

At the sink, she brushed her teeth and splashed water on her face. Then she dabbed her skin lightly with a tissue to avoid displacing her makeup. She looked in the mirror, ran her hands through her hair and adjusted her blouse. She was the appearance of the consummate woman in grief. The whites of her eyes looked reddened and sore. Her lids were darkened, bloated and puffy. Her cheeks were hollow. Her mouth disappeared on her face—lips covered in a nude shade of lipstick to hide her expression from the people who would come to gawk at the mother who lost her young son.

*****

It was hot, and he really wanted to be wearing shorts. He hated being forced to dress up. The shirt collar bothered his neck and the pants were too plain and perfect—no frayed edges or stains or extra pockets. This wasn't him. This was the Adam who made a showing on school picture day, when parents turned their kids into people they weren't, for a picture that was supposed to chronicle who they were. It was all so fake.

And now he was supposed to pretend for his brother's funeral. Pretend that he was a well-dressed, proper ten-year-old. Pretend that he wasn't afraid about what had happened to Max and what was happening in his family.

Everything was upside down. His mom never spoke; she just cried and sobbed, or slept for hours. His dad was around all day, every day, after spending the last ten years at a place called work doing stuff Adam couldn't picture or understand. Both sets of his grandparents were visiting at the same time, which never happened, although his dad's parents were staying in a hotel instead of staying at their house like they usually would. The things he thought he understood about the world were all in question now. There were things he expected to lose in life—games, homework, keys, teeth, hair (if he took after Grandpa). But then there were things that had felt so concrete and permanent—Mom and Dad and Max and Sadie. They were always going to be there. At least that was what he had believed.

He dreaded going to the funeral. He would be surrounded by adults he didn't know, who would try to be overly attentive and helpful. They'd look at him intensely, trying to read his mind. *They're worried about how I'm handling this, but just look at Mom…. She isn't handling this at all. They think that playing a game of Monopoly is going to keep my mind off of Max just because they want it to. It isn't that simple. If they can't escape their sadness, what makes them think they can help me escape mine? We're all human.*

*****

"Honey? Lindsey? We need to go now," Jerry said. He had been back and forth talking to the closed door for the better part of an hour. She had a habit of making him wait whenever they went out anywhere, but she had never shut him out like this before. He used to come into the bathroom, sit on the edge of the tub, and make snide comments at her reflection about her lack of progress. Today, he felt entirely defeated and useless. He could give her nothing but space and it killed him.

The door opened slowly.

Lindsey was a vision before him. She looked stunning in a way that went far beyond beauty. The woman who had gone into the bathroom had been stooped and weak, shouldering a burden of pain and loss that only he could come close to understanding because only he had shared the distinct pleasure of creating and raising the beautiful and vibrant child they were celebrating today. To see the transformation into the tall and wisely understated woman who stood before him.... In another life he would have joked about the miracle that must be in the makeup bottles and cases she collected. But this was now, and the joke was over.

He pulled her close as she tried to brush past him and felt her body stiffen at his embrace. He kissed her temple and noticed the cold of her skin against his touch. He whispered, "I love you," and heard the silence in return. A shiver ran through him.

He wanted to look back into the bathroom for Lindsey. Maybe she was huddled in the corner of the room. This woman was put together and beautiful, but she was not his wife. This was not the same person he had cradled in his arms all night long.

In a few interminable days, Lindsey had gone from a state resembling catatonia when he first found her in the hospital, to clinging to him—to Adam—to Sadie—as if they could keep her from flying away. And when there was no living being to cling to, she was holding tight to Max's favorite stuffed animal—Floofy, the floppy bunny. She had been a warm body, wet with tears, just a couple of hours ago. Now her face showed the aftermath of those tears, but her eyes were dry. *Can someone run out of tears?* Her body showed no vulnerability. She was a sharp bag of bones to touch. It wasn't that her physical body had changed; it was more that every bit of emotion or feeling was locked away, leaving behind only hardness.

He wanted his grieving, sniffling wife back.

-8 Weeks-

Adam had always thought that the police or fire department or ambulances were first on the scene in an emergency. That is what grown-ups taught you; dial 9-1-1 and they will come to your aid. But it was actually the phone company—the guy in uniform who came running to try to help his brother while everyone else stood around dumb or afraid, like he was.

Life had always seemed so easy—safe and secure—experiencing it from within the bounds of his family. His parents had built a world around them that kept out the things that didn't make sense. He had glimpsed what other lives could be, on TV and at school, but he had felt distanced from all of that. He was just an average ten-year-old kid with two parents, a little brother and a dog. That was who he was and who he thought he would always be.

Then, six days ago, everything changed. Six days ago, he saw the crash—the cracked windshield—the dead body. Six days ago, when Max died, he became someone else. He was thrust into a new life where nothing felt safe anymore. He saw dangers everywhere—things he had never thought about before. He had been crossing the street alone for a while, but now every street looked like a highway with speeding cars. And when he left water on the floor in the bathroom, he threw a towel over it so no one would slip and crack their head. And he couldn't sleep at night until he knew that Grandma had blown out the candle she put on the front windowsill in honor of Max. Now, the sound of sirens meant more than the chance to glimpse racing, flashing emergency vehicles, it meant that someone was hurt... or dead at the end of that race.

He had dreams that Max was alive and they were playing, and then suddenly he would be gone all over again. Sometimes he would hear the screech of tires, or sometimes the sound of a gun. Sometimes it was a gruesome and bloody end. Sometimes Max would just vaporize to nothing like he had never been there at all. Sometimes he would wander off while they played hide and seek, and Adam would look and look and never find him.... The only thing that was the same was the way he would wake up—sweaty and panting, with his heart racing. He didn't tell anyone about these dreams. He didn't want anyone to know. He didn't want to know if dreams like that meant he was going crazy.

*****

There was a distinct bustle within the walls of the house. The dishwasher was rumbling downstairs. The clothes washer was swishing. The dryer was tumbling, and zippers were knocking and pinging against the stainless steel interior. It was the sound of Saturday mornings growing up, when she and her brother had hidden out of sight as long as possible to avoid their chores. It was the background music of life in a home—any home, anywhere. But all of that noise couldn't actually make things normal again. It couldn't soothe her heartache. It couldn't bring Max back. It was just a charade, and Lindsey knew that her mother was at the center of it.

The clock by the bed glared at her in angry red—11:12. She had missed breakfast and had hardly eaten anything for dinner the night before, but she still wasn't hungry. In fact, she was a little nauseous at the thought of food.

Somewhere below, she could hear murmured sounds of conversation; probably Jerry and her father talking.

What day is it?

70

Everything ran together in a smeared ooze of time, thick with the weight of each passing moment. She didn't know how many days and nights had passed since she stood in line at the funeral. It was all a blur of motions, giving hugs and handshakes as she accepted people's sympathies, collecting their cards and reading their words, taking their offered casserole dishes and handwritten instructions. She had done it all with a brave and stolid front, all while she was falling apart on the inside. She knew that in their efforts to offer sympathy and help, these people were searching for comfort. They wanted to do something—anything—that would help them make sense of the world and the tragedy for their own peace of mind. But other people's grief was different from hers. They felt guilt that they were not going through this, as well as relief that they were not chosen for such an awful twist of fate. They didn't have to live each day and each moment with this reality. When they left the funeral, when they retreated to their families and homes, they left the horror behind them.

She had done what was expected of her for as long as she could take it. She no longer had the strength to deal with other people. She couldn't deal with their level of discomfort in her proximity. She had no more empathy left for their feelings, and she'd had enough sympathy and help to last a lifetime. It was exhausting. She just wanted to be left alone—sit in the same underwear for days at a time if she wanted, allow the dishes to pile up to the ceiling, disregard the trash and let it spill over the edges of the can. She didn't want another casserole coming to the door. She didn't want another bundt cake.

Burying Max had meant burying a part of herself, and she had come home with overwhelming grief that was magnified by the emptiness. Even in a house full of people, there was too much space inside these walls without Max's vibrant spirit. In an effort to shrink that emptiness, she had closed herself off in the bedroom, hoping that confining the physical space would confine her emotional space as well. And there she had stayed, shades drawn against the sunlight that came back each day in an attempt to prod her into living again.

She stubbornly refused to be moved, so occasionally someone would come to the door and push food at her—food she didn't want. Max had been part of her balanced diet. Her family fed her soul, and without him she was missing vital nutrients that she couldn't get from any food or fancy pill, or from anyone else. She felt ill, and she wondered if this type of deficiency could actually kill her.

*****

"Are you going to come downstairs?" Jerry asked, his disembodied head hovering next to the door.

"Why is my mother doing laundry and dishes?"

"Because someone has to, and it seems to make her feel good to keep busy."

"The noise—God, it's so frustrating. The house seems alive with it."

"Lindsey, they're leaving today. Give her a break. She's just trying to do something for us... for you," he said, resigned to his place in the middle.

She knew she sounded like a spoiled brat, but she felt like she could crawl out of her skin from over-stimulation of her senses. It was just too much commotion.

"So, are you?" he prodded.

"What?"

"Coming down?" He was aggravated that he had spent the last several days making sure that her parents felt welcome, and she couldn't even come down and spend the last few hours with them and say a proper goodbye.

She looked at him blankly, like he had spoken in a foreign language.

"I know you. You'll regret it, Lindsey."

"I can't," she finally answered, carefully averting her eyes.

He retreated quickly and shut the door. Resentment was building and seething beneath the calm, congenial surface he had carefully measured for the past days. *What is this 'I can't' shit? I can't do this either, but I'm here anyway. I am doing what needs to be done. I am holding myself and this house together. 'I can't' is no answer.*

Jerry wondered about the vows they had made to go through the thick and thin of life together. In this threadbare moment, when they should be turning to each other, she was withdrawing into a hard, dry grief. He wanted to hold her—would hold her forever—if that would help make everything all right. He wanted to feel their pain as one. But this woman who no longer cried for their lost son seemed so angry—at God, at the driver, at him, at the world... he didn't know.

The woman in his bed now only resembled Lindsey. Gone was the wife and mother who had to run everything in her family down to the last detail. This woman didn't care about anything—laundry, meals, dishes, dust. Lindsey used to busy herself at every spare moment and was downright unyielding when it came to the needs of the house. She was adamant about beds being made, floors being swept, and the boys showering each day.... Now she didn't even tuck Adam into bed anymore—that would require that she leave their bedroom. She hardly spoke except for clipped, perfunctory conversations that always drifted to nothing, like she lacked the will to continue. She didn't ask after Adam. She refused to answer the phone, even when Shelley called. And she had entirely ignored her parents during their stay.

The shift in the house was so swift and so violent. One day they were moving through their lives at a nice clip, enjoying the ride, and then suddenly the bottom had fallen out. Jerry felt the pressure of all of the things that had fallen upon him in the past week. He was scrambling for his footing, trying to keep them on track, and he had lost his partner in the world. Seeing her as she was now, he couldn't help but question his decision to take Lindsey home from the hospital without having her examined. Maybe she needed something more than time and space. It wasn't like she hadn't progressed from that point, but she wasn't actually better—only different. He worried that maybe she was moving in the wrong direction.

He wasn't qualified to judge her mental state. He had never been through something like this before. The last of his grandparents had passed when he was just an infant. No one close to him had ever died—*how does someone grieve for his child? What is the right way? Who is to say that there is a right way? Who am I to say whether Lindsey is normal or abnormal in the way she is handling this?* He wondered if maybe he was the one who was acting strangely. Was he callous and unfeeling to be able to take care of the necessary steps society required regarding death?

Even thrust into the unreal world of planning his own child's funeral, he hadn't crumbled. Not when he picked out a small coffin for his son's body, or while standing in the middle of a sunny cemetery picking a plot for his final resting place. Not when he purchased a stone plaque and chose the final words that could never begin to sum up what Max meant to all of them. There were so many choices he had been left to make alone because Lindsey ignored his requests for help. He understood her not being able to handle going to the funeral parlor; that had been hard for him to do as well. But her disregard for making decisions about their child's eternity—what would happen one day when she finally came to and realized that she hadn't been a part of any of it?

He wondered if they would visit his grave. Would they go each day? Each week? On special days—birthdays, Christmas? Would they go each year on May 27th? Would they eventually stop going? What would it say about the importance of Max's life if they did stop going? What if they moved away? The questions were endless, and he could not escape them or give them voice. The only other person who shared the same stake in this tragedy wasn't listening.

He wanted to shake her out of her grief and tell her he needed her. He wanted to tell her that what happened wasn't fair. That it hurt, but that they were in it together—all three of them. He was scared. It terrified him that he would never see Lindsey again; that she would wither away to nothing while she still had a job to do. There were people in her life who needed her love and attention. Adam couldn't go on for long without a mother. It wasn't fair for him to have to see what was happening to her on top of dealing with Max's death.

*****

"Is Mom coming down for linner?"

"What?" Jerry asked, wondering if he had misheard.

"Is she going to have linner with us?"

"Linner?"

"Grandma says that's what you call a meal that is not quite lunch but way too early for dinner," Adam said with a smirk.

"Oh, linner." Jerry winked at his mother-in-law and gave Adam a one-armed hug. "I didn't ask Mom about linner, Sport. I'll give her a little time and make sure to ring the linner bell when the meal is ready."

"I hope she does. She hasn't eaten with us in days. Mom always used to eat every meal with us. She used to cook every meal," he said, to no one in particular.

He was worried. The house was full of people; yet it was so quiet all the time. Even when he was just walking through the room, he felt like he was making too much noise. He had resorted to moving on tiptoe, trying not to draw attention to himself. And he watched TV with the volume turned way down because the sounds of the cartoons he liked seemed way too happy, slicing through the silence like a knife.

It seemed like no one was ever going to laugh again. So far, when anyone tried, tears would fill their eyes at the first sound and it would turn into a cry. The grown-ups around him were his only means of direction as to how he should be acting. *Maybe this is just how it is supposed to be forever. Maybe things will never be happy and safe again.*

He had stood outside his parents' room many times over the past days, hoping to feel his mom's presence. Once, he got brave enough to crack open the bedroom door. He saw her peering out of the dark room into the unbearable brightness of the hallway, squinting through him. It was like she had become a vampire. He worried that she had been injured by what happened to Max. An injury that couldn't be fixed by bandages and medicine.

*****

Lindsey knew that she should go downstairs, and at the very least say goodbye to her parents. She owed them that. They had come the moment they first heard, and they had been here for her and Jerry and Adam, asking nothing in return, even though their grief had to be as great. But knowing and doing were two different things, and going down there meant facing a house full of family, without Max.

She had already cried immeasurable tears for the life that should have been. Her heart had broken for the bleak future that was still yet to be lived. What was left was a growing bitterness… and guilt. Now that the bone-chilling shock of losing Max had thawed, she could see it all more clearly. This never had to happen. She could have stuck to her usual schedule, and they never would have been in that parking lot at all. The lives that were upended on that day never had to feel this pain. Everyone who mourned did so because of her choices.

Her grocery cycle was down to a science, running out of one staple or another just as she was bringing in reinforcements. Her schedule was so perfect that pushing the shopping off by a day required rationing. On Thursday night she had served smaller glasses of milk with dinner so she could conserve and stretch what was left through breakfast the next morning. Jerry joked about feeling like a giant, but nothing more was said; he trusted her implicitly to manage the household. He didn't know that there was no good reason why she chose to move her shopping off by a day. It wasn't bad weather or car trouble or illness. She just *had* to clean out a stupid closet— nothing time sensitive, or life or death; yet that is exactly what that decision turned out to be. It would forever define her family, and she would regret it for the rest of her life. It wasn't worth the price they all paid for it.

She wondered how Jerry could even look at her anymore. She certainly couldn't look him in the eye. She had put into motion the events that decimated their family, and now she would never be able to hold his glance without seeing her guilt mirrored in his eyes. And there was Adam, his childhood ripped away from his grasp.... She let it happen.

Get a hold of yourself. Do the right thing and go downstairs. Life is too fragile to let them leave without saying goodbye.

*****

"So, are you planning to file a suit?" his father-in-law asked.

"I don't really know. I hadn't thought that far into it at this point," Jerry said, baffled by the prospect. He had never needed a lawyer before except for closing on the house. He wouldn't even know where to begin, beyond the ridiculous ambulance chasers who advertised on daytime commercials.

"Well, you get yourself a good lawyer if you're going to do it. Don't cheap out. And don't get one of those charlatans from the TV," he added gruffly.

At his periphery, Jerry saw the hollowed, pale face that had appeared like an apparition. She moved quietly, almost like she must have glided downstairs on air. It wasn't until she spoke that he could be absolutely certain that she was there and not just a vision his mind had hoped to see.

"We're not filing anything," Lindsey said from the doorway to the kitchen, her voice forceful.

"There's my girl," Frank bellowed, in a show of overexcitement, ignoring her statement.

"We aren't filing suit," she said again, her eyes alighting quickly on each face in turn and darting away just as fast, as if afraid to convey the full weight of her challenge.

Jerry was momentarily stunned by his wife's unexpected appearance, if not by her chosen words, but he quickly redoubled his efforts to maintain a calm and neutral environment. He wanted to keep peace while in earshot of Adam, who was confused enough by everything that had been happening over the past week. He could also see the strained look on Marie's face as she recognized the potential for her daughter's comments to start what would be a distasteful disagreement.

"We haven't had time to discuss anything yet, Frank," he said, attempting to push the matter to the back burner so everyone could enjoy a nice meal together before his in-laws got on the road home again.

"The police aren't pressing charges," Lindsey said, as if she couldn't read the clues he had left behind to drop the conversation. "I don't want to go after someone for an accident that had no criminal element. It won't change anything."

"It's a civil suit," Frank interjected.

"We can discuss this later," Jerry said, getting up from his seat to guide Lindsey to her place at the table and hoping to use osmosis to tell her to let it go for now.

"It isn't right. You all know that it wouldn't be right. What if everyone tried to capitalize on every little mistake people made?" Her voice was beginning to tremble, not with weakness but raw emotion. "I won't do it—"

"Okay," Marie cut in. "Okay, Lindsey. Why don't we call Adam in and sit down to have a nice meal?" She raced Jerry to her daughter's side and led her to the table.

"Don't patronize me." She shrugged off her mother's hands. "I'm not a child. I'm not some hysterical freak. I just want to leave my son in peace, and this would just—it would just add to the mess. That man didn't mean to do this. I think he is suffering enough." She walked to the table and plopped herself down. "There is already enough suffering. So now we can drop it—for good."

There was stunned silence around the table, broken by the sound of Adam coming into the room.

"Is it linnertime yet?" he asked.

Jerry's unsettled shock at Lindsey's intense reaction was eclipsed by his wonder at the simple inflection of Adam's question. Those four little words, spoken in the gap between moments, conveyed something so perfectly normal that he felt a flicker of hope for the future.

*****

Lindsey had gone back upstairs immediately after her parents left, as if anxious to escape from him. When he came in the bedroom after tucking Adam in for the night, he found her sitting on the edge of the bed facing the wall. He wondered if she had been like that for the past several hours, or if she had been preparing to get back up.

"I'm glad you came down to have a meal with everyone," Jerry said, busying himself with unbuttoning his shirt.

He received nothing in return—not even the slightest movement.

Bristling with annoyance, he said, "Lindsey, we need to talk." He deliberately kept his tone severe but his volume low, so his voice wouldn't carry down the hall to Adam.

She still wouldn't respond.

"I'm serious, Lindsey. I was just talking to Adam…. He thinks that he caused Max's accident because he wouldn't help him open his candy—because he refused to break the rules. Can you imagine a ten-year-old taking on that burden? It's bad enough that he saw it happen, but to think he believed—" Jerry stopped speaking mid-sentence. He had been unable to coax a response with his words; he wondered if she would react to the abrupt silence.

Nothing.

"Lindsey!" he snapped, making her body jump but still not gaining view of her face. "What the hell is wrong with you?" he demanded, anger mingling with desperation. "Your son thinks he's to blame and you have nothing to say?"

He saw her shaking lightly, weeping without sound.

"What happened to all your bold convictions about what is right and wrong, morally and legally? You haven't spoken to me about anything—*anything*—for the past week, and then this afternoon you come waltzing in and put your foot down like you're running this house—this family. So, if you're in charge, what about Adam? How do you heal his grief? How do you banish his guilt? How do you pick up the pieces of this family and go forward? Is the answer written somewhere on that damn wall you're staring at?"

He was the one who was working to keep the engine of the house running until the heart started beating again, and he felt impotent. He could not get through to her.

"What happened that day, Lindsey? I've heard it from Adam. I've heard it from the police. I've read it in the papers—hell, I've seen it on TV and heard from fucking strangers on the street who witnessed it. But I haven't heard from you. You're my wife! Talk to me! God, please…. I need you." He stared at the slumped figure, willing her to turn around and face him—say something to him. "I'm trying to be patient," he said, leveling his voice. "I am trying with all my heart to hold on here and be understanding, but you better wake up to the harsh reality that we are all hurting. You're not special in your grief. We *all* feel it."

-9 Weeks-

Two hundred million seconds. Thirty-one million, five hundred and thirty-six thousand seconds for each year—birthdays, holidays, vacations, bedtime stories, trips to space, swimming lessons… every moment, big and small. But there is no equating life in numbers. Like the center of a Tootsie Pop, no one knows how long it takes to get to the center of grief. The hurt was deeply entangled in her soul. It was her darkest enemy and her truest friend, remaining by her side day and night.

Tomorrow it would be Friday again. It was coming right at her, like a truck barreling down the highway with no brakes. There was no way around a day or even a single minute. She would never escape another week without having to live through another Friday, and she wondered if every one of them would approach saddled with the ghost of tragedy. Just like she wondered if every time the clock slipped silently through 1:17pm—the moment Max stepped off the curb and out of her life—her heart would stop for a beat.

There were so many questions floating around in Lindsey's mind, but no one to ask because she knew that no one else could answer them. Would she ever feel her family was truly safe again? Would the month of May forever bring with it an awful sense of foreboding? Would Mondays always remind her of the funeral? Would the associations ever stop? Honda Accords? Grocery stores? Skittles candies? Would there come a point when her head would explode from trying to contain all of the threads of tragedy?

Then there was everyone else....

There were those who never skipped a beat at the news of a six-year-old boy who died in the parking lot of the local grocery store—strangers who were immune to the wrenching grief that consumed her and others who had lucked upon knowing that little boy during his short life. She stared in wonder at those people, talking on their cell phones and running their errands, oblivious to the horrors that could await them and their families around the bend. They didn't know pain. And not even two full weeks ago, she had been one of them—an object of envy for her naivety and good fortune.

Harder for her to accept, were those who were back living their lives again. People who had held Max, loved him, talked to him, played with him, known him... were moving beyond him. They had ceased wondering how to move on and commenced doing it.

Lindsey watched with a mixture of relief and sadness as Adam became a ten-year-old boy again. She knew that it was important that he heal, and quickly. If he didn't, he could lose his childhood to this. He ran the risk of growing up too fast, pulling away and getting into dangerous and destructive behaviors. She knew that she needed to provide a home he was comfortable living in, even if their home now made her own skin crawl.

And Jerry. He had gone back to work suddenly and unexpectedly. She knew it was more to get away from her and the dark cloud that followed her than it was to get back to his life. He just couldn't deal with her. He couldn't look at her in the same way. She had lost their child. Max died on her watch, and he would always question that. Most marriages didn't survive tragedy like this. Before, she would have thought that they could survive anything.

*****

In his prior life, he would have chosen to be home over anywhere else on earth, but what used to be a sanctuary was now like a prison to him. Anything was better than being at home with the oppressive silence and constant reminders of a life that was gone.

When he entered his office for the first time, everything felt cold and untouched. Time had stopped here. Nothing had been touched or moved since the moment he walked out in answer to the call that unraveled his existence. His laptop still waited in sleep mode. The time sensitive notes he had scribbled on Post-Its a lifetime ago had lost all purpose but still clung to the monitor, phone and paperwork. The travel mug he had searched the cupboards for this morning had been here the whole time, waiting on his desk— complete with the leftover sludge from an ancient brew inside.

Co-workers were stiff and awkward upon seeing him, but after condolences and brief words of sympathy, any lingering discomfort gave way to the necessity of work—reports that needed to be written, research that needed to be done and calls that needed to be made. Here, he was able to observe and take part in normal life. He was able to be useful and productive. He had a purpose.

When he told Adam that he was going back to work, his son had looked back at him with pleading eyes as if he were abandoning him. And he was. Being at home was squeezing the life out of both of them and it wasn't fair that Jerry had found an out. He hadn't even thought that maybe Adam would rather travel the halls of elementary school over withering away in the stony silence of their home. He couldn't let Adam flounder while he regained his own footing, so they both reentered the world today, while Lindsey remained in the vacuum of grief that threatened to suffocate her.

He wondered if their progress would have any effect on her. She had always been so busy, taking care of the needs of the house or caught up in her creative whims for the house. She had never wanted for something to keep her brain or hands occupied. She had been the faithful presence and the beating heart of the household; her constancy made everything seem like home. Part of him feared that once they were out of the house, she would have even less will or reason to try to move forward and find that part of herself again. He worried that Adam might come home from school to find his mother still in bed—seemingly dead.

*****

He walked through the halls under the watchful eyes of his fellow students and concerned teachers. Everyone looked at him and whispered about him, but they were careful not to speak to him.

Do they think I'm going to break down and cry?

He wouldn't cry. He swore to himself that he wouldn't do it. He didn't want them to have any more to talk about. He didn't want to prove them right.

Adam was already aware of the social pitfalls of a school career. He knew that if you were too fat or had ugly glasses, or if you wore the wrong clothes or had a generally geeky exterior, or if you weren't into sports and were into something like collecting stamps, you were going to be an outcast. He had learned this from countless TV shows, the bus behavior of his peers, and firsthand accounts in the cafeteria and on the playground. He knew it as plain as day—don't stick out and you can get by. But having a dead little brother didn't fit into the puzzle. There were no TV specials about how people would treat you and how you should cope; about how even adults would be sickeningly sweet to your face and then whisper about you behind your back. Or how kids might avoid you entirely out of—*fear?*

He was no longer Adam Strane—Kickball King and friend to all. He had become the dead kid's brother. That's what Jimmy Plevin named him. At least Jimmy wasn't pulling any punches. It didn't matter to him that Adam's family had just suffered a tragedy; he considered Adam fair game and treated him the same way he treated everyone else. While others were busy tiptoeing around him and being concerned and careful, Jimmy walked right up and said, "Look, it's the dead kid's brother. Tell me, what did his dead body

85

look like? Was it all bloody?" Adam didn't skip a beat and said, "Like a dead body, Asshole. Ain't you ever seen one before?" An altercation like that would have landed him in the office a couple weeks ago, but with grief came a certain amount of immunity.

Next time Jimmy or one of his friends wanted to have a go at him, he had something else up his sleeve. There was the fact that he had ridden in the back of a police car like a criminal. Sure, it was the ride to the hospital, since his mom had been too upset to drive, and there was nothing cool about it—it was terrifying—but it was still something other kids in elementary school would have a hard time competing with.

*****

Lindsey's eyes swam over the wavy lines of cursive on the paper—the same type of list that she had last held when she had two sons. This was the first of what would be infinite trips to the grocery store throughout the rest of her life, and she wondered if they would all start like this. She felt like she was on the edge of a panic attack.

Up to this point, they had lived on others' goodwill—meals made and packaged for them by people intent on holding their own discomfort of death at bay. The few additional things that had been needed, like milk and juice and bread, had been picked up by her mother and father while they were still in town. Now it was up to her to take over the task.

The roiling in her stomach began again. The faint nausea that had followed her around since the funeral had put her in the bathroom twice already. Her vision doubled, and she fought to control her insides from coming out. The cold sweat across her forehead and a sensation of pins and needles across her skin made her question her ability to go ahead with this trip. Closing her eyes, she steadied herself. She repeated the same mantra over and over in her head—*you can do this—you can do this—you can do this.*

She had limited the list to the most basic items, hoping that a shorter trip would be less overwhelming, even though it would also mean that she would have to go back all the sooner. Honestly, she didn't know if she would even have the strength to walk through the entire store, let alone get a full week's worth of groceries. She feared the very real possibility that she would end up crumpled in the fetal position in the middle of some random aisle, unable to go any farther. *It's just coffee and butter and eggs and milk and bread. That's it. You can do this.*

It was only nine o'clock, much earlier than she usually went to the grocery store. Today she wasn't running all of her errands, though. She was only making one stop and she wanted to believe that altering her schedule would ease the memories and lessen the blow, but she wasn't fooling anyone.

She hadn't driven since the day of the accident, and the task seemed surreal to her. It was almost like she was intoxicated, her mind floating in a dream of reality. Thankfully, the store was only two miles from the house. But as she approached the entrance, a jolt of fear struck through her heart. She knew there was no way she could turn into the parking lot and walk across the asphalt where her child had taken his last breath.

There were people who would leave memorials at crash sites, revisiting the scene of their worst tragedy, but she didn't ever want to go back. It was hard enough being surrounded at all times by the things Max had touched and treasured while he was here on earth—tick marks on the doorjamb where he had attempted to measure himself, the initials he had carved in the deck railing outside, his beloved toys in nooks and crannies around the house. To even think about re-exposing herself to the worst moment in her life—the one that ended his—was unbearable.

She steadied her hands on the wheel, continuing down the main road another six miles toward the next grocery store in town. It was inconvenient and totally unfamiliar—exactly what she needed. But she knew she wouldn't be able to escape the triggers that would be in every grocery store—shopping carts, cash registers… red bags of Skittles.

Stupid little bouncing candies. God, why hadn't I made him choose something else? A candy bar would have landed on the ground at his feet. But he wouldn't have wanted the candy bar. She knew that as well as she knew Adam would never choose anything but a chocolate bar. *If not the candy, then just a few seconds of time—earlier or later. A few precious moments would have made all the difference in the world.*

Again, she found herself twisting and turning her thoughts into knots, trying to figure out the puzzle of which the solution was a happy family of four. *Max would be at school right now, if only….* But all of the wishing and "what ifs" were not going to change what happened.

Stopped at a traffic light, she perused the other drivers and the people walking in and out of stores around her. Did they know that at any moment life could veer off course and suddenly everything that mattered before wouldn't matter at all anymore? Did other people who lost cherished ones live like she did? Did they question the cause and analyze other ways events could have played out differently? Did they go through the rest of their lives wondering why the world crashed down on them and left everyone around them standing—an awful tornado that only picked off one house in town, ripping it to shreds? Did other people wonder why they would never be lucky enough to hit the lottery, but when playing the same remote odds on tragedy they could come up losing big? She wanted to ask them… *Do you feel small in this world?*

*****

"Mom?" Adam asked cautiously, coming closer to where she sat staring out the kitchen window. She had met him at the door when he got home but retreated back to the table soon after, to an open magazine she probably wasn't reading and a cup of coffee that looked cold and untouched. He knew the look on her face by now, like she was there but really not there.

At least she had made an effort to talk to him at first, while he put his school stuff away. She asked him about his day, though he knew she didn't really want to know how it was so he stuck to one-word answers like "fine" and "okay." Eventually he bored her enough that she left him alone.

Actually, his day had totally sucked. He didn't like the strange looks everyone gave him and the overly nice teachers around every corner. He didn't like the way they treated him special, telling him he didn't have to participate in anything that made him uncomfortable. What he really wanted to do was launch a kickball right at the teacher's head during the game in gym class. He wanted to upend a kid's lunch tray as he walked by in the cafeteria to see if that, too, was "okay" considering his grief. What he wanted most of all was to go back to blending in with his small group of friends.

But he wasn't going to say these things to his parents. Mom was a zombie. And Dad just wanted so badly for him to be doing well and getting better, that he wanted to be that well-adjusted kid for him—at least on the outside. On the inside, he felt like he had been punched in the gut over and over by Billy "Rats" Watson, who had failed fifth grade twice already and was working on his third year.

"Mom?" he prodded, even quieter this time. He wondered if it was better to just leave her be and get in trouble later for not telling her where he was going. He turned to go, figuring he could slip out of the house unnoticed.

She brushed his arm with a cold hand, making him jump.

"Hey, what's up?" she asked groggily, like she had been sleeping with her eyes open.

"I—I just wanted to know if I could go outside and play over at Justin's house until dinner." He didn't even know if the other kids in the neighborhood would let him play, but at the very least he could go outside in the warm sun for a while, rather than being stuck in the house with the quiet darkness.

"Did you do your homework?"

"Yeah, at school."

"Is Justin's mom home?"

"Yes," he said, exasperated. He didn't actually know if Justin's mom was home. All he did know was that when he got off the bus there were a bunch of kids playing jailbreak outside his house. Justin was in sixth grade, and he was hoping that middle schoolers would be mature enough to handle the fact that he was the dead kid's brother.

"I guess that would be okay, but no crossing the street. None," she warned. "I'll be out in the garden. I can see you from there."

"Got it," he lied. He heard her all right, and he understood that she meant what she said, but he also knew that the other kids were going to be freely running across and around and up the street, and he wasn't going to look like a wussbag. It was ridiculous that his mom would try to take away his street-crossing privileges because of what happened to Max. Even though crossing the street scared him a little now, he was going to have to get over it and take a stand. So what if he got caught. It wasn't like anyone was really going to punish the dead kid's brother.

The phone rang, saving him from further questioning, and he slid out from under her automaton gaze.

Lindsey thought of simply ignoring the call, but a part of her worried that it could be important. Jerry was either at work or on his way home now and something might have happened. She checked the display on the phone—the window to the other side of the line. It was Shelley. She hadn't spoken to her since the funeral, and her throat closed up as she thought about all of the things she hadn't said and didn't know how to say to her. She retreated carefully, as if she feared that her friend could see her. Five rings. She listened for

Shelley's voice leaving a message. The ringing stopped and there was silence. She had hung up. Lindsey knew she was on the verge of losing her best friend in the world, but she just couldn't pick up the phone.

*****

"Mmmmm-mmm, what smells so good in here?" Jerry called out, making a forced effort to be cheerful. Home was no longer a source for escaping the stress of the day, instead causing tension and a feeling of emotional claustrophobia. The relief that he felt having all three of them back in a semblance of their normal routines, even if in a limited capacity, was dampened by the interactions between him and Lindsey, which were perfunctory at best. The motions of daily life were being acted out, but there was nothing behind it all.

There was no response to his question, reigniting his frustrations with Lindsey's lack of effort to engage beyond the most basic conversation. At least he was trying each day to inject something more into his words, thinking maybe she would return the favor. He knocked around in the foyer, dropping his keys and wallet loudly into the bowl on the entry table and tossing his suit coat roughly on the coat rack, trying to communicate his building annoyance with sounds he hoped she could hear.

Sadie danced around at his feet, impatiently waiting for him to empty his hands and pet her. He squatted down close and scratched behind her ears, whispering, "How's she doing today, girl?" He wished that Sadie could answer him; act like a barometer of Lindsey's emotional state. He didn't know what to expect—sullen and unresponsive, or cold and civil. There were no other permutations of her personality these days. The mischievous nature, wry humor and sexual innuendo that had kept their relationship living and breathing all these years, were gone without a trace.

Jerry took a deep breath and went into the kitchen. "What's cooking?" This time he kept his voice monotone and his actions solemn, as dictated by the coldness in the house.

"Meatloaf," she answered in kind.

"It always smells so good. It's hard to imagine that it is just lowly meatloaf." He unexpectedly caught her eye from across the room and made his features spread into a soft smile in hope of spurring the same from her. It wasn't quite a smile, but he saw something. Maybe it was a tiny chink in the armor she wore.

Her eyes darted away as if afraid to hold his gaze.

"I'm glad your stomach likes budget food," she said.

"I love a bargain." He wanted to keep the conversation going, even if it was about ground beef. He could feel a tenuous connection that was just out of his reach.

*****

Lindsey dressed for bed quickly, trying to get under the covers and at least feign sleep before Jerry came into the room. Sometimes he would stay when he found her like that. They would spend the night avoiding each other in their bed that used to be small and cozy but had grown to the size of a canyon. Other times he would just turn around and leave, to the far reaches of the house, where he would fall asleep on the couch or slouched in a chair.

She thought of that split second their eyes connected in the kitchen earlier. Even that was enough for him to melt through her cold front, causing the tiniest give in her heart for half a beat. His gaze was searching, though—dangerous. If she wasn't careful he was going to see through to the truth of her raw insides where she harbored her shame and fear. He would see just how weak she was and know how easily he could destroy her. So she dodged his gaze, his touch, his conversation.

She deserved the awesome power of his grief unleashed upon her, but instead he handled her with kid gloves, making it easier for her to hide from what she knew he was really feeling. The only true emotion he had shared with her was that night after her parents left, when he confronted her in the bedroom. And he had been right. His words that night had mobilized her this far—gotten her out of bed. But then there were the words that still hung in the atmosphere between them, words they were unwilling to voice—the ones that put their son's life in her hands.

She wondered if the longer they went on like this—an emotional stalemate—the easier it would become. Maybe the heartache for love would subside, like the pain of grief was supposed to do, under the encouragement of time. But what about guilt and shame? Those didn't just dissipate; those festered.

Before this happened they had been each other's best friend. They had talked and laughed about everything. They had fought with passion. They had made love with passion. Now they went through the motions of a family, but they were no longer a couple united. What if eventually they would come to accept the space between them? Maybe she deserved that fate, but Jerry didn't.

-10 Weeks-

Usually, Lindsey woke with the intense weight of grief crushing her body against the bed. Her heart felt concave, deflated to half its size and pumping only the thinnest trickle of blood through her system to keep her alive. Her eyelids felt puffy and swollen like she had spent the night crying, even though she knew that she had dried up her store of tears weeks ago. It took everything she had to gather her courage about her and drop her leaden legs over the side of the bed, shuffle through the dark bedroom, and then on through the gray day that stretched before her.

And then there were other mornings, when she would awaken alert and bright with a nervous flutter inside that she couldn't pinpoint... and those days were even worse. She would go downstairs and begin the morning process, making lunches and setting out breakfast. The whole house would be alive with her motion. Then she would go upstairs to wake everyone and get sideswiped all over again by the awful truth of Max's death—his empty bed, his toys that had an air of abandonment about them.

When that happened, she had to overcome the sheer force of the blow and rush back down to remove the evidence of her confusion. She didn't know if there was something really wrong with her, or if it was simply an attempt by her subconscious to protect her, if even for a short while, from the constant energy drain of her grief. No matter what the reason, she did not want Jerry and Adam to see the lunch she had made for Max with loving care, packed in his camouflage lunchbox. Or the extra bowl, spoon and juice glass she had set out on the table.

Once Adam had come down early and asked why the table was set for two. She just stared at the table blankly, like his question didn't make sense, until reality crashed down. She had to turn her head away quickly so he wouldn't see the intense wave of grief that swept over her. Then she sat next to him and choked down that breakfast, past fresh grief, just to avoid explaining things to her young son that he could never possibly understand and would only make him worry. He was already worried enough.

This morning was different. The grief was there, but she was wide awake and couldn't lie still. She was unnerved. Last night she had gone to bed with a bad case of indigestion and no culprit to pin it on—no eggs or onions. Now, in the light of day, the pieces were starting to fit together. Her nausea over the last few weeks and indigestion from benign foods suddenly made sense.

Oh, God, please no....

In another life, her first step would have been to call Shelley and tell her to come over—quickly. But they hadn't spoken in weeks, and Lindsey wasn't even sure if Shelley would come anyway, for what was at best a worrisome hunch. She would have to do this alone.

She hurriedly went about making breakfast and packing Adam's lunch, and then busied herself folding laundry and ironing, all the while holding back a serious need to pee. It was agony getting them out the door to work and school. Jerry seemed to be in no hurry to get on his way. He even offered Adam a ride to school, which prolonged her torture since they didn't have to leave nearly as early as when he caught the bus. By the time they finally pulled out of the driveway her eyeballs were floating.

She ran upstairs and stood in front of the bathroom vanity with her legs crossed. *Please, please, please be in here*, she begged, as she furiously dug through the drawers. She struggled with the twisted mess of travel toothbrushes, hotel soaps and shampoos, and an exploded container of floss—Max's impish grin flashed in her mind and made her snort a half-laugh through her nose. The spontaneous sound stopped her in her tracks for a moment, its notes so foreign. Then she saw the white foil package she was looking for, grabbed it, ripped into it and dropped herself on the toilet in one choreographed movement of hands and legs. Uncapping the stick, she held it in the stream, feeling both the comfort of release and the trepidation of her potential new reality.

I can't do this right now. I can't do this again.

She finished peeing, capped the stick and stared intently at the plastic handle. She had never before watched her destiny appear in the tiny window, fearing that it would jinx the result. This time she stared the stick down, willing the answer she hoped for. In defiance, the stick turned a deep angry red, where a blushing pink would have had many women jumping for joy. The speed it registered and the depth of color were alarming—*how far along am I?*

Lightheaded, she put her head between her knees to stabilize herself on the toilet. She felt ill and wondered if it was her raw panic or morning sickness. When the nausea subsided, she looked around the bathroom as if hoping to find answers there, or an escape hatch. But she couldn't hide from this. There was nowhere to go.

When she found out she was pregnant with Adam, Jerry had been right there. They were so happy—so totally taken that they feared it couldn't possibly be true. They forced themselves to temper their excitement until her doctor confirmed the diagnosis. Even though they hadn't planned to have a baby right then, their joy was unabated. When Max came along they had been trying, so when her test was positive, she hadn't even been able to contain herself until Jerry came home that night. She blurted it out over the phone. And now, here she was in stunned disbelief. The moment she saw the plus sign she felt the small insistent seed of the child within her, though she knew it was impossible to feel a pregnancy in its early stages.

There was no joy in her heart or excitement about her news. She had never felt so certain of her fate, and it filled her with dread.

She sat alone in the middle of the family room couch, frozen by the harsh injustice of the situation. This baby was something they had both hoped for and wanted only weeks ago. They had been trying and failing—aching for it—but then the world crumbled and they hadn't been with each other since. And she never wanted to try again. She couldn't do this again. But the baby that at one time they had so desperately desired was already inside her. *What am I going to do?*

Lindsey knew what she *should* do. She *should* tell Jerry, and she *should* go to the doctor and confirm the result. She *should* feel blessed.

*****

"Mom, guess what?" Adam asked with excitement.

"What?"

"Guess!" he demanded, unable to contain himself.

"You don't have any homework tonight."

"Actually, I don't… but it's better than that. Try again."

"Um… someone ate a slug at recess."

"Uh… no." He was caught off guard by the guess because it was an old-Mom kind of guess. "Last try."

"I'm all out."

"One more try?"

"I've got nothing."

"Only one more week of school and I'm officially a sixth grader!" Genuine excitement dripped from his words.

It had suddenly hit him that he was finishing elementary school and leaving behind the baby stuff that came with it. This school year would be over, and then there was summer vacation, and next year there would be new kids from other elementary schools all in the same middle school. Maybe by then he would no longer be the dead kid's brother. Maybe he could be Adam Strane again.

Lindsey smiled tightly at his excitement. It was good to hear joy in the house. It used to be the prevailing sound each afternoon when the boys came home from school. It sounded strange to her ears, but good just the same. And though she couldn't match his mood, she liked seeing Adam so unabashedly happy. He was proving to be pretty resilient to the pressures of grief that were overwhelming her. She was proud of his strength, which he must have gotten from somewhere else.

Looking at Adam, she could hardly believe her eyes. It was like she was seeing someone she hadn't seen in years. He was no longer a scrawny little boy. His body was bulking up and filling out, probably preparing to shoot up even taller. The T-shirt that was way too big for him early in the spring was just about perfect now. His face was maturing, and she could already see the young man he would become peeking through. He was growing up right in front of her, and if she didn't snap out of it she was going to miss it.

*****

"So, slug eating…. Is that what all the kids are doing these days?" Jerry asked, as he entered the den where Lindsey sat facing the door but looking intently at the computer screen.

Her cheeks colored to a healthy pink at the mention of her earlier conversation with Adam. "I was just joking around," she said dismissively.

He could see her eyes darting, and her finger madly clicking the mouse. He came around the desk toward her.

"What are you up to? Checking email? Shopping?" He kept his tone light, trying to goad her into conversation.

"Nothing." She made a move to get up from the chair.

"You don't have to leave. I won't bother you." He put his hand out benignly to settle her.

"No. I'm done. Have at it."

"I wasn't coming to use the computer," he said to her back as she rushed out of the room. "I was coming to talk to you," he grumbled under his breath. He had hoped that her mood with Adam today would mean a shift in her attitude toward him as well, but she reacted like a cornered animal.

*****

The small chintz loveseat she perched nervously on looked like something from Great Aunt Eva's living room. Soft classical music was being piped into the waiting room to create a calm and comfortable setting that was a stark contrast to other doctor practices. It was more like the lobby of a bed and breakfast, instead of a place you waited before succumbing to the ultimate violation of the female anatomy as condoned by doctors and health associations. Even though she had been here many times before, she still cringed at the thought of the exam that awaited her.

She had stalled through two long days before placing the call. It was an interminable amount of time spent avoiding—the truth of what was happening inside of her, the reality that she had to make an appointment… and Jerry. She didn't really want to see any of the doctors or nurses who had guided her through two pregnancies and deliveries before, not with what she was considering doing. But there was a defiant part of her that insisted she go through the proper motions before making a drastic decision that would upend everything she believed in. And there was still a slight chance that she wasn't pregnant, that there was some other gynecological reason for the feelings in her body right now.

She jumped when the nurse called her name, as if she had been caught thinking unacceptable thoughts in a place where they specialized in the pursuit of life. She blanched, looking guiltily at the woman next to her on the couch. Her neighbor was demure, her eyes veiled to hide her reason for being here; maybe she was having trouble conceiving. Lindsey averted her eyes and stood up to follow the nurse, clutching her purse to her stomach as if hiding her truth.

Lindsey walked through the maze of rooms used by the various members of the practice and their patients. She provided a urine sample and closed herself in the examination room she was assigned to. No sooner had she disrobed and put on the paper gown, when there was a knock on the door.

Her heart sank when a nurse she recognized entered the room. Nurse Jane was probably in her late forties, a mother of three, and she had assisted at almost every OB visit Lindsey had ever had. She felt the guilt welling up inside as she realized that she was exposing herself and her unwanted pregnancy to people who knew her as a loving mother of two little boys—children they had helped bring into this world safely.

"Lindsey! How great to see you! Don't tell me you're pregnant again."

"Well… possibly," she mumbled.

"Took a test at home?" Nurse Jane asked knowingly.

"Yes." She carefully avoided her eyes.

"Well, you know they're pretty accurate."

"Yes."

"A woman of few words, huh? How are your boys doing?"

"Well, they're—" Lindsey started, taken aback by the question. She hadn't been prepared for it. Max's death had come to define her so much that she thought she wore it on her face and in the movements of her body. She thought it could be heard in the tone of her voice. It never occurred to her that she would run into people who didn't know—people who would ask about him. She felt tears burning in her eyes.

"Is everything okay?"

"I just didn't realize...."

"What? What's wrong?"

"Max passed away. An accident... three weeks ago...." Lindsey choked out.

"What? Oh my God, Lindsey. I'm so sorry. I didn't know.... I never would have—"

"It's okay. How could you have known? Really... it's okay." But she was trembling.

"Let me just get your blood pressure and ask you a few questions. Then I will send the doctor right in," the nurse said quickly, as if anxious to get out of the room where grief was sucking the oxygen out of the air and making it hard to breathe.

Lindsey was relieved when she was once again alone. She sat on the end of the examination table. It seemed docile in its condensed state, inclined to look like a large chair. Her eyes wandered aimlessly around the stark, pale lavender room. The same furnishings, supplies and equipment were in every room she had ever visited in this office. Through her years as a patient, she had been in at least five different ones, and each one was exactly identical. There was a set of cabinets with a counter and sink, a blood pressure cuff in a wire basket on the wall, an examination light on the end of a moveable arm... a chair with a metal frame and sparsely cushioned vinyl seat that Jerry should be sitting in right now. There was the plastic diagram of a baby in the womb that made her imagine the one inside her, growing and pulsating.

Maybe I'm not really pregnant at all. Maybe I have some kind of infection... or a tumor—now I'm hoping it's a tumor? What is wrong with me?

There were cotton balls and tongue depressors in glass jars on the counter, neither of which had ever been used by the staff on any of her previous visits, making her wonder just what their purpose was. Farther down the counter she saw a set of silicone breast examination boobs. Throughout her prior pregnancies, Jerry had accompanied her to every visit and claimed that they were left out for the fathers to play with, like the blocks and books in the corner of each room were there to occupy young children. The thought brought a small smile to the edges of her lips that never had a chance to fully materialize before there was a sharp knock on the door.

Dr. Wallen stepped into the room, flipping through her chart as he came. He was in his late forties and ruggedly attractive. Over the years he had only gotten more handsome, his hair going from black with a touch of gray, to more salt than pepper. His mustache and attached goatee had aged the same way. His deep brown eyes were clear and soft, perfect for someone in his line of work. He was the kind of doctor you looked forward to seeing, at the same time you dreaded just how much time he spent looking at your least attractive parts.

"So, I see that you are pregnant again, Mrs. Strane. That seems to be the only reason you ever come to visit me." He looked up from the folder and winked over his glasses.

Her results were exactly as expected. She focused on his mouth moving and tried to believe that he couldn't read her mind to know just how unwelcome this news was.

"Mrs. Strane?" he asked gently. He spoke again only when he was certain he had her attention. "I wanted to let you know that Nurse Jane told me about your loss. We are all deeply sorry. Under the circumstances, I think that we are best to take extra precautions with your pregnancy because of the stress and difficulties you might find yourself experiencing this time around."

Lindsey gave a brief nod when he stopped speaking. She hadn't consciously heard what he said, but she knew that he was waiting for a response.

"We are here for you," he stressed. "Whatever you need. We consider all of our patients—mothers and babies—members of our family. Please, do not hesitate to get in touch if you have any questions or concerns as you go forward."

Again, she nodded and Dr. Wallen continued, "Now, do you know the date of your last period? It's not—"

"What?" she interrupted.

"Your last period?"

"Oh, I don't really remember. I've never been very regular."

"Well, in order to get a more accurate due date, we really should do an ultrasound at this time. But first, why don't we check out the heartbeat?" There was sun in his voice.

Mothers are supposed to love this part....

As she lay back on the table, she heard the sound of the metal transforming into the ugly device of gynecological nightmares. Nurse Jane came back into the room as the doctor put a dollop of clear gel on her flat stomach and then pushed the small microphone into it. It didn't seem possible that there could be a heartbeat in there, but within moments she heard it.

Tears welled in her eyes and cascaded down her temples, trying to escape and hide in her hairline. The sound brought the truth crashing down on her. Anyone who saw them would have thought they were tears of relief and joy, not her true emotions of regret, guilt and sorrow.

-11 Weeks-

The oppressive humidity had settled in to stay for the summer, but from her bedroom window all Lindsey could see was the bright blue sky. For most people, a sky like that would signify a day of promise. Not a dark cloud in sight; yet she had an unshakeable feeling of trepidation inside. It looked too perfect out there, too much like that perfect day when her life ended.

A wave of nausea rushed over her, filling the void of unidentifiable worry with an immediate need to throw up. She ran to the bathroom on rubbery legs, wondering if this was her punishment for not wanting this pregnancy. She had never experienced morning sickness before, so something that clinically looked like normal early trimester symptoms seemed to her to be a form of judgment for the thoughts and emotions running rampantly through her.

The appointment was made. It surprised her just how easy it was, easier than finding a dentist on short notice. It seemed unreal that one could find a contract killer in the phone book. That was really what it amounted to; her target was a nameless, faceless, helpless victim. She felt like the worst kind of person, yet the casual voice on the other end of the phone accepted her choice like it was the decision to get a haircut on Thursday at 10:30am, condoning her behavior without question. So on June 30th it would be over, because she couldn't allow January 12th to be the beginning.

She watched herself in the mirror while she brushed her teeth roughly, trying to remove the bitterness of her shame. The woman looking back at her was pleading with her eyes, for understanding and for hope. *A reflection is just a sham of a person*, she reminded herself. She reached out and touched the impermeable glass, wondering how the fraud had come to live on this side of the mirror. She snatched her hand away as if she had gotten burned, backing away from the eyes that could see right through her.

*****

Jerry knocked lightly on his own bedroom door before opening it. When he entered, he checked his spirit at the threshold because there wasn't room for the two of them in there—the unspoken grief was too great.

"Hey, I just wanted to let you know that I'm leaving," he said, not thinking that Lindsey even cared but feeling obligated to say as much.

She was sitting on the bed, staring into her own lap in another emotionless pose.

"Adam left a while ago. I told him to make his own lunch, but he said we didn't have any bread left, so I gave him a few bucks to buy something."

Still no response.

"Are you going to be able to get to the store today?"

"There's bread in the freezer," she answered absently.

"You sure?"

"I put it there."

"I didn't think to check."

"I always freeze extra loaves."

"Oh, well, now I know," he said coldly. He felt the familiar frustration of having to fill in where she was falling down. They both had jobs to do in this family.

"Do you even live here?" she asked, peering up at him slowly.

"What?"

"I have been keeping bread in the freezer for... I don't know, *years*?" she challenged.

He looked at her, shocked.

What is that... defeat in her eyes? Is she defeated by my ineptitude? Like she is the only one who could do this right, even though she is the only one who couldn't seem to get up and do anything this morning.

He fought the urge to bite back with his opinion about her uselessness. A fight was not what he wanted from her; he just wanted answers. She had been going through the motions and doing what needed to be done, and now here she was hiding away again. If she was going to oscillate between entirely shut down and hardly getting by, this was going to be a very hard road.

"I'm going to leave now. Maybe you can find the time to get dressed while I'm gone," he said, unable to quell the fire of his anger entirely.

"Jerry." Her voice was hesitant. "I'm sorry for being this weak. I'm sorry for not stopping this fr—I should have stopped it."

It was a glimmer of real emotion that came and went in a heartbeat. Before he could even open his mouth to coax more conversation, she got up and escaped into the bathroom.

*****

"Shelley, I have a problem." Her voice shook. They hadn't spoken since the day Max died. She had shut her friend out completely, and now she was afraid it was time for the return treatment.

"Lindsey? Wait... you're cutting out on me—is that really you?"

"Yes."

"I can hardly hear you, is everything all right?"

"No, not really."

"What happened?" Shelley's voice bordered on panic.

"It's not an emergency or anything...." She didn't have the strength to say anything more over the phone.

"Lindsey, are you still there? You're really breaking up," she said, mistaking the silence for phone issues.

"I'm here. Can you come over?"

"Of course. Whatever you need."

"Thank you, Shelley.... Thank you." All of the weeks of not speaking suddenly fell away. Her friend was still here for her in spite of everything and without the anger or hurt that she deserved to feel.

Lindsey sat in the living room, looking anxiously out the front window. She didn't even know where Shelley was when she called—around the corner, across town, across the state? Wringing her hands in her lap, her eyes darted back to the clock again. It had only been ten minutes, but it felt like an hour. She caught movement in the corner of her eye. A red car pulled in the driveway, slowly and carefully, and she immediately wondered what senseless asshole was coming to sell her something—religion or freshly butchered and flash-frozen meat—when she was in the middle of a crisis. It wasn't until she saw the blonde head emerging from the car door that she realized it was Shelley.

She rushed to the front door and threw it open. "I didn't recognize your car, or your driving for that matter. When did you get this?" Lindsey hardly recognized the voice coming out of her own mouth. Seeing her friend, she was immediately transported past her tragic existence, to their usual style of conversation. She didn't feel the stilted discomfort that she felt with everyone else.

"A few weeks ago. We traded in the Expedition for something a little less, well, big."

"And you got a Mustang? Just in time to start driving *slow*?"

"Yup. I figure it's all about the *appearance.* The car suits me better." Her eyes flashed with mischief. "Don't you think? Hot mama and all that?"

Lindsey stared at her in wonder. She would never understand how Shelley did it. She was full of enough life for five people. There was just something entirely enchanting about her.

"Ooh, Lin, I'm sorry. I just wasn't thinking. Somehow, every time I see you, I just revert back to high school giddiness."

"No, it's okay. I'd rather that than you looking at me like you're trying to assess whether you need to lock up all the kitchen knives to save me from myself."

"Do I?" she gasped in mock horror.

Lindsey felt a grin spread on her face. It felt tight and probably looked a bit pained, but it was there if only fleeting.

"Well, that's better than nothing," Shelley chortled, in response to the attempt at a smile. "We can build on that." She put her arm around Lindsey's waist and guided her back into the house.

"Thank you for coming so quickly." She leaned heavily into her friend's embrace, for physical and emotional support. "I wouldn't have blamed you if you decided to write me off."

"And why would I do that?"

"A lot of people would have written me off by now."

"Those people are just assholes. They're people who can't get beyond themselves enough to notice that it isn't *your* job in *your* grief to make *them* feel better by graciously accepting their need to help you. Screw 'em."

"You always know what to say."

"It's a curse, sista."

Lindsey went in the kitchen to get them each a soda and kill some time. She felt her palms starting to sweat as she thought about the real reason she had called her friend. This was not simply an overdue reunion but a favor. She took a deep breath to settle herself before walking back into the living room, where Shelley had already flopped on the couch like she owned the place.

"So really, a Mustang?" She settled on the couch next to her friend. She couldn't believe that Shelley had bought a car in the time since they had last spoken, while she had a hard time just taking a shower or doing a load of laundry.

"I was looking for a car a few months ago, remember?" She brushed the past away with her hand, like it was a gnat flying near her head. "Anyway, we decided that it was finally time to do it. We don't need anything that big anymore now that we don't have to bring car seats and baby stuff everywhere we go."

"Good for you," she said, although she felt her insides constrict at the mention of baby stuff.

"What is it? You just went from pink to green on me."

"Oh, Shelley," she cried softly. "It's so hard to do this."

"Do what?"

"This," she lamented, sweeping her arm at the house around them. "Anything and everything I used to do is so hard now. I just don't have it in me." It pained her to admit that the person she used to be was missing.

"Well, I didn't want to say anything, but really, the sub-floor look is so last year," Shelley said, motioning at the unfinished plywood underfoot.

"Thanks for your professional opinion." She smiled through tears—her facial muscles more comfortable with the motion this time.

"That's what friends are for. Especially friends with impeccable taste. I've never steered you wrong before—"

"Shelley, I'm pregnant," she blurted out, as if the words were so big and distasteful she could no longer contain them inside.

"What? Seriously?"

"Yes."

"Then you and Jerry have been out of touch because you've been...." Shelley arched her eyebrow knowingly.

"Actually, no. We haven't been—"

"What exactly are you telling me?" she interrupted.

"I'm saying that I am about three months along and Jerry doesn't know… and I don't want to tell him." Her voice got quieter with each word.

"What do you mean you don't want to tell him? He's going to notice."

"I want you to help me."

"Help you?" Shelley prodded, forcing Lindsey to say it.

"I need to get rid of this baby," she sobbed, gagging on the words.

"Lindsey, do you know what you're saying?"

She stared at her lifelong friend for a moment, hesitating on the precipice of the person she had been for their entire relationship and the woman she turned into the day she lost her child.

"Seriously, Lindsey, do you realize what you're talking about here?"

"I need an abortion, Shelley. I have an appointment. I just need you to help me."

Lindsey had always been the moral compass of their relationship—the good one who never cheated or lied or did anything wrong—but now fate had turned the tables.

"No, this isn't a simple abortion. This is deceit. This is betraying your husband. It's Jerry we're talking about here…. Jerry."

"I thought you of all people—"

"You don't want to go there," she cautioned.

"But I was there for you—"

"We were fifteen, Lindsey. *Fifteen!* And you said it was wrong back then."

"But I helped you anyway."

"Yes, you did. But *you* aren't all alone."

"Yes, I am!" she cried.

"No, you're not." Shelley grabbed her and hugged her, holding her tight.

"You don't understand," Lindsey whispered into her shoulder.

She pulled away and looked at her. "I don't get it, Lin. I don't get you at all. Jerry is your life. What you have—"

"What we have is dead. It died when Max died."

"What are you saying? I saw Jerry that day. He was worried about you. He loves you. He was there for you—for Adam. He was there for Max."

"We just coexist," she said through sobs. "If this had happened on Jerry's watch, I would have blamed him. I don't even know if I would have been able to look at him again let alone live with him. To think that he could feel that way about me, terrifies me. And the fact that he might not feel that way about me, angers me. I could have done something to stop this. I know that I could have stopped this from happening!"

"God, Lindsey, do you hear yourself? You haven't even given him a chance! You've done this to yourself, and to him."

"Didn't I just say that I'm to blame?"

"I'm not talking about Max. I'm talking about your relationship with Jerry. You shut him out before he could shut you out. He's not the enemy."

"... I never told you that we were trying to have another baby," Lindsey smiled slightly through her tears, picturing their life before.

"No, you didn't, and I would like to kick your ass about that," she said sternly.

"When it didn't happen, I didn't want to say anything. I didn't want the added pressure. And then, when Max—when he died, I was relieved that we never conceived. I've been afraid ever since that Jerry would still want to have another baby, so to avoid talking about it or risking it, we just stopped."

Shelley looked back at her dumbfounded.

"I know that sex is important, Shell. It was always important in our relationship. I miss him. I miss Jerry in every way.... I just can't."

"Can't what?"

"I can't have another baby. I can't raise another child. It hurts too much…. And I've already hurt Jerry so badly…. I can't tell him. You've got to help me."

"I can't. I won't do that to your marriage. I won't be a part of it," she said, shaking her head. "You can never come back from this decision, Lindsey." She looked at her for a moment, tears mingling in her lashes.

When Shelley walked out of the house, she knew that her friend was walking out of her life. There was no way to rally from this. She had tried to use her. This would be between them forever. If this could destroy their friendship, she could only imagine what it would do to her marriage.

*****

"Did you see Shelley today?" Jerry asked, undisguised hope in his voice that his wife was finally turning a corner. But what he saw on Lindsey's face told him differently.

"Why would you ask that?" she bristled defensively.

"Because I ran into Rob at the store and he mentioned that Shelley came over here today."

"Oh."

"What did you two girls talk about?"

"Nothing much."

"Nothing? Seriously? You usually have all kinds of shenanigans to talk about when you get together," he prodded, again trying to start a lighthearted conversation. "She's not thinking about getting a tattoo again, is she?"

"Nope. Nothing." She shrugged and turned back to the book she had been reading when he walked in the door.

Jerry watched her reading and turning pages, hoping the weight of his stare would turn her attention back to him. He was trying desperately to understand why he was being frozen out. He didn't know what else he could say or do to bring her back to him. It seemed like she was coming back to everyone *but* him. Jealousy coursed through his veins at the fact that he wasn't the one she was turning to. He needed her to need him. He wanted to be who they used to be together.

Six pages later, she still hadn't said a word or glanced in his direction. Wounded and disheartened, he turned to go.

Only then did she chance to breathe deeply again. Fear had gripped her as soon as he mentioned Shelley's name. Her friend would never vindictively share secrets. *But what if she told her husband?* Lindsey used to share *everything* with Jerry. It was only now that secrets were being kept that were pulling them apart.

Her son, her husband, her best friend—piece by piece the foundation she had built her life upon was crumbling. There probably wouldn't be a building left at all by January 12th; there would be nothing to bring a life into.

She looked around the living room at the unfinished walls. In another life, she had brushed splashes of five different shades of off-white onto each wall to see how the light reflected throughout the day. The sample cards that designated the colors hung below each swatch from long, wrinkled and smudged strips of scotch tape—Max's job. He had carefully pulled the tape off the roll and across the plastic teeth, making unwieldy lengths that he manipulated from one hand to the other until he finally stuck them to the wall, unintentionally immortalizing his fingerprints. She remembered how he asked why every color looked like each other, and how she tried to explain that in different light each one would show its true self. He had accepted the explanation, but really thought they should be painting the room blue instead—deep, dark blue like his favorite shirt with the fighter jet on the front.

In the past month she had spent hours staring at the paint samples, paying little attention to the colors. That tape meant that Max had been there. He had put his mark on this place. Painting over the walls he had touched felt like an attempt to bury him.... She didn't have any interest in finishing any of the projects she had started when Max was still alive and well and their family was whole. Projects halted—life halted. Even the almost complete dining room sat frozen in suspended animation, with naked molding on the walls begging for an elegant white finish. Somewhere there was a key to get it all started again, but she couldn't find it.

-12 Weeks-

"Shelley!" he called out, catching her on the way out of her house.

"Jerry?" she asked, confused.

"I need to talk to you."

"But I was just—"

"Seriously, Shelley. I just need a minute," he said grimly. He wasn't trying to sound hopeless, but at the same time he felt like she might be his last lifeline to his wife.

She stopped trying to get past him, but her body language showed that she was relenting against her better judgment. She looked like she wanted to be anywhere else.

What the hell does she know?

"I'm not trying to ambush you, but I don't know what else to do," he said honestly.

The color suddenly drained from her face, like she had just seen a horrible sight in front of her. Her mouth tightened like she was trying to hold back an explosion—*words, screams, vomit?* He didn't know how to read what he was seeing.

"You told me at the hospital that day—" He tried to clear his throat of the emotion that threatened to drown his words. "—you told me to talk to Adam. You said I needed to help him understand, but I wasn't really listening. I should have paid attention to what he was going through from the moment it happened. It wasn't until a week later—" He paused again, swallowed back the tears. "—he went a

115

week thinking, worrying, *believing* he caused the accident that killed his little brother."

She was shaking her head lightly, tears welling in her eyes to match those in his.

"You knew. You tried to warn me. Adam told me what you said to him. All I can say is thank you," he said earnestly. "You were there for him when I wasn't.... You were there for all of us."

"Jerry, it's not—"

"No." He held his hand out to stop her. "I have to say this, and at the same time I have to ask you if there is something I need to know—something I need to say or do for Lindsey. You were right about Adam. Now I need you to help me save my wife," he pleaded.

"She just needs time, Jerry." Her voice was shaky and hesitant. "She's shredded inside and it is going to take—"

"Time?" he demanded. "That's what I've been giving. I have given her time and the space to use it, and I don't know that any of it is going to bring her back. I thought that since she finally reached out to you, maybe she was starting to come around. I thought that maybe she would find her way back to me. But she seems even worse these days. I can't keep doing this."

The pain in Shelley's eyes was obvious, but he didn't know who she felt it for. For him? For Lindsey? He was afraid that he was going to be left in the dark forever.

"She loves you. There is no question of that." Her voice was clear and unfettered.

"There was a time when I never would have questioned that," Jerry said almost wistfully.

"Don't."

"Don't what?" he asked in frustration.

"She loves you," she said, more forcefully. "She will find her way back, Jerry. I just hope—"

"Mom?" The voice belonged to the blonde head that poked out the front door. It was Shelley's fifteen-year-old daughter.

The spell had been broken. He had been able to taste the moment, heavy with a clue to what was going on with Lindsey, and now it was over. He saw relief on Shelley's face—her daughter, a welcome distraction from the conversation she didn't want to have.

"Hold on, Lacey!" she called toward the house. "Listen, Jerry, I really do have to go. I need to pick up a dress from the dry cleaner that she just *has* to have for tonight." She rolled her eyes like a schoolgirl.

"Yeah, sure," he relented. Suddenly he was right back where he started.

*****

The silence was thick as usual at the dinner table. He dreaded sitting down every night and staring at his food to avoid eye contact just so he wouldn't have to see his parents' tortured faces. The runt had left an awesome hole in the family, and he wondered if he would ever get big enough to fill it. *Would it have been like this if I had died and Max was left alone with Mom and Dad?* He didn't want to be dead, but he didn't want to think that his life was going to continue like this.

Adam remembered the days when there was constant conversation at the dinner table—his parents talking swiftly and certainly about politics or current events, or prying information out of him and Max about their days at school. Meals would drag on simply because no one could eat too fast with the amount of talking. Now, he just wanted to shovel the food in his mouth as quickly as possible so he could leave the table.

He lifted his gaze from his half-finished plate of baked chicken, rice pilaf and mixed vegetables, wanting to mention how Max would have considered two-thirds of the meal inedible. He wanted to talk about his brother and remember him, not pretend that he never existed. But it seemed like his name was off-limits. Both of his parents had their eyes focused steadily on their own plates. He wanted to scream, but he wondered if the house could handle the strain, or if it would crumble on top of them from the unexpected sound. This was the beginning of a long summer—his summer vacation—and he was miserable. He had to do or say something if only out of self-preservation.

"I found a snake in the backyard today."

"Really?" Jerry asked quickly, thankful for the distraction from his own thoughts.

"Yeah, I don't know what kind it was. It got away before I could catch it."

"You remember what we talked about," he reminded Adam, referring to their discussions about which indigenous snakes were harmful.

"It wasn't anything dangerous. I just would have liked to catch it and find out exactly what it was."

"Well, maybe next time."

Adam noticed that his mom had remained silent, but she had at least raised her head to focus on him. It was a far cry from her usual reaction to slithering things, whining like a little girl, but it was a start.

Time to take the conversation to the next level.

"Are we going to take a trip to the beach this year?" Adam asked innocently. This was a loaded question, and he lacked the courage to follow it up with eye contact. He focused back on his plate and attempted to look very busy eating his vegetables.

Every sound outside of the fork and knife on his plate stopped short. He put his utensils down. *So this is total silence....* His life was lonely and quiet, but there had been a constant background noise of basic living—pages turning in a book, someone chewing, the coffee maker perking, a cough, the dog licking herself. He had stopped the world in that moment... at least his little world.

He heard his dad clear his throat, but he was afraid to look up. Instead, he quickly grabbed his fork and shoveled more vegetables in his mouth with the ones he had yet to swallow. He could hear his mom cough quietly around her own mouthful.

Jerry couldn't believe his ears. It wasn't that the question was unacceptable, but it was so unexpected. He had gotten used to Adam not asking for anything. He hadn't asked for so much as a drink of water in the last month. And then to whip this one out into the open—*what am I supposed to say? Damn us for taking trips to the beach each year, for attempting to make any memories. It hurts to remember.*

He heard the choked sound coming from his wife and glanced over at her as she grabbed her milk to wash down a mouthful of food, or an unvoiced response. She looked stricken enough that she was either going to freeze in that position or start babbling incoherently. He knew at that moment that she was not capable of fielding this question.

He thought guiltily about the money they had already put down as a deposit on the house they had rented last year. They had set up their vacation months ago, and he had been avoiding thinking about it. He hadn't even broached the subject with Lindsey, fearing anything that might shatter her fragile state. He was prepared to take the thousand dollar hit—a sixty percent deposit—and cancel the rental, but for some reason he hadn't done it yet.

"Adam, I don't think this year is good for us to take a big trip like that." The words felt harsh on his lips. He knew how much courage it had taken for his son to ask, and he just trounced all over his spirit.

"I was just wondering," Adam said, shoving some chicken in his mouth and refusing to look up.

It killed Jerry to watch his son take one hit after another. Big and small, this kid was covered with bruises by this point.

*****

Lindsey stared out into the yard beyond the kitchen window. Her hands were in the here and now, busily scrubbing pots and pans, but her mind and heart were elsewhere. In better days, she'd had a bird's eye view from this spot; Adam and Max together, playing on the swing set or kicking a soccer ball around. She used to love washing dishes. This window once offered the perfect view of the perfect life. But the yard was empty now, Adam disinterested in playing out there without his playmate around.

Sometimes she braved a look at Adam's face when he wasn't watching TV or hunched over his PSP or eating dinner or drawing, but when he was just staring off into space—oblivious to the fact that she was invading his private thoughts as they skimmed across the surface of his features. That was when she was at her best, unheeding of her own selfish interests. When she could see how much this thing called "getting on with life" was not about her. It was about a young boy who had lost as much as she had—perhaps even more, since innocence is so precious. She had proudly watched Adam thrive from infancy, reveled in every milestone and moment, and now she was turning a blind eye as he floundered. *What kind of mother have I become? I lost a child, ignored a child, and then made plans to kill a child....*

Her hand went instinctively to her stomach, where she felt the insistent presence inside her, growing. It had to be her imagination or her conscience, but it felt real, like a physical presence, straining and fighting her at every turn, rooting deeper and taking hold— *demanding to be.* But she was a coward—afraid to be a mother again and afraid not to.

Now she was slipping out of her first trimester, and every day was a day closer to the truth being exposed. She was disgusted with herself and the world at large. People waffled about what kind of eggs to eat for breakfast or what kind of shampoo to use or when to buy and sell stock. This was life and death; the answer should be simple. *If it were my life in the balance, there would be no question.*

But this baby doesn't know what it will do to me. A baby doesn't have to worry about... anything. It's all on me, to care for and protect a helpless person. I'm not qualified. She thought about all of the things that had haunted her the first two times. There were so many concerns about feedings and SIDs and vaccinations and tumbles downstairs and strangers and crossing the street; it all seemed so impossible, like her heart would give out. And now she knew that those concerns weren't unfounded. Bad things do happen. *Why do we put ourselves through the pain of loving someone so much that it destroys us?*

That was what she was thinking as she sat in the parking lot, not eight hours ago, mere steps from ending her fear of new parenthood—conquering it. Her mind saw freedom on the other side of the door into that building, but her heart beat loudly and insistently in her ears, drowning out the message.

She saw a few other cars in the lot and wondered if they were doctors or nurses or women who were braver than she was. Someone pulled in the lot and parked and got out and walked to the door. Less than a minute and that young woman, little more than a girl, was swallowed up whole by the building. She didn't hesitate. She didn't sit in her car juggling mangled emotions. She just did it.

So Lindsey went in. A grown woman, a wife and mother of two—almost three—soon to be one child—followed a perfect stranger into her chosen future. This is what her life had whittled down to, making choices based on magazine horoscopes and fortune cookies and the wisdom of a teenager. She went to the reception desk and was asked to fill out a form, asked if she had her own pen because they were out. *This is supposed to be a doctor's office, and they don't have any pens?*

Her hands trembled as she searched through her purse for something she could use to sign away her baby's life, like a nail file

121

to nip her own vein and use her own blood. She lied to herself, insisting she wasn't forsaking motherhood. She still had Adam to raise and love and release to the world at large. Wasn't that asking more than enough of her shattered heart?

Hopelessness reigned, and those thoughts and feelings scared her. She was alone but for the one person who mattered the most in the decision, who wasn't being allowed a say. Her hand closed on some crumpled and folded papers at the bottom of the bag, and she pulled out the slip for today's appointment and the ultrasound picture of the fragile peanut she held within her. She felt nausea skirting the edges. She had shoved her baby's picture into the bowels of her purse like an empty gum wrapper that had no purpose to her. She had become callous and unrecognizable. She was so angry about losing Max that she had come to question the value of any life. But if she put an end to the pain of the unknown tortures of raising another child, she would drown in the pain of the known... that she had thrown away a life—a piece of her and Jerry.

-14 Weeks-

Jerry passed by Home Depot and drove the few extra miles to Ed's Hardware. Lindsey was the one who shopped here, supporting her home improvement habit, while he had always been content to pick up odds and ends at the more convenient chain store. But today he found himself here, looking for light bulbs... *and my wife—have you seen her?*

At the checkout, Ed stood behind the counter. Jerry recognized him immediately from the descriptions Lindsey had made over the years, when he teased her about the affair she was having with her hardware guy.

"You ready?" he asked, motioning at the small packages of halogen bulbs Jerry held.

"What?" He looked down at his hands as if he didn't know what was in them. "Oh, yeah, I'm ready."

"Can't interest you in anything else?"

"Nah, just this stuff."

"And how would you like to pay for this?"

"I hate to charge such a small amount," he said, closing his wallet and patting the cargo pockets of his shorts in hopes of finding a few spare bucks.

"Ah, no problem," Ed said, waving him off.

Jerry handed over his credit card and ID.

"Whoa," Ed exclaimed, rubbing his forehead, "You're the infamous Jerry. Where is that rambunctious wife of yours?"

"I wish someone could tell me," he grumbled under his breath.

"I haven't seen her in… oh… two months or so. I was thinking of sending out a search party." Noticing the wince of discomfort on his face, Ed continued quickly, "Although you probably don't mind her staying away from here. Saves you money."

Jerry had been pretty certain that Lindsey hadn't come here since Max died, but a part of him—the part that drove him here—hoped to find that she had started making plans again. It was one of the pieces of her that he missed terribly, the mischievous wild spark in her eye that told him she was up to no good.

"Actually… we have… had a death in the family." He almost choked on the large lump in his throat.

"Oh no!"

"It—it was our youngest son… Max. He was killed in an accident."

"I had no idea." The old man looked stunned and embarrassed.

Oddly, Jerry was relieved to run into someone who didn't know what had happened. It was heartening to see that, to people who weren't privy to his family's pain, he looked like any average guy out shopping. He had begun to wonder whether there would ever come a point when he could function again without an obvious cloud of grief hanging over him, real or imagined.

"I never would have—"

"Don't… it's okay, really."

"I'm truly very sorry."

"Thank you."

During a brief moment of awkward silence, Ed looked him over as if he was sizing him up. "Your wife used to come in here every week; sometimes more than once."

"Believe me, I know." Jerry rolled his eyes with exaggerated annoyance.

"I miss her… energy."

"Yeah, well, that's one way to put it," he chuckled lightly.

"No, really, she always had such a zest for all things in the home improvement realm. She was like a burst of excitement and possibilities, always believing she could tackle anything.... And if not her, you could." Ed pointed at him with a craggy finger that looked like it had been broken at least once before.

"She had more faith in me than my skills demanded."

Ed swiped his hand in the air, pushing his comment away. "You know, I don't put a lot of stock in that ADD bullshit, but if it does exist, Lindsey has it in spades—at least when it comes to home projects."

"You're telling me," Jerry snickered. "She always had something new up her sleeve."

"I hope to see her again soon. Tell her my company stock is plummeting."

"I'll tell her," he said, thinking a fat lot of good it would do. "By the way, thanks, Ed. I needed that."

"Always like to give a little extra with every sale. You take care now."

*****

"Your mom sent you something." Jerry dropped a thick envelope on the counter in front of her as he passed through the kitchen and into the family room with the rest of the mail. His tone was devoid of all feeling, cold and impersonal, like he worked in the mailroom and she was one of the executives.

Lindsey looked at the envelope, the address penned in her mom's careful hand. She felt a twinge of guilt at how she had been deliberately avoiding talking to her, but her mother seemed to be all-knowing. It had been practically impossible to keep secrets from her, even as a teenager, when keeping secrets from parents was supposed to be like some kind of sport. Marie Toll was an optimist and a busybody, and she had strength that Lindsey couldn't even begin to quantify. Her mother would never question how to get on with her life. She would never consider ending a life. She could never begin to understand the dark place her daughter had found.

She opened the envelope and found a curt note enclosed with some pamphlets:

Dear Lindsey,

I came across some information that I thought you might find helpful for the summer.

Love, Mom

She stared at the pamphlets for a moment, uncomprehending. It was such a heavy-handed gesture. She felt like the butt of a cruel joke—an addict at her own intervention. She held the pamphlets tight in her fist and stomped into the family room.

"Have you been talking to my mother?" she demanded.

"What?" Jerry looked up from the electric bill, shocked by the unexpected blast.

"She sent me summer camp brochures in the mail. What the hell is this about? She knows we don't do summer camp."

He stared at her blankly.

"Well?" she prodded.

"I don't know what the hell you're talking about!" he hollered back, as if she were hard of hearing.

"I'm talking about the fact that my mom knows how I feel about sending my kids—" She stopped, realizing they only had one kid to talk about these days. The word was *kid*—my *kid*. "I have always said that summertime is—"

"Time for family," Jerry cut in, reciting the rest of the slogan she had coined in response to all kinds of requests of their summer over the years.

126

"So why is she trying—" But it wasn't Jerry; it was Adam who had talked to Grandma a few days before.

"What? What is it?" he asked, noticing the fight had suddenly gone out of her like the wind out of sails, leaving her languishing.

She looked closer at the brochures. They were for a grief camp, mixing summer activities and counseling. *Point made, Mom.* This was her mother's way. She would gently nudge you in a direction you didn't want to go, just to get her point across—you need to get your head out of your backside and start thinking straight. This was supposed to be Max's first real summer vacation after his first year of school, so Lindsey had been avoiding recognizing summer at all. She was denying Adam the summer he needed and deserved because Max wasn't here. She thought about the memories that a beach vacation would conjure up—*happy memories.* They all lived with memories of Max every single day in everything they did. There was no escaping him. Their life was full of Max, and it was a blessing and a curse that he was around every corner and in every room. *What is there to be afraid of then?*

When she turned to Jerry, her gaze was soft and apologetic. "We need to go to the beach like Adam asked. We have the house. I think we should use it."

*****

"Hey, Bud," he said, keeping his voice low. He could have spoken louder; he was among those who understood. As it was, his words carried only so far in the gentle breeze before they tumbled free and dissipated to nothing. "We are going to the beach this summer. Maybe we'll see dolphins like the ones you saw last year.... You know, Adam is going to miss having you there to build the moat around the sandcastle and catch the little fish to put in it.... We all miss you terribly."

He came every day at his lunch hour. Here, beneath the umbrella of a mature cherry tree with thick low branches reaching away from its center trunk—a climbing tree, Max would have called it—he could be closer to his grief and love than anywhere else. Just sitting here, he felt at peace. And when he talked to Max, he narrated his days, making small careful steps through his sorrow. He couldn't talk about Lindsey here, or the gulf between them now, but he could find what he sought personally with his son—something he couldn't find in the stifling atmosphere at home.

Jerry considered the rows upon rows of people around him; their stories imprinted on marble plaques—dates that told of a just and long life or one cut tragically short. He looked sadly at the fake flowers adorning some of his son's neighbors. In an effort at a show of beauty that wouldn't wither away, people had taken a shortcut past death and into the realm of never having lived at all. At least cut flowers represented a life that once was.

The first several times he came to sit with Max, he came with empty hands, beseeching some answer about how to move on. He didn't know what treasure to bring, even though it saddened him to see the bare grave. Then one day he stopped at a roadside nursery where a potted perennial caught his eye. Perched at the head of his son's grave, that pot full of tiny, clustered yellow flowers brought a smile to Jerry's face, if only fleeting. Now the cycle of life would continue above Max.

"I love you. I know I'm the only one who comes right now. They just aren't ready yet, Bud."

*****

"I got your message, Mom," Lindsey said.
"Oh really?" she asked conspiratorially.
"Loud and clear."
"Good."

"You know, the camp actually looks like a pretty great program, if it was local and a day session thing. But I could never send Adam away—not now."

"I know," Marie said simply.

"Thank you… and Mom?" she asked softly.

"What?"

"I just wanted to apologize for everything I have… and haven't been since—"

"Lindsey, you don't—"

"Yes, Mom, I do. I need to say something. I have been really awful to you." Her voice was shaking with emotion. "I've been rankled by your attempts to help. I've ignored your kindness. I've avoided your calls. I've been unfair to you in your grief."

"You do know that I never expected anything from you," her mother prodded seriously. "I was just trying to be there for you no matter how you needed me. I wanted nothing in return. Lindsey, I can't offer you much. I haven't been tested in this way. I haven't experienced the level of grief that you feel right now. It wouldn't be fair for me to judge, and I never dreamed of it. I just wanted to make sure that you kept breathing long enough, until it became involuntary again. I didn't want you to thank me or pat me on the back for my good deeds. I did what I did because that is how I handle things that upset me. I keep my hands busy. I keep my body moving. That is how I cope."

"I couldn't even think about getting out of bed."

"This is not about comparisons, Lindsey. I don't expect you to be me. You are your own person. You are a good person. You are a wife and mother. I consider you a success."

"But I—"

"You what?"

"I lost my son."

"It was an accident."

"But I was right there. I saw it happen." Her voice was practically a whisper.

"And you would have done anything humanly possible to stop it."

"I just feel so guilty. I feel like I should have known. I should have *felt* something. How can I be the vessel that held my child for nine months in this world and *not feel* when his life is about to be yanked away? People talk all the time about feelings—not getting on a plane because they had a feeling it would crash—"

"Oh, cut it out, Lindsey! How often do people do just that and the plane *doesn't* crash?"

"But—"

"And sometimes it does. Sometimes a lot of things happen. But life happens in split second moments. Who is to say how many different choices and actions have to line up to bring us triumph or tragedy? You can't make up an alternate universe where this didn't happen, Lindsey. It isn't healthy to live in the 'what if,' not when you have a son who is very alive and hurting. You can't keep your family from growing just because you don't want to face the future."

After she hung up the phone, her mother's words still rang in her ears, making her think about herself and Jerry and Adam. All of them had lost a most precious piece of their family. They were all hurt deeply, but that hurt and its triggers were different for each. Grieving in close quarters was difficult. She realized that she couldn't just shut herself away until the world made sense again. That wasn't working. She needed to scratch and claw and *find* sense again if there was to be any hope of holding her family together.

-15 Weeks-

Adam noticed only two place settings at the table. Immediately, memories of dinners with Max came to mind. Mom used to feed just the two of them when Dad was going to be late coming home from work, and then the adults would have a meal together later—something peculiar with mushrooms and wine sauces. Adam loved those early meals with his brother because Mom made them special, fun foods like cheese stuffed hot dogs in crescent rolls and macaroni and cheese out of a box. She would fill the compartments of divided plates with all their favorites, including their dessert, and let them eat in whatever order they wanted to. Max always ate his dessert first. Adam always saved dessert for last. After he gobbled down his own dessert, Max would pick at the rest of his food and stare longingly at Adam's. Once he asked the little freak why he ate his dessert first since he always ended up wishing he had waited, and he said, "If I don't eat dessert first, I might not have room after everything else." But tonight the table wasn't set for him and Max.

"Where's Dad?" Adam asked cautiously.

"He's working late tonight," she replied, as she poured the pot of steaming water and noodles into the colander in the sink.

He couldn't put his finger on the last time his dad had worked late. He'd been home at dinnertime every single night since—

"Hey, Adam, why don't you wash up and help me get the last of the dinner ready for the table. You can pour the milk."

"Okay," he mumbled uncertainly.

Meals had absolutely sucked since Max died, but being alone with Mom seemed even worse than the usual dinner of stony silence between his parents that made him afraid to breathe. His dad had been really sad for a long time now, but at least he still saw glimmers of his old dad in him. His mom was unrecognizable. She did all the same things for him that she had always done, at least when it came to the necessities, but she was different. He washed his hands, slowly, drawing it out to avoid the inevitable.

As he came back around the corner to the kitchen, he saw the divided dishes out on the island.

"Do you mind if I use this one?" Lindsey asked, pointing at Max's royal blue plate.

He shook his head, haltingly, in stunned disbelief.

"Good, because I haven't had a meal like this in a while, and I need this special plate to make it just right." She smiled at her son's surprised face.

Even this tradition was hard for her to follow through on, making her heart ache at the thought of trying to get through birthdays and holidays to come. Finding a way to celebrate special times without Max was going to bring a new level of difficulty on top of the numbing discomfort of simply knowing that normal daily life would no longer include his goofy humor and lopsided grin and perpetual bed head. And what about Max's birthday? *How do we celebrate his life, without recognizing the years?* It all seemed so daunting viewed from here. But this was just a single meal, and it was important for Adam.

She skirted around him where he stood, in the middle of the kitchen, uncertain and waiting for direction. Adam used to be so sure of himself, but it was like he didn't know how to be around her anymore, like he feared she might be seconds from flying off the handle or falling apart right in front of him.

God, I am so screwed up.

It was clear to her now, just how much she had disregarded Adam's feelings while focusing on her own. She needed to help him heal even if it meant that her own wounds stayed fresh a bit longer. What she had been doing to the two men left in her life wasn't fair to either of them. They didn't deserve the brunt of her guilt or her grief. She had to stop the collateral damage that she was inflicting on them while she was trying to punish herself.

She appreciated that Jerry had made every effort to be home each night to be with them, but his unexpected call this afternoon was a welcome opportunity. The silence at dinner was killing her, too, and the tension was thicker when Jerry was home because of all that had gone unsaid between them for so long.

"I put the glasses on the table already," she said, putting a smile in her voice as well as on her face.

"Okay." He walked to the refrigerator to get the milk.

"Bring me the milk when you're done, please."

He finished pouring the milk in the glasses, wondering at the change in his mom's tone. As he brought the jug back to the counter, he saw the blue box of macaroni and cheese. And he definitely smelled hot dogs.

"Can you mix this together while I get the hot dogs out of the oven?" she asked him, as she poured some milk in the pot on top of the noodles and butter and powdered cheese.

The swollen knot in his throat that was almost always with him these days, especially when he was home, started to shrink in size. His heart started to lighten.

She dished up a hot dog for each plate, some sweet corn with butter and salt, a huge helping of macaroni and a brownie for dessert.

"You're eating this?" he asked in shock.

"I love this stuff!"

"But I've never seen you eat stuff like this," Adam pointed out.

"That's because I like the other stuff too. And this was *your* special meal—you and Max."

He nodded his head solemnly as he thought of his brother. It struck him that this was the first time he had heard his mom say Max's name since the accident. And she was smiling; he could see tears in her eyes, but she was still smiling.

"You know, when your dad and I were younger, we used to live on stuff like this," she said, motioning to the meal in front of them.

"We should eat like this more often."

"You know what? We should. I used to do this for you boys when I wanted to make something really special for Dad and me. Since you've always been so good about eating whatever I feed you, I didn't realize just how much you like this type of thing. Max was always so picky that I *had* to feed him stuff like this just to get him to eat, remember?" Her voice cracked with emotion and her heart ached.

"I didn't mean to make you think about Max again. I know it makes you sad."

"Oh, no, honey, I like to think about Max even though it makes me sad. But what makes me sad right now is knowing that I haven't been thinking about you enough." She looked him straight in the eye so he knew she really saw him.

"I make you cry?"

"Knowing that I hurt your feelings and made you worry about talking to me makes me cry. Adam, I have been wrong for a while now... but I promise you can talk to me about anything you need. I'm here for you."

He was silent, mulling this over in his head. Then he finally spoke. "I miss Max."

"So do I."

"I miss playing with him and even fighting with him."

"I miss it too."

"Even though you used to get so mad when we didn't get along?"

"Of course."

He looked her over, as if assessing the truthfulness of her words. Satisfied, he turned his attention to his dinner.

"So, where do we start?" she asked.

"Well, Max would start with dessert—always."

"In honor of Max." She brandished her brownie in the air.

He touched his brownie to his mom's like they were clinking glasses in a toast. Then he took a big bite and swallowed it down with ease. Something was definitely missing, and it felt good.

*****

Beyond where she sat in the small circle of light thrown by the lamp next to the couch, the family room was steadily graying as night moved in. She held a book open in her lap, but she couldn't remember what she had last read or even if she was still on the right page. She felt herself drifting off and let it happen. Sleep was welcome wherever and whenever it chose to come, since in the dark of the night, sharing the same bed she had always shared with the same man she had always loved, she spent her time lying awake worrying. She worried that Jerry would want intimacy that she wasn't ready for; at the same time she wished he would cradle her in his arms and just hold onto her. But he never tried anymore. She worried about how she would ever live the rest of her life without Max in it. She worried about her ever-tightening clothes and what that meant—what she still had to do.

She was roused by the key in the lock and the squeak of the front door on its hinges, signifying that Jerry was home. Then she heard Sadie, scratching at the back door, furiously trying to get inside to her master and properly welcome him. Lindsey hesitated. She never used to question going to her husband to welcome him home, but these days she didn't know what he would read from that or even if he would respond to the gesture. She wondered if he stood on the front step each evening in a similar predicament, uncertain how to enter his own house. For all intents and purposes, they had reached a standoff; neither was willing to cross the invisible line between them.

She closed the book in her hands without marking her page. If she was ever going to really understand it, she was going to have to go back and read it from the start. She went to the back door and released the hound, then slowly followed Sadie into the kitchen just as Jerry was coming in from the foyer.

"Hey," she said softly, stretching.

"Did I wake you?"

"Not really. I just drifted off reading. What time is it?"

"It's about nine," he said, checking his watch.

Lindsey scratched her head, looking out the nearest window and wondering how that much time had passed her by.

"Are you okay?" he asked.

She couldn't help but see the look on his face, like he was trying to gauge her mood and mannerisms on some "crazy scale" to determine if she needed professional help.

"What? Oh, I'm fine. I guess I was a bit deeper asleep than I thought."

Jerry spared a glance at the kitchen stove and counters, clean of any signs of a meal.

"Adam and I ate early tonight," she said, as if in answer to his unasked question.

"Oh," he said awkwardly, wondering what that meant for him.

"I saved you a plate in the fridge if you're hungry," she added quickly.

"Thanks."

"Do you want me to heat it up?" She was trying to be helpful and light, putting herself out there carefully.

"I can do it."

"No, I'll get it. You relax—better yet, go up and see Adam."

"Is he in his room?"

"He said he wanted to draw for a while. I haven't seen him since," Lindsey said, already busying herself in the refrigerator.

Jerry stared at her backside as she jostled things around on the shelves. He could feel familiar stirrings inside. As basic and stilted as the conversation had been, it had been the most normal interchange they'd had in a while. Something was definitely different, starting with the fact that she had initiated it.

Upstairs, he found Adam in his room. It was the room he had shared with Max. They had been moved in together because of the renovations, and Jerry often wondered whether this living arrangement had made Max's death harder on Adam—confronted with the loss more personally and constantly because both his roommate and brother were gone. But Adam was proving his resilience. He was adjusting better than the adults.

He took a soft breath as he stood at the cracked door. He could hear Adam inside, lightly shuffling papers around, and he could just make out a halo of brown hair over the foot of the bead. The bed was bathed in the warmth of his reading light, while the room beyond was cast in a strange red glow from the thumbtack shaped lamp in the far corner.

"Hey, Sport," he said, grazing his knuckles lightly on the door to coax it open as he entered. He cautiously avoided looking toward the other side of the room where Max's bed lay vacant. He had wanted to remove it months ago but Adam refused.

He looked up from his drawing and smiled. "Hi, Dad."

God I love that face.

"Whatcha drawing?" Jerry asked, sitting on the edge of the bed.

"Stuff."

"What kind of stuff?"

"Dad, why do you call me Sport?" Adam asked suddenly.

He looked at him blankly for a moment, surprised by the question.

"Well… because when you were really little and fussy, I could sit you down with me to watch sports on TV, and you would always calm down." He smiled at the memory.

"Really?"

"Yeah, really."

"That's actually kinda cool."

"I always thought so."

"So why didn't you call Max, Dork?" Adam smirked.

"He was a dork, wasn't he? A loveable dork."

"See? Perfect name."

"But you know why I called him Bud?"

"Why?"

"Because from the moment we brought him home, he was your buddy. When he was fussy as a baby, all he had to do was look at you—watch you playing and doing all the big kid stuff you could do—and he calmed right down."

"Wow." Adam chewed on that for a moment. "I never knew that."

"Yup. That's pretty cool, too, huh?"

He went back to drawing, and Jerry observed his deep concentration. He couldn't see the paper, since Adam had his knees drawn up as a makeshift aisle, hiding his view.

"Well, Sport, I'm going to go back down—"

"Dad, why did God want to take Max away?" Adam asked, still focusing on the paper in front of him.

Jerry stopped for a moment and bent his head in defeat. This question had been eating at him for months now, and he still couldn't get his own head or heart all the way around it. He wondered if his faith just wasn't strong enough. When he raised his head, he saw Adam was looking at him, hoping for an answer that would make everything right again.

You don't know how much I wish I had that answer. What I would give to make this make sense for you—for all of us.

Jerry began haltingly. "I don't know that he wanted to take him away, Adam. Sometimes things just happen... and God is there for you when they do. He is there for Max in heaven, and He is here for us on earth. Whenever we need Him, He can guide us and help us."

"At the funeral people said that he was in a better place. But what better place than right here? This is where he belongs," Adam said, tears in his eyes.

"I like to think that we all go peacefully to God whenever that time comes, as long as we live our lives with respect and love for the gift life is. We need to enjoy each day and be thankful for our existence. And I think that Max definitely enjoyed his life. He loved being a part of this family. He loved you and Mom and me without any question—" His voice broke under the weight of emotion.

"So he did everything right?"

"By the book."

"But he's still gone."

"Yes."

"Don't you wonder why?"

"Yes," Jerry said truthfully, wishing he had a better answer.

"Thank you, Dad," Adam said, a brave smile on his face in spite of his tears. "I just wondered if I was missing something."

"No, you're not missing something. It hurts and it sucks. It's always going to suck. But we are going to be okay," he said, hugging his son tightly, ignoring the sounds of crumpling paper between them.

"Wait, don't crush this one," he yelped.

"What is it?"

"It's me as a superhero," he admitted, embarrassed.

"Cool! What powers do you have? Flying? Invisibility?"

Adam's voice went down several notches as he said, "I would bring people back to life. Not corpses from the grave, but people who have only been dead a short time—you know, so their bodies aren't all gross and decomposing like zombies."

*****

Lindsey stood outside of the room, listening to her husband trying to comfort their son, answering questions she was still having trouble answering for herself. Her heart softened as she heard them both putting the emotions she felt into words that made sense. She put her hand on her stomach, beginning to wonder if maybe it wasn't just about her strength. Maybe their family was strong enough. She felt the familiar sting of tears.

At the sound of creaking bedsprings, she quickly tiptoed down the hall and back down the stairs, avoiding the fourth one and its awful squeak. *That needs to be fixed*, she thought, as she almost tumbled the rest of the way down. Her hand flew protectively to her stomach. Once she steadied herself, she quickly descended the rest of the way. By the time she reached the kitchen, her heart was racing from two near misses. She went to the sink to make herself look busy.

"I've heard tell of hotdogs in the house," Jerry called out as he came into the room with Adam in tow.

"And who would have told you that?" she asked, wiping her eyes quickly with the paper towel she'd been drying her hands on. She didn't want to destroy the lighter mood with tears they would mistake for hopelessness and sorrow.

"I told him about our great dinner tonight," Adam said matter-of-factly.

"You did? That was a secret," she whispered.

"But I saw you putting a plate of leftovers in the refrigerator."

"Maybe I was saving them for a midnight snack."

"Yeah, right. Besides, I smell them right now," he said, as he continued through the kitchen toward the family room and the TV.

"So, hotdogs and mac n' cheese. What's the special occasion?" Jerry asked, sidling up just close enough that she could smell his cologne, but a safe distance from invading her personal space.

"I just realized I hadn't made something like that in a while— too long actually. I thought that Adam would enjoy it."

"Well, you know I love a good hotdog, so I can't complain." He rubbed his belly.

They both stood in the kitchen uncertainly for a few more seconds until the welcome beeping of the microwave saved them from each other.

"Here, I'll get it." He made a move for the door.

"No, relax. Go into the family room and grab a TV tray. I'll get this," she said, waving the potholders in her hands.

"I'm not going to put up a fight if you want to wait on me."

"Enjoy it while it lasts," she snickered.

He put his hands up in surrender and went into the family room where she could hear him asking Adam what they should watch on TV, which was code for: let's find something other than the kid show you're watching right now.

As she approached with the plate of food, she gave him a soft, self-conscious smile. Jerry couldn't help but notice something different about her. There was a bright sparkle in her green eyes, and her skin glowed pink in the lamplight. Her chestnut hair shined and bounced in soft waves around her face, finally released from the ponytail she had worn for months. She looked stunning, wearing a simple pair of jeans and a plain T-shirt—her breasts pressing full against the fabric.

My God, she is irresistible.

As she leaned down to put his plate before him, her hair cascaded forward, sending a wave of vanilla scent into the air. Her hair and their relationship had been restrained for so long that he had forgotten this cue of their love. It was like he was suddenly home again, and he wanted to wrap himself in her fragrance.

"Oh, I forgot your milk." She turned to go.

He watched her retreat toward the kitchen, admiring the view and wishing he was the pair of jeans that was hugging and holding her curves. Shaking his head almost imperceptibly, he attempted to cool the fire that was building quickly. Something had definitely shifted inside him—inside this house.

It scared him to be too hopeful, but he wondered if they were finally coming out of this tragedy on the other side. He looked over where Adam sat on the other end of the couch, content watching TV, and prayed that he was right to even consider it.

"Hey, Dad, are you going to eat your dessert first?"

"What dessert?"

"The brownie," Adam said, as Lindsey reentered the room.

"Brownie?" he asked, looking questioningly at his wife.

"Oh! I forgot that too." She continued toward him and placed a glass of milk on his tray. "I didn't want to heat it in the microwave with everything else."

"So you weren't just trying to covet the brownies?"

"Why I never." She brought her hand to her chest in mock horror.

Oh, to be that hand.

"Well maybe not *never,* but at least not this time." She pushed her hair back behind her ear, betraying her embarrassment by fidgeting. Then she hurried back to the kitchen.

"So what's this about eating dessert first?" he asked, turning his attention back to Adam.

"Mom and I ate dessert first tonight in honor of Max," he said boldly.

Jerry blinked, looking toward the kitchen for corroboration. Lindsey was making a lot of noise just to get one little brownie. Yesterday, he never would have imagined it possible that his wife even mention Max in their presence, but today it seemed like anything was possible.

As she came back into the room, he caught her eye and she slowed her gait.

"What?" she asked self-consciously.

"I just heard about you eating dessert first tonight."

She looked over at Adam. "You weren't supposed to tell Dad."

"You never said," he piped up.

"Well, when in Rome," Jerry sighed, reaching for the brownie that was resting on a napkin in her hand. He held it up in the air for a moment, in a gesture of cheers toward heaven, and then took a huge bite, savoring the sweet and rich taste of love and comfort and hope—all the things that had been missing in their home for too long.

-16 Weeks-

The unobstructed sun peered down from the sky, bouncing off of the sand and making it almost seem to glow. She always forgot that part about the beach. She could see Adam off in the distance, playing Frisbee with Sadie, though that was definitely a loose term for what was going on. Sadie was hardly catching anything, just snapping at the oncoming Frisbee, missing it, and then frolicking in the surf where she undoubtedly noticed teeming little fish that provided playmates and a food source all in one.

When Jerry had brought up the idea to bring Sadie with them, Lindsey was grateful for the distraction. Usually, they would have left her at a kennel where she would have a miserable week with caregivers who didn't understand her persnickety ways. Instead, she was romping around on the beach, helping to keep Adam occupied, and generally lightening the atmosphere everywhere she went, like a little kid experiencing something new. She was a welcome change to the family dynamic that helped to ease the discomfort of missing Max. Nothing could entirely erase the obvious—they were at the same beach and in the same rental—but Sadie's sparkling personality helped.

Being here felt good, but preparing to go had been especially difficult. She was packing for the trip when it hit her that there was one less suitcase, which meant much less she had to do. Max was notoriously difficult when it came to packing. Left to his own devices, they would arrive at their destination to find he had a couple bathing suits, his favorite T-shirt, the clothes on his back and possibly an extra pair of socks in his pocket. His suitcase would instead be filled to bursting with small toys and books and every action figure he owned—his essentials. The task of packing up Max's things and limiting the toys he brought to a manageable amount of car storage space had always left her spun out, especially in addition to packing her own suitcase and boxing up the household and food stuffs they needed to bring. This time she found herself painfully prepared, with idle hands and too much time to spare to think about a long ride in a car that was too empty, and a week of family time without their whole family.

Now she was taking the week off—no guilt and no blame allowed. She wanted to wallow in good memories even if they made her sad. She wanted to drown in new happy moments. And she wanted to allow herself to truly understand what she held so deeply and safely within her. The baby was a constant presence to her now, not just an imagined seed inside. She would feel the sensation of butterflies in her stomach at unexpected moments and she knew that it was making itself known, asserting its right to be here. She had been vacillating for weeks between her better judgment, and the stark fear of reclaiming the responsibilities of parenthood with an infant, toddler, first grader. Time was constantly pushing her forward as if trying to out-pace her decision. Maybe she would find the answer here.

Lindsey leaned back in her chair and defiantly thrust her chin toward the powerful sun, challenging it to do its worst. The unrelenting heat was soothing to her, just like the stiff breeze and crashing water. The beach was so alive that she couldn't help but feel injected with life herself.

*****

145

She looked downright sexy sitting down by the water. Her skin already had a touch of color and a sheen that he imagined smelled like tropical coconut butter. Her hair was windblown and tousled in a way that could only be achieved by beach breeze and salt spray. The deep chestnut had already lightened with golden highlights after only a few days.

The desperation he had felt about his relationship with his wife was dissipating, replaced by fragile hope. After what they had experienced over the last couple months, he never would have believed it possible, but one day Lindsey came back to him. She was a softer and more tentative version of her old self, quiet and reserved in a way that made him feel like they were teenagers just beginning to date, but it was definitely her. They spoke lightly and carefully with each other, both cautious not to go into the choppy waters of their recent history, which was too raw. But civil words had turned into light, friendly banter, and they were getting to know each other all over again.

He could see her curling her toes in the sand. Her arms were now white side up on the armrests of the chair. A gauzy cover-up clung to her body over top of her bathing suit, leaving little to the imagination. He turned away quickly, feeling the stirring as his body and mind tried getting the better of him. They hadn't reached true intimacy yet, and he feared the risk of pushing too fast and scaring Lindsey back into the darkness she had just come from.

He turned his attention to Adam and Sadie, who were fast becoming small stick figures in the distance. The beach was dotted only occasionally with umbrellas and tents, giving them a broad range to play and roam, but he still wanted to keep them in identifiable sight. It was a big change from prior years, when he spent much of his time double-fisted with kids. He was the main beach patrol guy, taking the boys in the water, playing games, and catching crabs and fish. He had always kept them safe at the water's edge. Even up until last year, Max was still small enough that an errant wave could have knocked him down and dragged him out to sea, making vigilance necessary. Now, he felt the familiar sadness that always settled over him when he saw how his family was changing as they learned to live without Max. All of them had more freedom this summer. It was a change that would have happened with time anyway, as Max grew up—*why now? Why did it have to happen this way?*

*****

It had taken forever to get here—long enough that he wondered why he had ever brought up the trip in the first place. He hadn't realized how much of the drive time he usually spent either playing or fighting with Max. His iPod helped to pass the time, but not as well as playing the alphabet game or Punch Buggy, or having slap fights with his brother. And now there was no one else to complain about the trip with and take turns calling out, "Are we there yet?" to Mom and Dad every few minutes until they threatened to turn the car around. Sadie wasn't nearly the same type of car companion—she just sprawled out on the seat and slept almost the whole way.

But at least he had Sadie. Every year Adam begged to bring her along. He thought every member of the family should go on a *family* vacation, but his parents had never bought on to that reasoning. He knew why they decided to bring her this time. They were all afraid to go on vacation without Max. Bringing Sadie was like plugging in a nightlight when you were afraid of the dark. She wasn't better than just turning the lights on full blast, but she was a friend and playmate he could count on.

He watched her running into the waves and realized she was the most resilient of all of them. He wondered what she thought about Max's death—if she thought about it. Did she feel the change in the house now that he wasn't around? Did she even remember him? Did dogs grieve too? For a few days after Max died, Sadie had refused to

147

eat her dinner. *Maybe she was mourning.* And sometimes she looked downright mopy, lying around the house with such a pitiful look on her face that he imagined she must be missing him. He hated to think that Max didn't matter to her at all.

The beach stretched before them like it went on forever. At some point he just couldn't see it anymore, but it didn't mean it wasn't there. He wanted to keep walking and see if he was right— see just how far the beach went before it dropped into the ocean.

"Hey, Sport, what's up?" Jerry called, out of breath from his run to catch up.

"I was just trying to play Frisbee with Sadie, but she can't keep her mind on it," he said, rubbing his feet in the hot sand.

"She never was very good at catching or fetching. How about you and I play instead?"

"Sure!" Adam brightened.

"I'm just warning you, though; I'm pretty good at this. You better bring your A-game."

"Dad, it's *Frisbee.*" He shook the disk in his hand as a reminder.

"So, who says we can't have a competition?"

"Okay…. What are we playing for and how are we scoring it?"

"Keep it simple—each catch is a point. Loser—"

"Loser gives Sadie a shower." Adam pointed at the dog. She was busy rolling her wet body in the warm, dry sand. So far, the job had been his. He had to wash himself and Sadie in the outdoor shower each afternoon before they were allowed in the house. If Max had been here, it probably would have been all three of them in the shower at the same time—Max would have loved that.

"Ooh, that's a steep bet."

"If you don't have it in you—"

"No. I'm in."

They played to twenty-one. Adam quickly took the lead by purposely tossing off his mark so his dad had to dive for the Frisbee.

"Man, you slaughtered me! My old bones can't take that kind of abuse!"

"Anytime you want a rematch, I'm here," Adam said, cocky.

"Sure you are." Jerry grabbed him in a headlock and delivered noogies.

"Wait! Wait!" he protested. "I won! You should be the one getting the noogie treatment."

"I have to shower the dog. That's punishment enough for losing."

"Dad?" he asked, suddenly serious.

"What?"

"I'm glad we came."

"Me too."

Adam looked at him intently, as if he were sizing him up before sharing a secret. Then he dropped his eyes to his feet like he had decided to keep his mouth shut.

"How about—" Jerry started, attempting to fill the awkward silence.

"Some girl had a stupid necklace on the last day of school.... It broke, dropping these... little plastic multi-colored beads everywhere in the hall. She was crying and trying to pick them up as they scattered on the floor, and everyone was kicking them around on the way to their classrooms."

Jerry felt his blood run cold as he began to understand. He watched his son toe at a broken shell in the sand like he was hoping to find the courage to continue underneath it.

"It scared me. It was like I was back watching Max in the parking lot, picking up his candies.... I hate Skittles. I would throw up if I ever tried to eat one."

Jerry put his arm around Adam's shoulders, giving himself as something steady to hold onto in this world.

"He ran right around Mom," he said in disbelief. He looked up, eyes glistening with tears yet to fall. "She always held out her arm like a barricade that he was supposed to stay behind. But that stupid candy was so important.... Mom would have gotten him a new bag. I know she would have. Or I could have shared my candy bar. He could have had all of it.... I just want him back with us."

He felt every bit of Adam's anguish.

*****

They sat on the deck, staring out at the ocean—shades of night that glistened with moonlight. It was a powerful image; the sea never stopped moving. It didn't get tired or sad or overwhelmed, just like her heart kept functioning even when she felt like it couldn't possibly stand up to the pain anymore. Her heart was always present and always faithful, even when broken.

When the sun had gone down, the relentless beach wind had grown cold, prompting her to put on a sweatshirt. Now Lindsey wished she had pants on as well. The cup of coffee she held kept her hands warm, but the rest of her body couldn't escape the chill. She wanted to slide into Jerry's chair next to him and share his warmth, but she didn't want to upset the spell of calm between them. No words were being spoken and yet it felt right for the first time in a long time. The air seemed charged with something other than tension.

She turned her head to soak in the view of his strong profile. It was her great fortune to have him here with her. She knew that she had almost lost him to her grief and sadness, and the secret between them now threatened to destroy them all over again. She felt the quickening in her stomach again, agreeing with her. She wanted to put an end to the charade. She wanted to tell him about the child she had been hiding from him, like a smuggler hiding illegal drugs from the law. But to tell him would be to accept her fate, and while she was softening to the possibilities of regaining a future, part of her was holding back. The part that said another unexpected tragedy in her life might actually kill her. As soon as this child entered the world, she would be powerless all over again.

*****

"It's time, Sport," Jerry called out from the doorway as he came in the bedroom.

"What time is it?" Adam asked groggily, peering through sleepy eyelids.

"It's time to get up, sleepyhead."

"Aw, come on, it's summer vacation!"

"And before the heat of the day, we need to get up and at 'em."

"Seriously?"

"Totally."

Adam literally rolled out of bed and onto the floor, pulling on the clothes he had dropped there the night before when he slipped into bed.

"Don't let your mother know you're dressing like that," Jerry said, shaking his head. He remembered being that age; dirty clothes were just clothes as far as young boys were concerned. But Lindsey was definitely not on the same page. "It's your head if she finds out."

He shuffled out of the bedroom and directly into the bathroom, and Jerry followed.

"-o, --eally, ut's oin' o-?" he asked around the toothbrush in his mouth.

"If I tell you, I'd have to kill you."

Adam grunted and rolled his eyes.

*****

She watched Jerry come into the kitchen. The beach took years off of him. He looked so cool and laid back in cargo shorts and a loose camp shirt. His brown wavy hair framed a tan face that was punctuated with bright white teeth. Being here was good for him.

"So what's all the commotion? Why'd you wake Adam up? I would have stuck around here and let him sleep in."

"We aren't sticking around here—none of us. We have places to go."

Lindsey looked at him questioningly.

"It is high time we had some forced family fun."

"Oh no," she said, clutching the dishtowel in her hand against her in mock fear.

"Oh yes. It isn't a proper vacation if we don't have a family challenge. Loser buys ice cream."

"Can you float me a loan?"

"What? Already giving in to your fear?" he joked.

"I'm just hedging my bets since I don't know what this challenge is. If it's something like baiting hooks, I'm totally screwed."

"Hmmm, baiting hooks… that's an interesting idea."

"Don't, Jerry," she warned, laughing nervously.

"Okay, I'm here, 'sup?" Adam asked, tilting his head up at the end like he was some kind of street hood.

Jerry observed his son, amused.

"Your breakfast is on the table, Adam," she said, passing him in the kitchen doorway and planting a quick kiss on his head. "I have to change before we go."

"Where are we going?" he called after her.

"She doesn't know, Sport, so don't even try," Jerry said, ruffling his hair as he passed.

"Come on, Dad, I need to know so I can be properly annoyed or disgusted by the prospect."

"Practicing to be a teenager?"

"Maybe."

"Well, you don't need to start that quite yet, do you? Can we get through today first? I was planning a Strane family triathlon—three events and the cumulative totals decide the winner." He pointed at himself. "And the loser buys ice cream." He pointed down the hall toward the master bedroom.

"You're kidding, right?" Adam asked, trying to read the joke on his dad's face.

"What? You have a problem with that plan?"

"No. I just thought that we were done doing stuff like that," he said quietly, pouring milk on his cereal.

What the hell have we been thinking? The truth of Adam's words cut deep. He lost his brother, and then piece by piece they dismantled his family entirely, to the point where it had become unrecognizable. Every moment was studied control—an attempt to hold it together. *We sucked every last bit of carefree joy out of the atmosphere around us. We have forgotten to live!*

-17 Weeks-

He came into the room in a rush. "Damn it, I meant to get up a few minutes early. I have to stop for gas, and I have a meeting first thing." He went to the coffee maker and pulled a travel mug out of the cabinet above.

Lindsey immediately felt the tension that swept into the room with him. She got up from the table, wanting to help but not wanting to get in his way. Whatever had been there last night was missing this morning. Now she didn't know what to do…. Talk to him? Make his coffee? Hug him? So she did nothing but stand next to the island, helplessly watching him ignore her.

He brushed past her on the way to the refrigerator for creamer and again on his way back —contact more suited to strangers on a crowded train. He snapped the lid on the mug and turned to go, calling over his shoulder, "Could you put that back for me? I've really got to get out of here."

Her insides tightened with concern and sadness. She thought what had transpired between them last night—the glances, the heat, the gentle sparring—meant something. And when he got into bed, he had spooned around her in a comforting cocoon, waking every nerve in her body with his presence. Eventually, she had fallen to sleep with his breath soft against her neck. She felt the stirring of desire even now as she recalled it. It was the closest they had been in months. She had wanted to turn over and talk to him—to love him— but she stopped herself out of fear that he would reject her. There was no way to simply jump past all the unsaid. It had grown high like an emotional mountain between them.

Just going that far had stretched their emotional limit. Now this morning they had snapped back into baseline civility. She wondered if Jerry was really rushing toward something or if he was just trying to escape. The longer their emotions were denied the harder it was becoming to pull out of the mess she had made of their relationship. She missed how they used to act on impulse, not questioning every moment and wondering about every thought. They used to live as if they were one, possessing each other fully.

*****

"Son of a bitch!" Jerry yelled. "Shit that hurts." He moved as much as he could within the confines of his seatbelt, trying to pull the hot fabric of his pants away from his groin with one hand while navigating through the heinous knot of traffic with the other. A lap of hot coffee seemed a fitting wake-up call. "What the hell else is going to go wrong today?" he asked the dashboard, just waiting for the engine light to turn on in response.

Four hours of sleep—hard-fought hours he achieved only after nursing another awful case of blue balls that had practically become a permanent condition. This wasn't going to cut it. Last night had been the worst. Lindsey had been so close, her body up against him. He could have thrown something through the wall with all the pent-up sexual frustration coursing through his system.

Life isn't all about sex, he reasoned. *Although that is how life starts.*

Perhaps it wouldn't be so hard to deal with if they hadn't had such a healthy sex life in the first place. The fact that it had gone from total satisfaction to absolutely nothing made every aggravation in his life that much greater—running out of toothpaste, being late for work, losing his pen, spilling his coffee. The house was just too damn small. Lindsey was always nearby, yet out of his reach. Her breasts looked fuller and riper than he ever remembered, and the closest he had come to them was to graze against them "accidentally" when he was spooning her last night. Just the thought of her awakened desire all over again. He was like a teenager who was unable to quell the mechanisms of his body. He couldn't understand how she could just shut that part of herself down, or why she would want to.

Marriage had always been easy. Even their occasional fiery fights were more like blips on the radar, never challenging their union. He thought they truly knew each other, but the first big test of their relationship had annihilated them. When Max died, so did their dreams for their family, home and future. Even the slow progress and faint glimmers of Lindsey's healing heart weren't enough. The gears in their relationship weren't catching, so they weren't able to get anywhere together. It was as if she was afraid to find joy again, refusing herself anything good because—*why?* Did she think she didn't deserve it? Did she think that her life had to be over because Max's was over?

What he wouldn't give for the woman he knew mere months ago. He ached for her. He even missed Lindsey's wildest dreams of home improvement glory—the crowning achievement, a spread in *Better Homes & Gardens* magazine—which had overwhelmed him at times. Her exuberance had drawn him to her in the first place. She was utterly adorable and obsessively terrifying all at once. There were times he used to wish for a moment's peace from the ever-growing, eternal list of things she dreamed up to do. Now that he found himself in a place where his wish had come true—living in a house that was not being shifted or altered in color or design, with a wife who was totally complacent to her surroundings and entirely undemanding—he realized that it came at a huge cost. The true spark that was "Lindsey" had gone out.

*****

"You know, Adam's birthday is only a week away," Jerry said, by way of greeting. The words felt like acid on his tongue, and he saw them hit their mark as her face tightened in response. She had always taken great pride in planning and preparing for events in the household, so he knew it would hurt her to have him point out her shortcoming. He was hoping to incite her anger or frustration—ignite some passion. He was fed up with playing this game, trying to be nice and calm and careful, and not getting anywhere with her.

"Well, hello to you," she said icily, folding clothes out of the dryer. "I didn't hear you come in." She motioned at the washer that was loudly filling up with soapy water.

But Jerry was suspicious that she purposely found things to do to keep her occupied during the time that he was expected home, just to avoid having to interact with him on his terms.

"So what is the plan for his birthday?" he asked, purposely needling her.

She paused in mid-fold, staring at the wall for a moment before sliding her gaze to him. "Well, Jerry, I don't know…. What do you think we should do?"

"This is new. You're always the one with the plan."

"Honestly, I hadn't given it any thought," she responded, defeated. "I just—it's hard to think about celebrating."

"Lindsey, birthdays are going to happen. You can't hide your head in the sand and just hope they don't."

"Do you think I don't know that, Jerry?"

"I'm beginning to wonder," he grumbled under his breath.

"Now what the hell is that supposed to mean?" Her voice was suddenly strident.

"You've had your head in the sand so long now, it's like you don't even know you're upside down anymore!"

"I know that the calendar is changing. That events will happen. That I have to make peace with the fact that Max won't be here for them—"

"*We* have to," he corrected. "You seem to forget there is a *we* here—three of us—and all of us have to come to terms with this. Adam can't pay the price for his mother's inability to cope." He watched the tears come to her already sad eyes, and it made his heart ache.

Lindsey dropped the shirt she was folding. It fell effortlessly into the washer, quickly soaking up water and sinking below the surface. Blindsided. *Where is this coming from? Is he purposely trying to pick a fight?*

The lump in her throat seemed insurmountable, so she was surprised when she actually heard her own voice, "Maybe *you* don't feel *enough*, Jerry. Did you ever think that maybe this thing we had thrust upon us should hurt you more? Did you ever wonder why you could go back to work so easily, so soon after losing your son? Your *son*, Jerry!"

She was so angry, hating the fact that he was right about her, wanting to lash out at him and make him hurt too. She wanted him to feel as guilty as she did right now.

"How dare you! I can't believe you would ever—ever try to insinuate such an—" He stopped, trapping her under his smoldering glare. "Losing Max cut my heart out."

She had never seen hatred in his eyes before, and it scared her. She had gone too far and yet she hadn't wanted to stop herself. She squirmed under the weight of his eyes. It was the slightest movement, just enough to break his concentration, and he stormed out of the house.

*****

158

Adam sat on the stairs, listening, and when he heard his father's heavy footsteps coming into the foyer, he retreated quickly to his room. The front door slammed at the same time he closed his own door softly.

His parents' argument had rumbled through the vents to his bedroom. His ears weren't used to hearing raised voices in the house. Everything had been spoken in hushed tones for so long; he had begun to imagine that he lived in a library. He had gone to the stairs to get a better listen, and now he wished he had stayed in his room with a pillow over his head. He didn't want to be in the middle of whatever had just happened. He didn't really want to have a birthday party anyway. It wasn't like anybody was going to want to come. He had left his friends behind when school ended in June. None of them had paid him much mind after Max died anyway. *What does an 11th birthday matter?*

He looked around the bedroom, where he spent so much of his time now—escaping. His brother's side was perfectly preserved. He remembered how Max always left the sheets rumpled underneath the comforter when he made his bed. When Adam had come home after the funeral, he remade Max's bed carefully, straightening the sheets, so his little brother would rest in peace. He also cleaned up the toys because seeing them out, like any moment Max would be coming home to play with them, had been too much for Adam to take. But he had drawn the line when his father wanted to remove Max's things and pack them away or give them away. It seemed like he would be erasing his little brother from his life. Now he realized that they were just things. He was about to turn eleven, maybe it was time to take the little kid stuff out of his room. And what good was the bed Max had slept in? Nobody was ever going to sleep over at his house again, and certainly not in his dead brother's bed. Maybe it was time to grow up.

-18 Weeks-

"So, when is your friend, Greg, supposed to get here so we can get this party started?" Jerry asked, making an embarrassing attempt at club dancing moves.

"Uh... he isn't coming," Adam said, bewildered. He had assumed that his mom told his dad about it already.

He knew why his friend wasn't coming. It was the same reason none of his friends wanted to come here anymore. He was the dead kid's brother and they were all freaked out by him now. They treated him like the grim reaper. But he carefully avoided telling his parents about anything that was going on in his social life. His mom was still screwed up and his dad just wanted everything to be normal around the house again. He didn't want them to worry or muck things up any more than they already were.

Adam saw his dad looking at him expectantly, like he wanted more of an answer about Greg, so he quickly changed the subject. "Oh, Dad, don't do that move in public," he said, wincing like it physically hurt to watch.

"What, this?" Jerry asked, dancing even worse this time.

"Yeah... that," he said with teenage-style disgust.

"You think that's bad?"

"Yes."

"But these are the moves that hooked Mom."

"Really?"

"Absolutely."

"She really had bad taste," Adam laughed.

"I always thought so," he agreed.

✶✶✶✶✶

"So what's this about Greg not coming?" Jerry asked, sidling up close to Lindsey at the kitchen counter to make sure Adam didn't hear the conversation.

"He told Adam he couldn't come. That's it," she said simply, focusing on frosting the chocolate cake.

"Did he give a reason?"

"He doesn't have to give a reason. This isn't school or work, there aren't any unexcused absences," she said sarcastically.

"But don't you think it's odd?"

"I tried not to think too deep into it."

"He was the only kid Adam wanted to invite. Without him...." Jerry motioned at the empty space and lack of celebration.

"It can still be a party," she said tersely.

"If it was one kid out of eleven invites, no big deal. But the *only* kid isn't coming?"

"What did you want me to do about it?"

"Well, did you ask Adam?"

"Of course."

"And what did he say?" Jerry prodded.

"Nothing. He didn't say anything."

"So, did you call the parents? Maybe there was a misunderstanding."

"Jerry, I've been doing birthday parties since his very first one," she reminded him. "I have never checked up on people who say 'no,' and I'm not going to start now."

"Well, considering Adam was counting on a special birthday with this friend, I think something should have been done."

161

"Then you do it." She whirled around with the frosting spatula still in hand and looked him hard in the eyes, challenging him.

"I will. What's this kid's number?"

"It's in the address book."

"And what's his last name?"

"Trent. It's Trent," she said, exasperated that he was so oblivious to the daily routines, schedules and friends that had been around the house for years.

He reached for the phone.

"At least go to the study to do it, so Adam doesn't hear. You don't want to embarrass him."

"Point made," he said, walking out of the room with the address book in hand.

Jerry couldn't understand why she saw nothing wrong with this. He could only imagine the heartbreak Adam must be feeling that his best friend wouldn't be coming to his birthday. It was like she was entirely dead to the actual real world around her and too sensitive to the emotional world inside herself.

The phone rang in his ear only once. *Well, they obviously weren't busy doing something else today.*

"Hello, Cynthia?.... Yes, it's Jerry—Jerry Strane—Adam's dad.... Thank you, I will tell him you wished him well.... About his birthday, that's what I was wondering. You see, Greg is the only person Adam invited.... Is there any chance you would reconsider?.... But it is really important.... What are you implying?.... You know, Cynthia, we're doing fine here... You make it sound like we're crazy—we lost a child!.... You mean you don't want to expose him to us.... You know, it isn't catching.... Well, maybe they shouldn't be playing together at all, would that ease your worries?"

He pressed the off button and slammed the phone down on the desk. *The nerve of that woman to judge us!* He wanted the satisfaction that only came from throwing something—like a fist through the wall. Instead, he yanked on his hair with both hands, trying to release the frustration he felt as a man boxed into this awful place—dad of a kid who died. Every moment of his life was defined by this reality.

He breathed deeply for a few seconds, trying to calm down. Jerry knew that he was the one with the nerve. If the shoe were on the other foot, he would have been just as apt to want to protect his child from the horrors others were experiencing—heck, he would change the channel away from the news when his kids came in the family room, just to avoid them hearing about the awful crimes that happened in the large city that overshadowed their small town. Yet he had been unable to protect Max. And he had been unable to shelter Adam from seeing it happen or experiencing the torment that has unrelentingly shadowed them since that moment. He would have done anything to keep his children naïve to death. Life—pure and simple—nurtured the young; this blackness was parasitic, sucking hope away.

And he was lying when he said they were fine. Their family *wasn't* all right. They were still bleeding every day. The hurt was still strong. This was only the first celebration without Max. *God, where will we be come Halloween? Thanksgiving? Christmas?... Max's birthday? That woman had every right to protect her son. I'm the one with the problem here.*

*****

"Are you sure this is what you want to do for your birthday?" Jerry asked, turning around so he could see Adam buckled in the backseat.

"I'm sure," he replied, trying to sound braver than he felt.

Lindsey sat stoically in the passenger seat, holding her feelings close to the vest.

They drove the twenty miles quietly. The trip seemed interminable, slowed by the weight of unspoken fear and grief.

Adam stared out the window at the passing world. He had only ridden this route once before, but that trip was burned into his mind—the little pale yellow house with blue shutters and an American flag out front, the boarding stables complete with five horses in a corral, Pat's Donut Shop with a donut-shaped sign on top, the tire store with stacks of tires in the front and on the sides and out back, the county library, Grover Park, American Legion Post 536 with an ancient tank out front, a statue of some guy on a horse stationed in front of the gold-domed city hall, Waxman funeral home where he had sat for what seemed like hours staring at the small coffin and feeling claustrophobic, the empty shell of an Eckerd drugstore, the yellow caution sign on a tight curve that someone sprayed to make it eighty-five miles per hour, O'Rourke's Used Car lot that was famous for live animal commercials, the ReMax realtor offices built out of the same brick as the fencing for the cemetery next door.

As they reached the entrance and turned onto the one-lane road that weaved through the quiet grounds, Lindsey felt a moment of panic. She didn't even know where Max was buried. Nothing looked familiar. She had been so intent on getting through the funeral that she had tunneled her focus on that one thing. The visual cues that she would normally pick up regarding her surroundings were entirely missing. *What kind of mother doesn't even know where her son's grave is? What kind of mother takes this long to visit?*

Jerry pulled to a soft stop where he always parked, at the edge of the road, leaving just enough room for other visitors to squeeze by. They got out, all three avoiding each other's eyes out of respect for the emotions that were undoubtedly betrayed there.

It was a relief to finally reach this point, led by Adam to a place Jerry believed they needed to be. He was touched that Adam felt it important to share his birthday with his brother, who had always made every birthday brighter. And he only hoped that this visit would be whatever Lindsey needed to help her come to terms with her grief.

She straggled behind them, husband and son walking hand in hand. In a normal situation, Adam would have shrugged off such a gesture, but here and now he knew to welcome the strength and support his dad offered. *If only I could do the same*, she thought, admiring his courage.

As they topped a rise, she saw a beautiful tree up ahead and was enveloped by sudden warmth in her chest. Max was beneath that tree. She remembered looking at the branches, arching gently over toward his grave, dappling the light that fell on it. She remembered thinking how beautiful and fitting it was that a cherry tree would stand above him, weeping thousands upon thousands of tears for him each spring when its pale blossoms fell gently to the earth.

She came up beside Jerry and put her hand in his free one, kissing it gently with lips that were wet with tears. He had found this place for Max while she was far away, trapped in selfish grief and pain. He had done this for their son. He had fought off the darkness and made sure to see that their child was at peace.

"Max?" Adam said, breaking the silence. His voice was shaky. "I didn't want you to miss my birthday party. I'm eleven today...."

*****

It was hard to keep the smile on her face and light the candles and sing the song. Every piece of the birthday puzzle was heart-wrenching. Every step conjured memories—

Max singing loudest of all.

Max blowing out the candles before Adam could get to them all.

Max plucking candles out and sucking the frosting off of each one.

Max wearing bows on his head while Adam opened gifts.

165

Max exclaiming with delight over everything his brother got, saying, "I'm gonna ask for one of those for Christmas."

He was indelibly linked to every aspect of the family even though he had been a member for the shortest amount of time. He was the lifeblood of the group, the one who had operated on untarnished joy at being alive.

Adam had always been more cynical and analytical, and Max had tempered that. It was sad to watch just how serious Adam was now, without his character foil by his side. There was no levity from his brother to loosen him up. And as parents focused on bills and work and their own issues of loss, they were hardly capable of being the fresh air their son needed. He was holding up well, but he was growing up too fast—hardening to the world. He had gone past childhood on that fateful day and it was a one-way door.

Lindsey knew that other kids must be unnerved by the change in him, if not outright frightened by what he had gone through. She imagined them whispering about his story, making him feel so small under the weight of their stares. That was why she hadn't pressed him on the birthday party issue. When he wanted to invite Greg, she thought that it was a great idea. He hadn't told her until the day before that Greg wasn't coming, and the expression on his face cautioned her not to ask. Perhaps Jerry was right; maybe she shouldn't have left it alone. Maybe she should have facilitated the situation and gotten to the bottom of things. But—right or wrong— she had tried to respect Adam's desire not to share.

At the end of the evening, when Adam was tucked up in his room drawing with his new shading pencils, she turned to Jerry on the other end of the couch. The rest of Adam's gifts were spread between them, a messy but welcome barrier. Standing hand in hand by Max's grave, listening to Adam talk to his brother about lighthearted things, eased some of the tension that had been thick between them since the blowup about planning the birthday party.

Maybe they were both ready to let go of the ugly things that were said—*she* had said.

"So, what happened when you talked to Greg's mom?"

"Oh, nothing," he said, raking his hand through his hair and yawning in defeat and exhaustion.

"Did you tell her off?" she joked lightly. He looked at her crossly and she quickly added, "I just wondered. So I know if I should give her the evil eye at the next PTO meeting."

"Actually, there are going to have to be apologies," he smirked.

"You didn't!"

"I really should have thought before speaking," he admitted.

"How embarrassed should I be?" Her eyes betrayed the humor she found in their dysfunction.

"Pretty embarrassed."

She let out a deep sigh of breath that she must have been holding for a week. Now that the first birthday was over and she was still in one piece, she actually felt a sense of calm settling inside her.

-19 Weeks-

It was like the traffic gods were punishing her with every red light along the way. Patience had never been Lindsey's strong suit and coupled with nerves and a full bladder, she was ready to blow. She had been drinking water since the moment she got up, and now her eyeballs were floating under the pressure. She squirmed in her seat and tapped her hands on the steering wheel to release some of the nervous energy that was flooding her system, trying to think of anything but fluid of any sort.

When she reached the lot, she found the only space left—way in the back forty. She didn't want to make the headlines for peeing herself in the middle of a public parking lot, but a screeching stop in the fire lane or stealing a handicap space probably couldn't be explained away by her type of emergency. She parked, judging the distance to the door as somewhere around impossible, wondering if she could run and cross her legs at the same time.

It was as if her body had decided to burst forth with the truth overnight. Suddenly she had a small protruding stomach and a lot of additional strain on her bladder. *How do they expect me to hold this much water in my system?* She reminded herself that this had been no easier the last two times, the difference being that Jerry had been there to laugh her through it. It didn't seem nearly as funny all alone. No, it was just sad. She needed a bathroom—ladies' or men's—immediately.

She plowed into the building and past innumerable doctors' offices and milling patients, in dire search of a restroom. She didn't care who she bowled over, old or young, this was an issue of potential humiliation.

Thank God!

The picture of a triangular stick figure on the sign up ahead made her want to cry. She sealed herself in the first stall and danced in place while she fought her way out of the pre-maternity pants she had put on this morning. They were part of the problem, adding to her woes by putting additional pressure against her abdomen.

Ah… the sweet ecstasy of relief!

By the time she made it the three floors up to the doctor's office, she already felt the beginning urges to pee again and knew it wouldn't be long before she felt like she was holding back Niagara Falls. She had uncorked the whole fluid waste operation, and her body was going to want to evacuate all of it every five minutes. She checked in at the desk and sat down, planning her escape to the bathroom and back again without being missed or found out. They said you were supposed to drink all that water and not pee until *after* the exam.

When she heard her name called, she was suddenly too terrified to think about anything as paltry as needing to use the bathroom. Closed off in the solitude of the exam room, she undressed quickly and put the gown on. Then she knelt at the side of the examination table, intertwined her hands and leaned her head down against them to pray. She knew she would look like a sight if anyone entered and saw her in her pink paper gown and stocking feet, but she suddenly felt the need to have an honest conversation with someone she hoped would still be ready to listen to her after all this time.

Please, let everything be okay. This baby deserves so much more than what I have given. This little person can't come to be without me, and I have been trying to deny that for so long. I avoided providing anything but the bare minimum, refusing to see a person

169

but rather a threat to my selfish needs. I have hidden from life and refused to accept the truth, that love brings true feeling—happiness and pain. I tried not to love because it hurts. I tried to get rid of this child. Can you ever forgive me for that? Can my baby forgive me?.... I don't need anything for myself. I ask only for this helpless and innocent child, for Jerry and Adam. Please let this baby be healthy and strong and thriving—

"Excuse me, Mrs. Strane?" the technician asked, as she stepped in the room furtively. "I'm sorry. I knocked and didn't hear you answer. I didn't mean to interrupt."

"Oh... no," Lindsey said, coloring slightly. "I'm sure you have walked in on worse than this." She stood up and brushed absently at the wrinkles in her gown, hoping she was right.

"Actually, this is probably the best thing I've walked in on in a while," she said with a smile. She was an older woman—short and slender, with strong gray hair that was kept trim and elfin features that would belie her true age forever. There was an awkward silence before she continued, "So, you are at about nineteen weeks now?"

"Yes, I am." Her lips trembled around her smile.

"Well, let's see what we can see. I'm not making any promises."

"Is that disclaimer a part of the training?" Lindsey joked, remembering her earlier pregnancies.

The technician nodded, absently, looking closer at her chart, "I see that your chart is a little light."

"Oh, that—" she started to explain, ready to come clean to this total stranger in a way she would never be able to with her own husband.

"Is everything okay?" the technician asked pointedly, looking straight at her like her eyes were a lie detector.

Lindsey held her gaze. "Yes.... Actually, everything is really good now."

"Have you been taking your prenatal vitamins without fail?"

"Yes, I have." And it was the truth. She had never missed a single vitamin. It was as if a part of her had never even entertained the notion of not keeping this baby, and that part had finally banished the other out of her system.

"Good. Glad to hear it. The doctor will certainly have more to say about skipped appointments, but I just want to get a picture of this baby. So let's get to it."

Lindsey watched the screen next to her anxiously. She worried about what might appear. Her shame could show up on that screen in the form of a baby stunted by lack of love. She had given it such a hostile environment in which to grow that she didn't know if a fragile life could have the strength to fight the forces of her disregard. But there it was... the living, breathing image of her child—two arms, two legs, fingers and toes, one beautifully large head.

"It's a girl," the technician said, a smile in her voice.

My daughter looks perfect.

Part of her wanted to covet this moment for herself alone; the other wept for the desire to have Jerry with her—to tell him. But now that she wanted him to know, she feared what he would say. How would he take finding out she was four and a half months pregnant? Where did the time go? She needed him now more than ever, but the distance between them was a gulf that she had created, and she didn't know how to bring him back into her life again.

*****

The parking lot of St. Andrew's Church was desolate in the middle of the week, and it was neutral territory. She didn't know what their meeting was going to be like after what had transpired between them last time, but at least her friend had agreed to come. It was a start.

Shelley pulled to a graceful stop, perfectly within the lines, right next to her.

"I'm glad you called," she said, getting out of the flaming red mustang.

Lindsey pointed at the lines on the pavement. "What's this?"

"What? I parked perfectly."

"Yeah, that's what I mean. Are you taking lessons?"

"Lin, don't you think that maybe I went through a lot the last several months too?" she asked seriously.

"Well, I—"

"After what happened, don't you think that maybe I looked at myself and thought that I could have been the one? What happened to Max.... I could have hurt someone like that. I was always so reckless, and we just laughed about it. I never knew just how un-funny it really was."

She had noticed the change in her friend's driving immediately, but she was so caught up in her own nightmare that she had never taken the time to think about why. This woman, with her raucous and carefree exterior, really had a heart that bled. She had turned something tragic into a life-altering lesson. Max had saved her from herself.

"I really needed to talk to you... to apologize," Lindsey said, approaching her friend and giving her a hug. She held on tight, welcoming the physical closeness that she had been shunning from everyone for so long.

After a few moments, Shelley tapped her on the back. "People are going to get the wrong idea."

"Let them. I'm not quite done yet."

"You know, maybe lesbians have a point, this boob to boob hugging is extra soft and comforting," Shelley giggled.

"Leave it to you to turn something beautiful into something sexual," she chided. They pulled apart and she looked at her friend. "I'm truly sorry, Shell."

"What the hell are you talking about? Did you sleep with my man or something?"

"Can you ever be serious?"

"Once or twice a year."

"I have been a crap-ass friend," Lindsey said, bowing her head.

"That I can agree with, but I figured I could give you a pass."

"I shouldn't have ignored you for so long. And I shouldn't have tried to manipulate you into—" She stopped, unable to say the words. "I never should have asked you."

"Lindsey, I'm glad you trusted me," she said quietly, as if afraid that God would overhear. "You needed to be able to tell someone about it—"

"About her," she cut in.

Dawning quickly spread across Shelley's face, along with a smile. "Her?"

She nodded.

"You mean you didn't go through with it?"

She shook her head.

"But I just figured—when I left you were so certain. I just assumed—"

"And what did Mr. K always say about that in driver's ed?"

"You make an *ass* out of *u* and *me*," they said in chorus, laughing with relief to have found each other again.

"So, what does Jerry think of this? He must be over the moon!" Shelley crowed.

"Actually…"

"Lindsey! You have got to tell him. Someday he is going to figure this out. And he can't be the last one to know. You're just lucky that you haven't popped like a Christmas goose already—which, by the way, is a whole other reason for me to hate you, seeing as how I pop at conception, and here you are at number three going on five months! What the hell kind of freak are you?"

"First of all, I *have* popped."

"Yeah, right. If that's called popped, then I must be pregnant now too."

"That's beside the point, Shell." She refused to relish in her fortunate physique when there were more pressing issues. "I know I need to tell Jerry. Believe me, I was going to. The other day we had this moment—"

"I'm going to stop you right now and ask if this 'moment' is about sex."

"No," she said wistfully.

"Well, honey, if it's not about sex, Jerry isn't caring about the 'moment' you think you had."

"No, really—"

"No. He's not. You have this man wound so tight by now that he doesn't know which end is up. You have got to get back on his horse and now."

"But you were always the one saying that Jerry and I are different. That our relationship is something more. You talked about it being deeper," Lindsey reminded her.

"Yeah, yeah, I know what I said. But these are dire circumstances. After living in a relationship with ample sex, and then stopping cold turkey, even the most sensitive guy on the planet is going to start humping the furniture," Shelley lectured.

"God, you make a pretty image."

"I can't help myself. It's an art."

"Pornographic art, maybe."

"Potato—potäto."

"But what if he turns me down?"

"Possible... but unlikely. You just have to make him an offer he can't refuse," she said, slipping into a bad impression of a mafia boss.

"It's been a long time. I don't want to make it tawdry," Lindsey said, embarrassed.

"You don't have to be a dominatrix or anything. I just mean you need to, at the very least, give him an opening. If he doesn't take it, then you need to take the chance and *come* to him—preferably naked. And then you get to *come* again, hopefully…. It *has* been a while," she joked.

"I just thought that it would happen naturally as we healed. But just when things seemed to be improving, he shut down on me."

"I'm not saying you *tried* to hurt him while you were grieving, but you cut him out of the process entirely and it *did* hurt him. So, just like you apologized to me, you need to go to him," she enunciated slowly and clearly.

"I was afraid you were going to say that."

"I'll tell you one thing, Lin, you do seem much better. Even if you are hopelessly fucked with your man. So turn it around now and hopefully be fucked *by* your man."

"You're nasty."

"I'm just saying."

*****

A small speck of hope floated by in the air, and she grasped hold of it—a mere moment to realize she had forgotten to be sad today. Max was with her. His memory was strong in her heart. She had talked about him today. She had thought about him today. And yet she failed to be sad. Or maybe she finally succeeded in being happy.

After months spent chained by the weight of an awful deception, suddenly she felt full with a wonderful secret she wanted to tell. Her skin almost crawled with the desire to let it out, like it was going to burst through her pores. Her daughter was thriving. Her prayers were answered. The key to open her heart again was inside her. It had been there all the time; she just refused to see it. She had life to share.

But her happiness was tempered with nerves. *What will Jerry think? What will he say? Will he believe me?* She couldn't call him. No, he deserved to hear this face-to-face. She had waited an entire day already; she reasoned she was strong enough to make it through another. And then maybe, once he knew, he would forgive her everything. Maybe the joy of a new daughter would be enough to erase the months of torture.

Lindsey wandered the house like a caged animal with energy to burn and nowhere to use it. Her eyes searched the space around her and suddenly reality popped into view, in full color, no longer obscured by her selfish pursuits of fear and shame. The house she had taken refuge in, attempting to hide from life, was suspended in disarray. There were tools gathering dust where they had collected during the last project they were working on before the bottom fell out of their world. And beyond that she saw new things that needed to be done.

She stood in the foyer at the bottom of the stairwell, a point from which she could see the upstairs hall, foyer and living room all at the same time. *I need light! More light...everywhere!* Outside the sun was bright and the sky was clear; yet the house seemed impenetrable to the rays. She wanted to banish the shadows from every corner. In the stairwell—a skylight to welcome the day inside and make it seem less confining. In the foyer—sidelights and a transom around the front door. On the bare wall at the bottom of the stairs—a small ornamental window to bring in the light and change it, redirecting it with bevels or ripples of water glass... something to make the light dance with life. Her eyes drifted to the living room, and her body followed. So much sunlight came in the front windows, light Sadie lazily basked in all morning. But now, as the day moved toward afternoon, Lindsey could see the boxes of light were shrinking into slivers across her fur. Facing the fireplace, she looked at the walls on either side where she had always imagined floor to ceiling bookshelves. *Thank God, Jerry never agreed to them.* Now, a shorter set of shelves, and above them more ornamental windows to bend and extrude the light so it dazzled as the afternoon waned toward evening. This way they could capture the life of the sun all day long.

It was all so obvious. How could she not have seen the gloom everywhere? She felt her fingers practically burning with the need to get into something. The part of her that had lain dormant for months, the creative force inside that had always itched to do something more and make the house something more, was rubbing its eyes and stretching out of what had seemed a bottomless slumber.

*****

She took a deep breath of the scent of cedar and looked around. Nothing had changed in her absence—

"Miss Lindsey, as I live and breathe!"

Her eyes darted around quickly, trying to find the source.

"Earth to Lindsey," he said, approaching her quickly.

"Hi, Ed." She smiled softly, awkwardly.

"Oh, come here!" He pulled her into a hug.

She stiffened for a moment—their relationship had never been on this level—but then she settled into the comfort he offered.

As he pulled away, he gazed at her. "You look good," he said, satisfied. Then he corralled her with his arm and guided her further into the store. "I was a little worried that you weren't going to grace me with your presence anymore. I was worried about you."

"Oh, I'm fine…. Just haven't had much want or need for working on the house for a while," she said, putting up a brave front.

"I hoped that I would have the chance to tell you that I am so sorry for your loss. I know where you've been these last months," he said earnestly. "I understand. And I'm glad that you are finding your way back."

Lindsey stopped and looked at the kind old man who was standing before her. She had seen him countless times. She had talked to him. She had joked with him. But she had never looked past the blue of his eyes, to the gray depths, to see the pain within that she saw right now.

"How—"

"My Sammy." He patted his hand lightly over his heart. "It's been... oh... forty-one years now, and I still feel him. He was too young. We were all too young." His eyes shined with tears unshed. "It is so hard to find joy. It's hard to find *peace* again."

"I never knew," she whispered, tears beginning to fall from her own lashes.

"That's probably the worst of it. It's hard enough to be around people who know what kind of pain you've experienced. But to think about those you will meet who will never know who you *had* been. They will never know that this earth was a better place for the short life of the child you lost. It breaks my heart."

"You've had a good life since." Her tone was a hopeful question.

"Oh, I muddled through. My wife and I divorced a few years after. She never came back from the brink; that much I know. I was there with her at first, but I found my way back. I found something I love enough—this place." He nodded toward the space around them.

She stared at him, wondering at the fact that she would never have known his history—that he lost his precious child—but for her own dreaded circumstances. He didn't wear it on his face. Maybe it was hidden somewhere among the wrinkles of life that graced his kind visage, but no one would know without a map. His wounds were on the inside, where his scarred heart continued to beat.

But the lacerations on her heart were still new, and they itched as they attempted to heal. When she scratched them, by accessing memories of Max, they broke open again. She wondered if they

178

would ever stop bleeding. Maybe some people were just stronger than others, like Ed was stronger than his wife. *And Jerry is—*

"Lindsey."

"What?" She shook her head to clear it.

"You *will* find your way back from this," he urged.

"But you said your wife—"

"My Cara was a good woman, but she was troubled, even before Sammy. She had difficulty immersing herself in the pursuit of life. Sammy was the glue that held us together. And the only reason we stayed together after is because I feared for her well-being. It was only when I realized that she was going to drag us both under—drown us both in her grief—that I parted with her."

"But weren't you afraid for her?"

"Of course I was afraid for her, but I couldn't bring her out of it. She wouldn't turn to me or lean on me. I couldn't live like that. She was going to kill us because she couldn't bear to live without him."

The man standing before her could be the spirit of Jerry's future. Everything he said set off warnings in her heart.

"Now, I'm not going to pretend that I know you any better than a person who spent hours of his life going over paint samples with you could. I know I'm just your handy hardware guy, guiding you through your projects—*years* of projects. But since you could have gone somewhere else long ago, and instead chose to put up with an old guy like me, I have something important to say."

Lindsey nodded her head in submission.

"You are stronger than your grief. You can hurt and you can mourn, but you *have* to go forward and find happiness. I know simply from the fact that you haven't been in here in a while that things are not normal inside you. You will never be the same… but you can find a good place in life again. It may seem impossible, but you *can*." He gave her a reassuring wink and squeezed her arm gently. Then his voice levitated to its normal tone. "Now that my public service announcement is complete—what can I get you to buy from me today?"

Lindsey smiled through her tears. She felt lighter all of a sudden, like Ed had taken some of her grief off her heart to lessen her burden. "I'll start with a couple gallons of paint for the living room," she said, following him to the counter.

"Certainly. Did you choose your color already?"

"Sort of. I was really looking for a second opinion, though. You were right about how different a color can look from one place to another. The porcelain bisque was perfect in the dining room, but when I put a swatch of it in the living room, ugh, it was awful."

*****

The familiar sounds transported him back to the days when he and Max would come home from school to find Mom covered in white sheetrock dust or splattered with paint. The stagnant silence that had engulfed him every time he stepped in the house since had vanished, overtaken by blessed commotion. Loud music filled the air, accompanied by the sound of a sanding block.

Adam couldn't believe how the day just kept getting better. First, he had been allowed to stay home alone for the first time ever, while his mom ran out to the store this morning—it seemed that being eleven years old was going to have its perks. Second, Justin had just asked him to go to the movies, which was why he had come home to find his house alive again—the third and most exceptional moment of the day.

Suddenly his heart was full of excitement and hope. His mom had finally come back. And he was going to start middle school soon, wearing the armor of a new friend who didn't give a crap about what had happened to Max. He and Justin had been hanging out more now that their year difference in age no longer bridged the huge gap from elementary school. Justin didn't look at him as the dead kid's brother. He saw him for himself and liked him anyway.

"Hey, Mom!" he yelled, coming closer and trying to compete with the stereo. "Mom!"

"What? What is it, Adam?" she yelled back.

"Can I go to the movies with Justin?"

"When?"

"Right now," he said anxiously.

"Really?"

"Yeah... it's the twilight show."

"Well, I—"

"Please?" His tone was even, but his eyes were pleading.

She looked at him for a moment, her head cocked uncertainly, but just when he feared that his day was going to come to a halt, she yielded. "When will you be back?"

*****

Jerry stopped just outside the front door, bracing himself for whatever he might find—sadness, pensive evenness, suffocating stillness. This had become part of his normal daily routine, an attempt to center himself in preparation for the difficult hours he spent at home. He shuddered at how much easier it was becoming to banish all expectations and hopes for his marriage and family. He was learning to accept this new world. Pretty soon he wouldn't even remember what it used to be like—what it should be like.

He swung the door wide and his nose was immediately accosted with the fumes of fresh paint, thrusting him down a rabbit hole to another world he thought he had left permanently behind. He dropped his briefcase on the floor and his keys in the bowl on the foyer table, following the sound of a fully loaded paint roller traveling up and down the living room walls. The paint samples had been removed and the swatches of practice color were a memory.

The room looked basically colorless, like fresh canvas, but where the walls met the trim, the color showed more truly, creamy beige. It was being transformed into living, breathing space again.

What is she going to ask me to do now? he wondered, with hope in his heart.

He caught sight of Lindsey at the same time the room exploded with the strains of Peter Gabriel. She had her back to him in the opposite corner of the room, unaware of his presence. He watched her work. She was beautiful in this setting, a vision of better times from their past and hopefully still to come in their future. Her head was tilted to the side as if she were looking at something much farther away than the wall before her. She had always tackled her projects with vigor and whimsy, and he saw both in her right now. He saw her eye for detail mingling with some faraway dreams of order and beauty that she would term "brilliance." And there was that small stripe of paint in her hair—probably from absently brushing her hair back with the hand she used to wipe up errant paint splatters—that made the moment perfect. She was a mess, but her body's fluid movements meshed with the music like she was the portrait of a tortured artist, entirely engrossed in her process.

"Hey," he said when the music died off, trying to get her attention before a new song started up.

She startled, almost losing the roller. Then she turned around with a sheepish smile and said, "Please don't kill me."

"For painting? Seriously, after all the times I've caught you painting when I come home? You would have been dead ten times over."

"No, not this." She waved the roller at the room, unleashing a few drops of paint onto the newspaper drop cloth at her feet. "This was just about damn time. I only hope I didn't go too light... too white."

"We've been living with the samples on the wall forever; they were all fine with me."

"Actually, I didn't use any of those. I went to the store and just decided to wing it."

"So we might be in trouble," Jerry said, chuckling.

"God, I hope not. I just couldn't make a decision from the ones on the wall. I thought maybe I was putting too much stock in those choices and figured I needed to open myself to a different option entirely. It's a gamble, but I really wanted to get something done today, so I took it—without testing the color out first. I was afraid I would end up in limbo again," she said, talking fast like she finally found her voice and had to get out the words that had been clogging up space in her brain for too long.

"So if the paint is not what you feared would push me into a murderous rage, what is it?" he asked, leveling a stern but playful look at her. He was so happy to see her looking and acting like the Lindsey he loved that he wanted to slough off all the hurt and anger and live in this moment.

"Brace yourself.... I just figured it all out." She encompassed the whole room with her arms.

"What exactly?"

"What we need around here."

"And?" he prodded.

"Windows!"

"What did you do?" he asked warily.

"Nothing. I just know what we need to do—what *you* need to do," she said pointedly.

"Ah, what *I* need to do." He nodded his head in understanding. "I see, said the blind man."

"That's what is missing around here," she said definitively.

"I was thinking more along the lines of the floor being what's missing," Jerry sparred, pointing at the bare plywood that peeked out from under countless newspaper pages. "Or is this the new look in all the magazines?"

"Very funny," she blanched. "The floor is obvious. I'm talking about the essence of the space."

"Oh, the *essence*," he mocked, easily slipping into their normal pattern of barbs like a comfortable pair of old shoes.

"Yes," she said curtly, like it was too obvious to require further explanation.

"And how much is this gonna cost me?"

"In blood or treasure?"

"Touché."

"So you'll do it?"

"I don't believe that's what I said," he chuckled.

"But it would make everything… perfect," she said wistfully.

"Promise?"

Their eyes locked, and he felt like he could really see her before him for the first time since their world stopped. He wanted to anchor her there to that moment, fearing it might be too fragile and fleeting—gone in an hour, a minute, a second, and plunging him back into icy uncertainty.

"Well, almost perfect. At least until the next stroke of pure genius that I have," she laughed, stepping toward him and wrapping her arms around him.

She tilted her head up to look at him, and he peered deep into her green eyes, searching but finding no ghosts and no darkness within. There was only light. *Maybe she's right. Maybe that's just what we need.*

Lindsey took in the fine lines in his skin that she hadn't remembered seeing before. *Max and I put them there.* She liked the character they brought to his handsome face. They showed that he was able to be moved deeply, just as other lines showed the capacity for unabashed enjoyment. Eventually those lines would be hidden among more lines and wrinkles collected over a lifetime of living— good moments and bad.

Rising on her toes, she kissed his lips softly. "You know you want to… do the windows," she whispered, melting her body into his and pressing her head against his chest.

"Yeah, that's exactly what I'm thinking about right now," he said huskily.

She felt his hands start to wander, and she pulled back slightly to see the dark agony in his brown eyes. Then she kissed him, deeply, guiding his hands to keep roaming. Pushing toward him, they maneuvered backward clumsily. And then she was falling on top of him.

"What the hell?" he called out in shock. "Where did this come from?"

She came out of the haze of desire for a moment, long enough to see that they had run aground on the infamous ottoman she had been hiding from him in another life. She had pulled it out this afternoon in hopes of having the room painted and pulled together enough to show him how great it all looked so far, and how much better it would be with a couple more windows. She figured the walls and the discussion of windows would entirely overshadow any confusion about a measly piece of furniture.

"Oh, this thing?" she asked dreamily. "This will work perfectly." It really would work on several levels, sex being the foremost on her mind. She straddled him with her legs and kissed him hungrily.

He came up for breath and said, "Lindsey, are you trying to—"

"Yes, you got me. I'm trying to distract you with my feminine wiles," she whispered in his ear.

Jerry pulled away slightly, his eyes traveling her face. "It's really *you*."

"Of course it's me, who else would jump you in the living room?"

"Well don't let me stop you. We can talk about this later," he said, patting the ottoman with his hand.

-20 Weeks-

It had been a humid spring day when her life changed forever, now finally that humidity was beginning to release its grip. The leaves on the trees were still green, and summer was holding on, but today the air felt crisper and clearer, like fall was dancing at the edges, eager to take over. And judging from the spunk in her step, Sadie felt it too.

They were zigzagging down the road at a stop-and-go pace, but she didn't mind being at the whim of a dog with a nose for all creatures great and small. As Sadie investigated the neighbor's mailbox, Lindsey took a deep breath—in through her nose and out through her mouth—taking in the signs of life that surrounded her: beach towels hanging on deck rails, toys smattered about in yards, flowers overflowing gardens, freshly manicured lawns—*when did the Klines get new garage doors?* They lived just across the street and she hadn't noticed. She wondered at all that she had been missing. Somehow she had shut off the periphery, tunneling in on a long life of sorrow before her. *People are living all around me, and I have been... dead to it. They love and laugh and move through the world finding joy and sadness, while I have been wallowing in pity and guilt.*

She walked to the side of the road and stepped up onto the sidewalk, taking in the flowers and butterflies some little girl had drawn in shades of orange and pink and purple. She smiled and touched her stomach, swollen lightly with the artist within her. She listened to the dogs behind the prison bars of their backyard fences, barking at Sadie's good fortune. She waved at people heading off to work in their cars, getting more than one look of surprise and many uncertain waves in return.

*****

He was sure that everyone knew. They weren't privy to his sex life, but anyone who had seen or talked to him yesterday and then came in contact with him today *had* to notice the transformation. They would say he must have gotten laid, but to him it was more than just physical. It was pure release from trying to walk blindly through his existence with no vision or hope for the future. He was finally out of the thick fog and able to see miles ahead. He no longer feared the unexpected danger that could be lingering, hidden but within reach. He had been through the worst and survived.

With her, he felt invincible. He could do anything. Lindsey had always had that effect on him. They were indelibly connected. They succeeded or failed together. They needed each other's energy and love to survive, and sex was their way to reconnect and recharge the energy source that supported them. Time and physical distance might have erased certain things, like the exact size of her breasts or the voluptuous curve of her hips, but it could not erase the memory of her love, or the way she touched him or held onto him, or how she moved or kissed. They were back. The gulf between them that had seemed insurmountable was suddenly bridged so easily.

*****

"Hey, Mom?"
"Oh no, what do you want now?"

He was momentarily stunned by the tone of her voice. He pulled the phone away from his head, staring at the earpiece like it was some kind of weird, voice-altering tool.

"Adam?" she called through the phone.

He held it back to his ear. "Sorry, Mom, I just wanted to know if it would be okay if I ate dinner here at Justin's. I know it is kind of last min—"

"Stop it!" she giggled into the phone.

"What?" he asked. Adam could hear talking and laughing in the background.

"Not you, sweetie. Sorry, I was talking to your dad."

"Dad's home?"

"Yeah. He just got here," she said, with a smile in her voice; he could hear it.

"Forget it," he said quickly.

"No, it's okay with—"

"I'll be home in a minute."

He hung up the phone before she could give him permission. Then he turned to Justin and said, "Maybe next time, man. I really need to call sooner. My dad just got home, and they already had a family dinner planned."

"Oh, that sucks! I feel bad for you," Justin commiserated.

"Well, next time I'll hit 'em up early, so I won't be stuck eating with them."

Adam rushed out of the house like he was late and about to get in trouble for it. Actually, he just couldn't wait to get home. What he'd heard on the other end of the line were two people he hadn't heard in a long time. If he actually believed in UFOs, he would have thought his parents were kidnapped by aliens and some kind of advanced robots had taken their place for the past few months. Now his real parents were back.

*****

188

Lindsey shielded her stomach protectively as she approached the bed. Her heart beat with fear and excitement, and she slowed her steps in an effort to calm down. It was their first chance for a truly intimate moment since they had broken the ice on the brand new living room furniture. Now it was time to tell him.

Jerry lay in bed, propped up against the headboard in a show of overt anticipation. "Don't tell me you're afraid to come over here," he said dangerously.

She blushed under the weight of his stare. She was wearing a short cotton nightgown with wide lace straps that rested on her shoulders, but his eyes seemed to burn right through it, like he could see all her soft and delicate spaces inside. She feared he would be able to search out that tiny kernel of doubt that had led her to consider putting an end to the life she held within her—the life that she was sure he would celebrate unconditionally. It was his unquestioning strength and acceptance of life that had led her to hide her pregnancy from him in the first place, because he could never understand.

"Come here." He beckoned with his finger, reeling her in.

She moved slowly, cautiously, still holding her hands in front of her, wondering if he noticed the blossoming nature of her body. It seemed like even the billowing cotton couldn't hide what was going on underneath. She felt her breasts pressed between her upper arms, fuller than usual. Angles were taking on curves now, in stark contrast to the harder, tighter qualities of Jerry's physique. She had felt it earlier, when he was holding her, as his body moved against hers— he had lost weight. His body had always been slender, but now he seemed to be nothing but muscle and bone. He was thinner, definitely, but his strength was still palpable, providing immediate comfort to her weak and uncertain soul.

As she reached the side of the bed, Jerry sat up, swinging his legs over the edge and enveloping her between them. He took her hands. "I want an unspoiled view," he said, pulling them away from her stomach and looking at her with hunger as she stood before him. "I haven't gotten a chance to see you in so long."

She felt heat burning within her as he pulled the straps of her nightgown off her shoulders.

"Jerry," she said breathily, feeling his lips on her chest, exploring through the cotton that had gotten trapped on her definitely larger breasts. A few months ago, the straps would have been the only thing holding the gown up.

"Lin, I've missed you so much."

"I've missed you too." She battled with herself to tell him before this went any farther, wondering what it really mattered if it waited a *little* longer.

He wanted to kiss and touch every inch of her body. After sixteen years of marriage, this past three months had been agony. He marveled at how true the song "Your Body Is a Wonderland" truly was. He couldn't imagine ever getting enough.

As his hands roamed, he felt the contours of her shape. Her breasts were only like this when she had her period on the horizon, and he wondered how many times he could slip in before that got in the way. She felt rounder, like a ripe piece of fruit, and he was hungry.

"Jerry, I really need to talk to you," she whispered in his ear, awakening the nerves and putting him further over the top.

"Mmmm," he responded, incapable of words.

"Really, Jerry, you're making this hard," she said, without much conviction.

"You're making me hard," he mumbled into her collarbone, as he continued to trail kisses everywhere, tugging at her nightgown to expose her breasts.

"Seriously, you have to know." She grabbed his face and lifted it toward her so she could look in his eyes.

"I'm listening," he said, still groping with his hands.

"I'm pregnant." The words came out softly, set before him carefully, like a delicate gift she was afraid to handle.

His hands stopped, rested where they were on her hips. His brain stopped thinking about getting inside. He just stopped.

"Really?" he asked, in awe, trying to remember when this could have happened, how it could have happened. "But we haven't—"

"It's a girl," she added quickly.

He blinked several times, trying to understand. His hands slid over her stomach, like he could find the answers there. He pressed lightly through the cotton gown, feeling what he had felt the day before, only now realizing what it meant.

"But how do you know?" he asked, struggling through the murkiness left over from raw passion.

"I just found out," she said tightly, hoping that he couldn't read the truth with his hands or his searching eyes. "I had been gaining some weight and feeling strange, so I went to the doctor."

"A little girl?" Jerry asked hopefully.

"Yes." She smiled through tears of joy, and his image wavered before her.

"God, I know we were trying... before—I just didn't—I never imagined that we had already succeeded." His voice was heavy with disbelief, but then he was pulling her over onto the bed, laughing and holding her close. "This is amazing," he said, with the excitement of a child. "When do you want to tell Adam?"

"I think we need to be careful telling him. We need to do it soon, but we have to be understanding that he might not be as thrilled with the prospect."

"Who wouldn't be thrilled?"

Lindsey's heart constricted at the thought.

"We need to get a move on around here. If we already know the sex, you must be... what, five months along?

"Close," she gulped, guilt filling the open spaces inside of her. She had almost stolen this from him. Months of joy had been lost to sorrow, and even worse, she had almost thrown his daughter away.

"There is a lot of work to be done if we plan to have a nursery prepared, and a safer environment for a baby in the house."

"Yeah, we aren't really baby-friendly around here." She almost choked on the truth of her words.

"We can fix that," he said, feeling a second wind that would carry him through life with a gusto that had been missing. He wanted to scream from the rooftops. He wanted to share his unabashed excitement. Their family had bounced back in a huge way.

He looked at his wife. He had wrestled her onto her back in his excitement. "You are a beautiful pregnant woman. I should have noticed earlier. You have an amazing glow about you—God, I'm just so happy! A little girl!"

He leaned in and kissed her deeply. But as he pulled back he saw a shadow flit quickly across her eyes, and trepidation streaked down his spine.

-21 Weeks-

"I love this room. I could live right here," Lindsey swooned, sweeping her arms through the air and spinning with abandon, like a young child. She tilted her head back to drink in the dewy glow from the large lantern above. It belonged in an outdoor vestibule, but she loved the cozy effect of its golden light shed through the seeded glass panels, and how the smooth white ceiling reflected it, accentuating a shadow design of the lantern's wrought iron scrolls. She beamed at the results of all her scraping, skimming, sanding and painting.

"Well, I'm glad that this is all you need to be happy. Myself, I would like to have working appliances and plumbing. But if all you need is a dining room, far be it from me to question your happiness." Jerry caught her eye and winked.

"You know what I mean," she moaned, chucking him in the shoulder. "I am just so happy to see something done around here. Completely done!" She allowed her eyes to wander over the three-quarter wainscot and plate ledge, the thick coved crown molding, the stenciled plaster detail, the perfect bisque on the walls. "It's exquisite, Jerry. It's exactly how I pictured it in my head. Now we need to fill it!"

"Wait a minute. Hold on. Can't we just enjoy the moment? Do we have to start moving furniture?"

She stared at him stubbornly, thinking about all the time that had passed. A project that had been slated to take weeks had gone from a room in honest transition to a neglected construction zone for months. At first, after Max passed away, she was so lost to reality that she didn't notice anything outside herself. When she finally woke up to the fact that life was still meant to be lived, she was afraid to come back in here. It meant immersing herself in the past— thoughts and dreams she had last been entertaining when Max was still traipsing through this house. But it turned out to be cathartic to finally finish a project from her old life.

"Jerry, I want to reclaim my dining room again," she said plainly.

He knew that she wouldn't let it go. He could fight it, but the moment he left the room she would be scraping furniture across the new walnut floors, trying to do it herself. For the sake of his sanity and their newly remodeled space, he relented.

"Where do you want everything?"

"Well, I'm not totally sure," she said, tapping her chin and looking around. "We might have to shift things around a bit to get it right."

He rolled his eyes and galumphed over to the buffet, readying himself on one end of the largest, heaviest piece.

"We should put this on the long wall between the windows," she said with certainty. "I think it's important that you see it as the main focal point regardless of which way you enter the room. Oh, and by the way, I don't want to use the hutch top. We can store it in the attic. I think it's too formal for the space here."

"But, dear, this is the *formal* dining room," Jerry said, exasperated.

"I just don't want such a structured look. The glass enclosed hutch makes the space seem so... untouchable."

"Correction—it makes the *plates* untouchable."

"I'm not going to let you get in the way of progress. The hutch top goes. Besides, that's why we have the plate ledge. That is what one would call built-in storage. The things we used to put in the hutch can go on the ledge instead," she said, proud of her choice to put the rational and charming decorative touch on top of the wainscot.

"But those plates are china. Why aren't *those* too formal for you?"

"Jerry, are you really going to go there? Because I'll tell you if you really want to know." She challenged him, knowing full well that he didn't want a lecture on home decorating—now or ever.

"Well, I hope you're not too much of a girl to get the hutch up the stairs and into the attic," he said, effectively acquiescing to her wishes.

"Bring it on."

One hour and several furniture shifts later, she appraised the results. "Perfect," she said, breathing deeply of the scent of crisp newness.

Jerry let out a purposeful and loud breath, like he had been afraid of her reaction.

"Now you may go and find something more enjoyable to do while I finish—"

But he was already gone. Like a kid finally released from the bonds of school or some other dreaded prison, he was out of sight in a flash.

Lindsey shook her head at the ridiculous thought that decorating was a painful chore.

She wanted to make the room model perfect, complete with place settings for six at the table. She felt along its gouged and battered surface. It had been in a naked and terminal state back when she won it at an antique auction, but the deep espresso stain and polyurethane protected and gave it new life, graduating it from a farmhouse kitchen workhorse into a true dining table. There were two matching armchairs for the heads, and four mismatched chairs in between. The unique patterns—shield, ladder, spindle—stained the same color as the table, added to her relaxed formal vision without being chaotic. She opened the drawer to the buffet that she had hand-painted and distressed herself, transforming it from waxed pine, to buttercream with a chocolate glaze. She pulled out a lace runner for the table and cloth napkins in a soft, dusty blue. She chuckled to herself as she placed three mirrored candlesticks along the table length, knowing Jerry thought they were hideous. She retrieved crystal napkin rings and candles from smaller, divided drawers. The final touch, her mother's china—white with a platinum ring and soft cornflower blue toile print along its scalloped edges—placed on pewter chargers. The effect was timeless and absolutely beautiful, a mixture of whites, creams, soft tans and browns in a variety of textures.

She dug two new buffet lamps out of the depths of the front hall closet, where they had been lying in wait for this day. The crystal lamp bases were definitely going to cause raised eyebrows, as Jerry would question why they weren't too formal for her taste. The lamp shades were eggshell white, with horizontal flat pleats that ran along the body. Sections of pleats on each panel were gathered and fastened in the middle with black fabric-covered buttons. The row of buttons down each panel reminded her of the buttons on formal menswear. Placed on either end of the buffet, they looked like waiter sentries.

It felt good to put all of the pieces together. So many treasured old and new things had been in storage for too long, tucked in boxes and pushed deep in the back of closets. To finally have everything out in full view, or nestled comfortably in drawers and cabinets awaiting the next occasion for use, made at least this one corner of the house just right.

There was still a lot of work to do, especially now that she had added new plans to the already extensive list of improvements. That meant there were going to be storage boxes and tools in the corners of many rooms well into the future, but at least projects would be moving forward again, and those tools would be getting regular use.

She could hear Adam yelling as the front door swung open wide, "Mom! Mom! You gotta see this!"

"I'm in the dining room!"

"I caught this lizard and—"

"Stop right there." Lindsey put her hand out to halt him before he stepped one grubby foot on the new wood floor, or worse—on the brown and cream damask wool rug. He had mud, caked and drying, up the sides of his sneakers, and there was no telling what the bottoms looked like. "Step away from the dining room," she said, in a mock police officer tone.

"But you gotta see this lizard."

"Where is the lizard?" she asked, trying to mask her exasperation.

"Right here." He held up his cupped hands in triumph.

"Why would you bring it inside?" Her voice quickly reached a fevered pitch that was hard to control. She couldn't help but wonder if this kid had any idea where he lived. She felt the faintest passing nausea at the thought of little reptile feet traipsing through her new room, or anywhere in her house for that matter. "You know that no *creatures* are allowed in here—you're lucky you're allowed to live here, to say nothing about Sadie."

She could hear the tags on Sadie's collar jingle as she heard her name, perking up her head from the spot where she lay at the living room window.

"I just wanted you to see the big red neck this guy gets. It blows up like a balloon!"

"Well that sounds cool, but outside, please." She calmed her tone so as not to startle the perpetrator into dropping the illegal load he carried.

"But he might run away before you get to see him."

"That's a chance we have to take, mister, because we aren't bringing that kind of nature into the house. Got it?"

"Yeah, I got it," he said, moping.

"Where is your brother anyway?" she demanded.

Adam froze.

"Oh my God!" Her hand went to her mouth as if trying to hold back the words that had already spewed forth, or the anguish that wanted to follow.

"Wow, you finished the room! The whole thing!" he exclaimed, overcoming his shock and trying to help by changing the subject. More times than he cared to count he had come in the house and gone up to his room, expecting to find his brother playing in there. He knew how naturally Max came to his own mind and heart and lips, and it actually made him feel better to hear his mom slip. *Maybe I'm not weird. Maybe it's perfectly normal to forget… especially when you're feeling happy, because when Max was alive we were all happy.*

She looked at her son, appreciatively, realizing he was trying to save her from herself. "Yes, it's about time. Completely and entirely finished from head to toe. Not even one piece of trim missing— that's a first," she added conspiratorially.

"So what are you going to work on now?"

"Hmmmm, we'll just have to see." But she caught herself before sliding back into her dreams. "Now get out before that thing in your hands tries to make a break for it."

*****

Adam woke with a start, flipping over quickly to check the clock by his bed—5:00. It was still early. His alarm hadn't even gone off yet. He had set it for five-thirty to give himself plenty of time to get ready and out to the bus by six-thirty. He laid his head back down and closed his eyes, but the squirming nervousness in his stomach that had woken him wasn't going to let him go back to sleep.

It was the first day of middle school. He was a sixth grader now, and he knew that this meant huge changes. He was actually looking forward to it, though. He would sit with Justin on the bus, which would insulate him from the eighth-graders who would rule the school this year, picking off the youngest and weakest. He would get a locker and change classes each period. And there would be so many new kids around that he hoped he would just slip into the moving current of people in the hall as Adam Strane—the boy with an untold story. It was a new world, one in which the shadow of Max wouldn't be able to follow him. Max had the elementary school to haunt. His brother would forever be too young to go where Adam was about to go.

He slipped into the clothes he had picked out the night before. To his relief, his mom had agreed to his newfound desire to choose his own style, with a warning that she had veto power over the dress code. If he really clashed or tried to wear something ripped or torn or stained that hadn't been purchased that way in the first place, she was going to strike it down. He turned off his alarm, so it wouldn't start belting out music to an empty room. Then he snuck by his parents' bedroom and into the bathroom, to get ready for school without waking up the rest of the house.

*****

Lindsey looked through the rack of tiny outfits in pink and yellow, marveling at how small humanity could be. Her stomach pressed up against the hanging clothes making them sway under her movements, and making her wonder why the racks weren't farther apart to accommodate people in her condition, who were their main source of sales income.

She already felt the growing urge to pee again, even though she had made a beeline for the bathroom when she first walked in the store.

"So what the heck happened to you?" Shelley asked, coming up behind her.

199

"What's that supposed to mean?"

"Girl you got faaaat."

"Thanks… thanks a lot," she pouted.

"You know what I mean. I just saw you a few weeks ago, and you still hadn't…." She made a rounded motion over her own, much flatter stomach. "It's like you pent it all up and as soon as you told Jerry your body let itself go."

"Yeah, well, you look like a hag," Lindsey said dismissively.

"That? Oh, that was an all-nighter with my man."

"Stop being such a slut all the time."

"Ooh, got your panties in a knot this morning? Oops, or is it that you just graduated to *maternity* panties?" Shelley jabbed.

"I swear if I wasn't a noticeably pregnant woman who is anxious to stay off the evening news, I'd kick your ass right here. Now, hold these so I can go pee, again," she groused, shoving the thermal crib blanket and outfits she had picked into Shelley's arms.

By now she really had to go, aided by the squirming figure inside of her. The fluttering had become insistent kicks and spastic jostling movements. This one seemed feisty.

After draining the tank, she washed her hands, silently talking to her reflection over the sink. *You've got to hang on here. This is going to be tough at times, but you can get through this, just like you got through two others.* But she knew it wasn't like the others. She found herself oscillating from contentment and even excitement about her daughter's impending arrival, back into a dark place where she feared her secret would come out; that her daughter or Jerry or Adam would find out she had almost willfully changed their family. *Will she know? Will she know I didn't want her?* Heat rose to her face, showing her guilt on the surface. She splashed water on her reddened skin and blotted it with a paper towel, erasing the shame. She was going to have to get a grip, and quickly.

As she left the bathroom, she walked right into Shelley, who— not one for rules—had crossed the "No Purchases Beyond This Point" sign while her arms were laden with stuff.

"I was coming to find you. Thought you might have fallen into the toilet," she snorted.

"Why do you joke with a woman on the edge?"

"Because it's more fun than joking with a woman in the center."

"Do you get this stuff from your kids?"

"I'm offended. I'm completely original," she said indignantly.

Lindsey rolled her eyes.

"So why am I here, anyway?"

"I need to start preparing the nursery for the baby, and I just thought it would be nice for us to do it together."

"Come on. You don't want or need my help preparing the nursery. Home décor is your thing."

"Okay, so I just wanted to spend some time with you, all right?" she admitted.

"How are things between you and Jerry?"

"Good." Lindsey shrugged casually. Then she opened her mouth to continue speaking, but shut it again silently.

"What?"

"Do you think that things can ever really go back to normal? You know, once something changes, can you ever recapture 'normal' again?" she asked, while she walked, rubbing her hands along the rails of the row of cribs on display.

"I guess it depends on the kind of change."

"When I was eleven, I got my first pantyhose—actually two pair, in those L'eggs eggs."

"I loved those!"

"I felt so grown up! When I got home, I rushed to my room and tried on a pair. I yanked them on like tights and put huge runs in them. I was so embarrassed and angry, and I put the other pair away deep in my drawer vowing never to wear them. They were like a sign of my coming womanhood. I remember that moment, feeling this horrible pit in my stomach that life was never going to be the same again. Everything had changed right then and there, and I couldn't go back to being a little girl." When she finished, Lindsey was standing before a crib outfitted in orange, pink, cream and brown, staring down over the bar at the embroidered flowers on the coverlet.

"Well, sure you can't go back."

"I had that feeling when Max died," she said, refusing to look at her friend.

"Of course."

"And it stayed with me all the time. It wasn't just a split second; it was there every time I looked at Adam and Jerry."

"You were grieving."

"And I had it when I found out about…" she trailed off, not finishing, cradling her stomach lightly with her hands. "You know, like you can't put the genie back in the bottle."

Tears came to Lindsey's eyes as she tried to take herself back. If she still had Max—if he was still on earth and a growing part of their family—this baby would have made every dream come true for them. As it was, Max was just a memory—forever linked in their minds to tragedy. Forever six years old. Someday, this baby would surpass her older brother in age. It was unnatural and wrong.

"You wanted another baby before Max died. You need to remember that this is not a replacement kid. This is not something you did in a moment of grief. You created this life," Shelley said, pointing at her protruding belly, "in a moment of *love and hope*. She's not a mistake. She's a blessing bestowed at a time when, believe it or not, you need her most."

Lindsey looked at her friend, questioningly.

"You need her, Lindsey," Shelley urged again. "Your whole family needs her. She will help you find the way."

"How do you know?"

She shrugged, like she suddenly realized she was being too heartfelt and philosophical and wanted to distance herself and go back to being crude. "I just do."

Respecting her friend's discomfort, Lindsey turned her attention back to the crib before her and said, "This is the one."

"The crib?"

"No, *that* I still need to keep looking for. But this is the perfect crib set." She pointed at the bumper and coverlet.

"You can always use my kids' old crib," Shelley offered, like it was a utilitarian decision that didn't really matter in the long run.

"Actually, this time around, I am more about the bells and whistles. You know, when I had Adam we were still kind of settling in to house and home, and then having a second boy it only made sense to reuse as much as possible. I think it's time for real decorating and all things 'girl'."

"Well, all right! Are these things going to have to be hidden or smuggled into the house, or is Jerry on board with this project?"

"Oh, he is so on board. Actually, it takes a *little* of the fun out of it, knowing that he has granted his approval in advance. I kind of like toying with the rules a bit—ugh, I've got to go pee again. Can you find the bedding set and get in line at the checkout? Then we can go to the furniture store next door, and I can check out their bathroom," she said, hurrying off.

*****

"So, shopping with Shelley? Am I broke?" Jerry asked with a smile, leaning against the island while Lindsey pieced together and frosted the brownie cake for dessert that night.

"Not yet," she said, matter-of-fact.

"But that is the plan?"

"Eventually, but I'm pacing myself. We do have a lot of years to go and girls are expensive."

"Case in point," he said, gesturing toward her.

She smacked him in the arm with a stray potholder off the counter. "I like to surround us with pretty things. Is that a crime?"

"In some states," Jerry chuckled.

"You're an ass—ortment of annoying adjectives," she said, making a quick save as she heard Adam's footfalls approaching from the foyer.

"Alliteration!" Adam said, by way of greeting. "Marvelous Mother, may we have marmalade and muffins for our meal?"

"Actually, Adam, I was thinking about artichoke hearts, asparagus and arugula antipasto," she giggled.

"Yuck!" he yelped.

"Hey, Sport, what's up?" Jerry asked.

He couldn't help marveling at the change in his son over the past few weeks. Adam had come out of his shell and away from his bedroom. He was in school again, and he had new friends and new interests. And it probably helped that his parents were no longer fighting or icily avoiding each other. Plus, Max had gone from a taboo subject to a common topic of conversation, especially focusing on his quirky and fun-loving personality. Life in their house was worth living again.

"Not much. I was hanging out with Justin," he said, shrugging his shoulders like it was commonplace.

Jerry took notice that "playing" was now "hanging" in the eleven-year-old's vocabulary.

"Dinner isn't quite ready; you didn't have to come in yet," Lindsey said.

"I know, but he had to go in and so did the other guys."

"Well, we need to talk to you anyway," Jerry announced.

She gave him a look, raising her eyebrows and mouthing, *Now?*

He nodded almost imperceptibly and then turned to Adam. "We have some news."

"If it's about getting a little sister, I already know," Adam said blandly.

"What do you mean?"

"I'm not a little kid. I can put it together. I mean, Mom was getting fat and all. No offense, Mom."

"None taken," she said, stifling a laugh the best she could.

"Plus, I saw some girlie baby clothes and stuff in the closet in the guest room, when I was looking for my sleeping bag to take to Justin's for his sleepover," he added.

"Well... so that's that," Jerry said, rubbing his hands together like it was a job well done.

"Actually, there is one thing. Do I have to share a room with her?"

"Of course not, Sport."

"Then I'm cool. It can't be worse than having a little brother follow me around, right?" he asked, eyes shining as he put on a brave smile.

"I know you liked having a little brother follow you around," Jerry whispered, while Lindsey was occupied washing out the brownie pan.

"Sometimes it sucked." Adam pointed out.

"Sure, sometimes."

"But usually—"

"Usually it was pretty fun, huh?"

"I didn't think so at the time. But now, yeah, it was pretty fun," Adam agreed.

"Well, you're going to be much older than your sister, so she won't really be able to follow you around all that much. But she will look up to you. That's a guarantee," Jerry said.

"That might be kind of cool."

"You know, Max looked up to you too. And part of that was why he wanted to follow you around and be with you so much. It wasn't that he wanted to make your life miserable," Lindsey said, turning off the faucet and reentering the conversation.

"But he was so annoying sometimes."

"He wasn't *trying* to be annoying. He was actually trying to be just like you. I know this because I have an older brother who I thought was so cool that I just wanted to be around him all the time. Sometimes he would complain to my parents that I was in the way, but I wasn't *trying* to be in the way," she pointed out.

Adam looked at her, confused.

"Your Uncle Will."

"Who's he?" he asked innocently.

"Well… uh…" Lindsey searched for an answer. It had come naturally to her lips to talk about her childhood with her brother. Those were good memories. But she hadn't thought about the questions it would open up for her son. *Why haven't I met Uncle Will? Where does he live? What does he do? Can I meet him?* She wasn't prepared to explain.

*****

Adam couldn't believe it. He hadn't been lying about putting two and two together, but to actually hear it straight from his parents made it more real. A little sister? A baby in the house? He hardly even remembered what it was like to have a baby in the house. He was only four when they brought Max home from the hospital. And at that point all he thought was that babies made a lot of noise and did a whole bunch of nothing for it.

But his parents seemed so much happier, so if this was what it took, then he was on board. He was tired of trying to avoid being a family. And as long as his room was going to remain his—all to himself, now that Max's stuff had been moved to the attic—then he could deal with sharing the rest of the house with a little sister.

-24 Weeks-

The phone rang fourteen times and still no man or machine picked up. She figured that no one could possibly be home with all the commotion she was creating on the other end, but her hands were too soapy and wet to hang up. She let the phone rest on her shoulder as she finished loading the washer with dirty clothes.

"Y'ello." The voice was brusque, like he had better things to do.

Lindsey froze, unable to formulate a response. She had been thinking about this moment for the better part of three weeks, since Adam had woken her to the realization that she *did* have a brother, while he had lost his. It had taken her this long to get up the courage to call.

"Is anybody there?"

"Hi," she squeaked out.

"I can hardly hear you.... I've got a bad connection or something," he hollered back.

"Will... it's me, Lindsey," she said, louder this time.

"Oh, yeah, how you doin'?" he asked noncommittally.

She hadn't expected that he would be excited to hear from her, but it didn't make this any easier.

When Adam had asked about his Uncle Will, she realized that she had no easy answer for him as to why she, who was lucky enough to still have a living, breathing brother, had no contact with him. Adam was simply too young to know the truth. He didn't need to hear about the drugs and alcohol that had run Will's life. He didn't need to know that no matter how much she had idolized her brother while she was growing up, she was thankful that she had been smart enough to see Will for who he was before she followed him down the path of self-destruction that he had chosen. He didn't need to know that she had made a conscious decision to freeze her brother out of her life, to protect her family—her young children—from his influence.

Yes, she missed him. When she was little, he had meant the world to her. He was never too busy to spend time with her, playing tickle monster or making her fried egg sandwiches or just listening to her when she talked. She basked in his glowing compliments when she was an awkward preteen, and he said she was going to make all the boys crazy soon enough. And she was thrilled when he agreed to give up his plans the night of her senior prom to act as her chauffer to the dance, driving their dad's Town Car and even wearing a suit.

It wasn't until years later that she realized Will had been doing drugs even in high school, but it spiraled out of control during college—so bad that he never finished. Their parents had tried everything to help him, but Lindsey had taken a different tact and cut him off completely. The only word she ever got was through the filter of their mother... and it was never good. A baby out of wedlock he never saw and had no contact with, rehab, back into drugs, rehab, bankruptcy, drugs and rehab again. Over time she had grown immune to the cycle. She believed that the brother she had known was dead. It was only through Adam's eyes that she suddenly saw that wasn't true. Adam could never have his brother back, but she could, even if it had to be limited to a phone call like this.

"Lindsey?"

"I—how are you doing?" she asked, holding off the inevitable reason for the call.

"I'm good," he said, and he sounded so normal. Not high. Not low. Just good.

It was time to give him what he deserved. "Listen, Will, I want to apologize to you. I shouldn't have treated you the way I did at the funeral."

"Lindsey—"

"No, let me finish," she insisted, growing stronger as she spoke. "I wasn't exceptionally kind to anyone that day, but I was *really* shitty to you."

She shuddered as she thought about the words she had said to him when he tried to speak to her.... *You don't know. You don't know about anything. Pain? You don't understand pain! Hell, you never lost a child! You gave up your child long ago without a second thought. Don't try to act like you care or even understand. I would rather die myself than be standing here right now. And you—you don't even deserve to be standing here. You've had your chances with your life, and you screwed it up over and over again. Your time should have been up long ago. You should be the one in there... not Max. Not my Max.*

Will was silent on the other end, either waiting for her to continue or weighing her words.

"I judged you unfairly, Will. I'd like to say that I wasn't in my right mind, and perhaps I wasn't, but that's no excuse. There's a time and place for everything. You know that I have no use for what you did with your life." She paused for a moment, expecting him to jump in and say something to defend himself, but he didn't. "I know you were just trying to be there for me that day. You were trying to do something selfless and good, and I trampled all over it, trying to kill it... and hurt you as much as I was hurting inside."

He took a deep breath, and Lindsey prepared for a maelstrom of anger.

"First of all, thank you," Will said smoothly. "And second of all, I have been a total bastard to a lot of people over the years, so you were right to keep your distance. You were right about a lot."

She was stunned. She had been prepared for a fight or to have to grovel. She had been prepared for him to be as unreasonable as she had been. She had been prepared for him to be high or drunk when she called and possibly have to accept the fact that she was never going to be able to clear the air, and that it might not even matter because he might still be entirely unreachable. But she hadn't been prepared for this.

"I stopped everything—all of it. The drugs. The alcohol. The lies. I stopped using—people and substances. I know you're probably skeptical," he snickered. "Hell, I wouldn't believe me. But it's true. And you know the best part? I stopped calling Mom and Dad. I love them, but I was destroying them."

Lindsey realized that it had been a long time since she had heard *anything* about Will. He used to be a standard topic of conversation when she spoke to their mother. Marie would say, "I know you won't have anything to do with Will, but I just want you to know that he's—" and then she would fill in the blank with the good, bad or ugly in his life at that moment. Maybe she had always hoped that it would get Lindsey involved, or maybe it was just a topic to talk about, like the weather. Whatever it was, it had stopped in the last few months. Lindsey figured it was the scene she made at the funeral that finally assured her mother that she wanted nothing to do with her brother, not this.

"I was the boil on the butt of our family, and I deserved a good lancing," Will chuckled.

Lindsey laughed. He'd always had such a great sense of humor—one of his best qualities. Drugs stripped him of that and made him a shell of the person he could be.

"So you're really clean?"

"Yes. Nine months," he said confidently.

Her hand involuntarily went to her stomach at his response, thinking about just what humanity can accomplish in that amount of time.

"I was actually already on the road to improvement *before* your little outburst kicked it into overdrive," he said with chagrin.

"So I was helpful?" she asked hopefully.

"Cruel. Very cruel. But helpful."

"I have to ask, what's different about this time?"

"I want it more. I realized that I was relying on Mom and Dad to step in and help me whenever I had problems, so with that safety net I never really hit the rocky bottom I needed to. I find that I am more motivated, suspended like I am now, over a ravine without a net. It works wonders."

"That's all I'm saying," she joked.

"You know, when I saw you at Max's funeral, I was just so torn up. You had always been so goofy and bright and obnoxiously excited about life, and there you were, a hollowed out version of yourself. I hated to see you that way. And I hated the fact that I never really knew this little person who obviously held your heart in the palm of his hand. All I could think was that he took your heart with him."

"That's what it felt like." Lindsey sniffed as her emotions overtook her.

"I wanted to be able to help you through it. I really wanted to, even though I knew that I wasn't the person I needed to be to do that. And you know what? I was jealous of you, too."

"What?"

"I have never felt the kind of love you feel for Max and Adam. I could only dream of the kind of love that would bring that much raw pain."

She sniffled again, wiping at her tears with an old dryer sheet, as if trying not to let him see her pain across the miles between them.

"You're right. I just gave up my kid like it was nothing. I never once thought any further about that decision... until that day," Will said somberly. "I've seen her, you know. Her name is Kaitlyn. She's eight now. She is absolutely beautiful."

"Have you talked to her mother?"

"Yeah, actually. We're taking it very slowly, but she is letting me into both of their lives little by little."

"That's great," Lindsey said, meaning it. She could feel the baby kicking against her hand, like she was begging to tell her uncle their news.

"I've screwed up a lot, with a lot of people."

"Tell me about it," she snorted derisively.

"But I'm trying," he said earnestly.

"I was talking about me," she clarified.

"Self-absorbed much? .... I'm saying that you're one of many people I want to—"

"*I'm* saying that I understand screwing up with people. I haven't been a picture of perfection these days."

"I think grief allows for a little—"

"Grief only goes so far. I almost completely screwed up my family—what's left of my family—because I couldn't see past my grief and guilt. I kept thinking that I was right *there*. That I should have been able to stop it from happening. Or that we shouldn't have even been there at all, and Max would—"

"Lindsey, you couldn't—"

"I know that, but it is hard to *really* know it. You know?"

"Now you sound like my thirteen-year-old sister," Will snickered.

"I was just so caught up thinking Jerry *would* blame me and *should* blame me that I shut him out. And I stopped focusing on Adam because he needed comfort I couldn't give, and I didn't know how to deal with it. And when I found out I was pregnant I—"

"Did you just say you're pregnant?"

She was silent.

"Lindsey?"

"Yes.... And I didn't want her. I tried to get rid of her. What kind of person—what kind of parent am I? I tried to get rid of my baby," she cried, unleashing her disgust and disbelief about who she had become.

"But you didn't."

"It doesn't change the fact that I thought about it. I never would have thought myself capable of even considering an abortion... and behind my own husband's back! I didn't tell Jerry about the baby because I thought I would take care of it without him ever knowing. I kept something wonderful from him because I was too weak to handle it. And now I will have to live the rest of my life knowing that I stole something from our marriage. Every time I look at Jerry and our daughter, I will know."

She heard a beep through the phone line, and then Will's clipped voice.

"—not the pinnacle of moral behavior, Lindsey, but I don't think you did anything wrong. *Thinking* is not—"

"Jerry would think so—" There was another beep. "—hell, I think so. I don't care about the argument that it's a woman's body and her choice, in my heart I know that what I was planning to do was wrong on so many levels. It wasn't fair to my husband or my daughter."

"Well, you feel how you feel, but I—"

"I had a child taken from me unexpectedly and against my will. How could I mourn and honor Max, and then *ever* justify purposely aborting a child? God, how could anyone in their right mind? We seem to think we have the market cornered on matters of life and death. It's sick."

*****

Jerry still didn't understand why they bothered to have call-waiting on their phone line when Lindsey never used it. He could imagine her, chattering away with someone and sneaking a peek at the caller ID when she heard the tone, weighing the importance and choosing to disregard his call in favor of the one she was currently fielding. Quite honestly, it hurt a little that she hardly ever switched over to him even just to say that she was busy.

He heard his own voice in his ear asking him to leave a message.

"Lindsey, I'm coming home early today. Thought that maybe the four—three of us could go out to dinner," he said, physically cringing at his slip. "I hope you get this before you start making something for tonight. I'll see you when I get home.... I love you."

He wondered at how even now, after months had put distance between their old life and their new one, he still found himself taken aback by little slips in his thoughts or words that reminded him of just how much their family had lost when Max left a hole in it. If he could have spared Lindsey the reminder and erased the message, he would in a heartbeat.

*****

"So the groceries made it in the door, I see, but they didn't quite put themselves away," Jerry joked, motioning to the island that looked like a volcano that had erupted grocery staples. Cereal, noodles, soup cans and cookies were mounded on the counter; while soda bottles, potatoes and dog food surrounded the cabinet on the floor.

"Ha-ha, very funny," she said snidely. "I put the cold stuff away and then I took a break. How was I supposed to know you'd be home early today, checking on me?"

"Touchy."

Actually, he didn't understand how Lindsey did it. He didn't know how she ever went to the grocery store at all, let alone week after week. He didn't think he would have had the strength to go after what had happened. He knew that she no longer shopped at the same store since the accident, but to think that she had to go through those same motions, over and over again.

"Where's Adam?" he asked.

"You beat him home."

"Really? His bus comes this late?" He looked at his watch like the time was foreign to him.

"Always has."

"How come I can never remember that? The bus comes at… four?"

"Just about."

"Don't ever leave me or I'll be lost," he snickered, making fun of himself.

"Don't say that."

"If something ever happened to you, I wouldn't know how to function around here. I wouldn't be able to pay a bill or put laundry away or find, well, anything."

"Please don't say that."

He saw the clouded look in her eyes. They had often joked about this type of thing, so saying it had come naturally, but now it cut to the bone. Mortality was all too real to them, and he should have realized that.

"Sorry." He tried to catch Lindsey's eye to convey the depth of his feeling, but she had her back turned, busying herself with the groceries.

"Listen," she said, brushing aside the moment, "why don't you and Adam go to the park or something when he gets home? He would really like that. I'll stay here and make some dinner."

"You really never check the messages, do you?"

"What's that have to do with anything?"

"I left you a message to let you know that I would be home early. And to tell you that I wanted us all to go *out* to dinner tonight."

She colored in embarrassment.

"Wow, now that's a guilty face if I ever saw one!" Jerry said triumphantly.

"I didn't know it was you."

"Yeah, right."

"Really, I was distracted. I didn't even look. Heck, I didn't even remember hearing the hitch in the line until just now.... My bad."

"Maybe we should just dump the call-waiting."

She looked at him in slack-jawed shock.

"Hey, it's not like I said we should cut off your right arm because you're left-handed. It's more like removing your appendix. You really don't use it, so why do we need it?"

Jerry moved to the phone to delete the message. He wanted to ride her about missing his call, but at the same time he was relieved that she hadn't heard what he left her.

"So what was so important that you couldn't answer my call, anyway?"

"Oh, I called Will," she said absently, while she went to work stocking the pantry.

"Your brother?"

"Well, you heard Adam the other day. It just made me think that maybe I should clear the air. I mean, through the eyes of a child who lost his brother and misses him, how can he understand me *choosing* not to have a relationship with my brother?" She remained focused on the groceries in her hands.

"Is everything all right?" he asked, knowing full well that something was going on with her. She was purposely evading him.

"Yeah, of course. It was just a phone call." She turned toward him and allowed her glance to skate over him as if that would prove it. Her eyes didn't come to rest again until they landed safely back on the groceries left on the island.

Jerry felt it in the pit of his stomach. There was guilt in her mannerisms. But why she would feel guilty about calling Will didn't make sense. As far as he was concerned, Will was an ass who wasn't worth anybody's time, but she shouldn't be afraid to call him. The only thing he had ever said was that he didn't want her dragging their family into his drama, and she had been on the same page about that. A phone call from eight hundred miles away was hardly something to be concerned about.

"So how is he?" he asked, not really giving a flying fuck how he was. He was making an effort to sound casual, but his frustration was building along with his certainty that there was more to the phone call than she was letting on. *Maybe he asked for money. Or maybe he got busted again.*

"Oh, he's good actually.... He's clean."

Jerry snickered, unable to contain his disdain upon hearing the same thing he had heard countless other times before.

Lindsey stopped what she was doing and turned to look at him, defiantly. "He's clean," she said purposefully.

He felt his stomach move unnaturally inside as he realized she had chosen sides. She had never stuck up for Will before. She had never believed him. She had kept him at arm's length and only occasionally talked about the fun times they had growing up. She had wanted nothing to do with Will, and suddenly she was protecting him.

"Listen," she said, softening, "I didn't think it was possible. I questioned him myself. But he sounds really good. He's stopped turning to my parents—*he* actually cut *them* off. He is back on track and I'm not going to undermine that."

"Well, I'm glad that you two have reunited," Jerry said icily, thinking that she sounded brainwashed.

"What's that supposed to mean?"

"That's supposed to mean that I've heard it all before, and I am a much harder sell than you, obviously," he said condescendingly.

"You can be such a dick," she said, keeping her tone as even as possible and making it sound like a matter of fact rather than an angry slur.

"How am I supposed to react when you sound like you're joining the cult of Will?" Acid was in his voice.

"Do you *ever* make any mistakes, Jerry? Or are you just perfect?" Lindsey spat.

"What the hell is that supposed to mean?"

Her words were vindictive—her tone, gearing up for a fight—but inside she was crumbling. This wasn't even about Will at all. It was about her, and the realization that Jerry would never understand what she had been going through for the past months. He was immovable and unshakeable in his convictions. He would never understand how she could keep her pregnancy a secret or how she could think about having an abortion, let alone scheduling one. He would never forgive these things... or forgive her for Max's death. That would be asking too much of him. She knew she either kept her secrets forever or said goodbye to her husband and family for good.

"Just what the hell do you mean?" he thundered.

"You don't know what it's like to be one of us," she said plainly.

"What are you talking about?"

"Most of us make mistakes in life. We hurt people. We hurt ourselves. We don't do everything right all the time."

"And?"

"And you can't accept that!" she screamed.

"What do you mean, I can't accept that?"

"I mean that you can't accept that people might screw things up."

"We are talking about a *chronic* screw-up. Will is a mess!"

"*Was* a mess. And you wouldn't like him if he had only screwed up *once*!"

"Because he made conscious choices that led him to his fate," he said evenly.

218

She felt a wave of nausea as she realized just what he would think about her conscious choices. She would be no better than Will in his eyes.

"I know that mistakes happen," he said, softening his tone and moving toward her.

Lindsey was fighting the nausea but knew that her discomfort was all over her face, reflected in his visage as he came to her side. "God, I made a mistake, Jerry. I've made a lot...." She doubled over in pain that she now realized was not brought on by guilt and fear, but something much worse. Something was wrong with the baby. "She knows I didn't want her..." she moaned softly, and then everything around her tunneled into darkness.

*****

Both of Lindsey's prior pregnancies had been entirely uneventful. Life up to now had not prepared him for the unfortunate possibilities of pregnancy complications. But life, until recently, hadn't prepared him for a lot of things. He had been lulled by two absolutely normal pregnancies into thinking nothing would go wrong in gestation. He had thought of life in utero as the ideal, safe environment. And now it seemed that danger might lurk there as well. He couldn't help but wonder if anyone was safe anywhere. *Are our children always at risk? Is life that precious? Our hold on earth that tenuous? How do we go on when we feel constantly barraged with danger?*

Now that Lindsey was in with the doctor, Jerry took a moment to take stock of the situation. He hadn't been back to the hospital since the day that Max was killed. He felt a twinge of dread every time he passed the building on the road, and here he was again, worried about another child who shared his blood. *If I were to lose her, would it hurt the same as losing Max? I don't even know her.*

Would she leave the same size hole in our family and our hearts as the vibrant soul of a six-year-old boy?

Stop it!

He couldn't let himself consider such a thing. *We can't take another hit. Please.... We are struggling as it is,* he pleaded silently.

He put his arm around Adam's shoulders, pulling him closer. "I called Shelley to come and get you. Mom might need to stay here overnight, and I think I should stay with her."

"I don't like it here," Adam said quietly, his voice muffled against Jerry's shirt.

"I don't either, Sport. I don't either."

"Excuse me, sir?" a voice called out.

Jerry looked toward the admitting desk more out of general curiosity than anything else. He caught the eye of a nurse who was beckoning him over. He patted Adam's shoulder and got out of his chair to approach the desk.

"Sir, I have your forms here. You didn't fill out the insurance information."

Jerry looked at the nurse, relieved to find that it wasn't the same one he had dealt with regarding Max. He needed no more harbingers of tragedy.

"Oh, I'm sorry. I didn't even notice. I—" Jerry reached into his back pocket for his wallet. "—shit, I forgot it," he swore, under his breath. He had shuttled them out of the house in a hurry, in a controlled panic but a panic nonetheless. Having his wife double over in agony and then fall limp in his arms, at six months pregnant—his wallet wasn't even on his radar.

Adam came up behind him and tugged his elbow. "Dad, I have Mom's purse if that helps."

He turned to look at his son, offering up the big leather tote Lindsey stored her worldly possessions in. "You brought Mom's purse?"

His eyes searched his son's honest, somber face—wisdom born of tragedy. Adam had seen things and experienced things that brought the reality of life's fragile nature crashing down on him, squelching that youthful naivety of mortality. He was all too aware of the possibility of death snatching life from someone's clutches in a single moment.

"Mom always says she needs her purse when we leave the house, and she's been *really* forgetful. She says it's the pregnancy. I grabbed it for her." He shrugged his shoulders, seeming embarrassed by his forethought.

"Thank you. This does help," Jerry said, dangling the purse in the air by the straps. His gaze slipped to the doors, which he heard sliding open to permit the entrance of the next unfortunate soul whose life had been turned upside down. What he saw was his savior.

"Why don't you go to Shelley and sit with her while I finish up here?" he prodded Adam. "It will only take a minute."

As Adam turned to leave, Jerry turned his attention to the nurse behind the desk. "Now, what is it that I missed?"

"You entered the insurance company, but we need the policy number, group number and phone number," she replied, quickly and efficiently.

"Okay, just a minute, I should be able to find her card in here."

He dug his hands into the bowels of his wife's purse. It felt wrong. He had hardly ever laid hands on Lindsey's bag, let alone gone through it. This was her space, and he felt like he was violating a trust by digging through it.

He found her wallet and opened it, expecting to find her insurance card tucked away safely in a slot just like her driver's license and credit cards. When he came up empty, he dug deeper in the recesses of the bag, where he found a compact umbrella, a toothbrush case and a weathered tampon. There were also a few ATM receipts intermingling on the bottom, folded in on themselves and old enough that the ink was disappearing from their faces. He opened a zippered pouch on one wall of the purse to find a bottle of hand sanitizer, which she always had with her. On the other wall of the bag, he found another zippered compartment. He pulled out some small papers folded around Lindsey's insurance card.

The nurse saw the card in Jerry's hand and thought he was offering it to her, so she took it to finish the paperwork. He didn't even notice.

He stood frozen by the picture that was left in his hand, fully exposed before his eyes—an ultrasound picture of what could have been a peanut resting in an orb of grainy blackness. His heart felt like it was suddenly pumping cold blood through his system. He had seen the ultrasound of the baby, taken the day Lindsey found out she was pregnant; she'd had arms and legs. He wanted to believe that there was a simple explanation, like she carried Adam's or Max's first sonogram around with her. But his heart wasn't in the story. He peered closer, at the date in the corner of the picture—June of this year. She would have been only a couple months along at that time. *I just found out,* she had told him.

He held the picture in his hands, the evidence. He wanted to crumple it up like it was a wretched lie he could squelch that simply, but this was his daughter. This was her first real picture. Instead he continued to cradle it, like it was her precious life he held.

Three nurses went by, rushing down the hall that led to the depths of the hospital. As they brushed past him, the photo caught their wind and blew up and out of his embrace, exposing the paper underneath.

TWC
342-555-6568
June 30ᵗʰ—10:30am

The ultrasound picture landed on the desk in front of the nurse who was finishing up with his insurance information.

"Oh, is this your baby?"

"It appears so," he said tightly.

The nurse gave him a strange look and handed his card and the photo to him.

He turned to go but was stopped by the nurse's words. "Um, sir, don't forget your… uh, purse."

If he hadn't already felt like less of a man—less of a husband and father at that moment—this was enough to rip the last vestiges of his self-worth out from underneath him. Lindsey had lied to him. She was keeping things from him. *Is it even my baby?*

Why else would she hide this from me?

"Thank you," he said, through gritted teeth, as he turned back to reach for her purse. He wanted to rip it apart right then and there, for merely holding the secret inside. Instead, he held it at arm's length as he walked in the general direction of the waiting room, blind rage blurring his vision.

"Jerry?" Shelley called out to him. "What is it, Jerry? What's wrong?"

He could hear fear in her voice, but he was in no position to calm her or put her at ease. He felt frustrated and defeated, feelings he had thought he was finally putting behind him. As his eyes honed in on Lindsey's best friend, he wondered what she knew about this. Maybe she was complicit in something.

"Do you know anything about Lindsey?" she asked hopefully.

"Probably not as much as you do," he said bitingly.

"Is the baby okay?" She ignored his response like she didn't expect someone in his position to make perfect sense.

He felt like a fool. "I don't know anything, okay?" His voice was cold, freezing her out.

He glanced at the ultrasound picture again, and then at the paper with a phone number on it. It looked like an appointment long past.

"Let me borrow your phone," Jerry commanded, figuring it was the least she could do for him considering she probably hid Lindsey's secret.

"But—"

"I forgot mine at home in my rush to get here."

*****

"Is she going to be okay?" Lindsey asked weakly. She was lying down on the examination table while Doctor Wallen and an emergency room nurse ran through an exam much like any regular pregnancy checkup. She had been fortunate to find her own doctor on-call at the hospital for the day, rather than seeing a random doctor who didn't know her personal history.

"Everything looks okay, but since we had a scare, I want you on strict bed rest for the next week."

"Is it something I did?"

"There was no immediate cause for the cramping, like an accident or injury, so it is just one of those strange things that sometimes happen. Everything looks good, but I want to step up our meetings to once a week just so we can keep a careful watch."

The tension and fear that she had brought this on herself began to ebb some and relief took its place.

"Now, Lindsey, you need to limit your stress and truly rest— full bed rest—until your next appointment. I am not kidding here. I will reassess the situation then," he warned.

"I will do everything you say," Lindsey said, lightened by the knowledge that her daughter was okay. She still had the chance to become the mother she could be... and wanted to be.

She stared at the ceiling tiles above her and said a prayer. *I screwed this up in so many ways. I don't know how I ever could have thought for even a moment about getting rid of this baby. Especially now that all I can think of is living for her and protecting her. She will bring love and life to our family, and the world will be a better place with her in it. I would give myself for her, even if she had to grow up without her mother. She is all of my best parts. If you really need to take someone, take me instead. Thank you for giving her life. For her. For Jerry. For Adam.... For me.*

*****

Jerry's hands were shaking as he slid the phone open to expose the keypad. He dialed the number on the paper, wondering if he had uncovered some tawdry affair Lindsey was hiding. Maybe it was a date with the father of this baby, to show him the picture of their love child.

At another time, he never would have questioned Lindsey's monogamy. Even in the recent months that they merely lived in the same home but seemed separated by miles, cheating never crossed his mind. He thought she was broken. That her heart was irreparably damaged when Max was taken from them. Not that she had found someone else.

For so long he had been frustrated that he and Adam weren't enough for her. As time wore on, he wondered if they would ever be enough. But when things had been at their most dire, her heart had started pumping again with more vigor. Slowly she had come back to him. Now he wondered if she had been sullen and distant with their little family because she was actually using up her life on someone else. Maybe that was why she had nothing left to give at home. Or maybe she had been mourning a lost lover and not their lost son all along.

The phone rang three times and then a voice answered, "Travis Women's Clinic, please hold." He sat in dead space for such a short time that the reality of his shock didn't fully register.

"How can I help you?" The voice was back, interrupting his scattered thoughts.

"Yes." His throat was dry and the words were hard to get out. "I was wondering what types of services you provide."

But in his heart, he already knew what he was going to hear.

*****

"Jerry!" she called out from the bed as she saw him coming in the door to her room. "Everything is going to be fine—she's fine," she said, rubbing her belly. Her eyes captured his image in a prismatic fashion, through tears of relief and joy.

He came slowly, his face hard set stone that seemed impervious to her happiness.

"What's wrong? Didn't you hear me? I mean, I have to stay here tonight, but then it's just some home bed rest—"

"I don't believe you," he growled angrily.

His eyes smoldered with hatred and deep hurt. It didn't make sense. Earlier, they had been fighting about her brother, but even though his anger had flared at her then, it wasn't the all-encompassing inferno that was burning through him now.

"What? What is it?" Her heart dropped, and her words were squeezed by fear that had settled in her throat as an immovable obstruction.

"This! What the hell is this?" he demanded, tossing the picture on the bed along with the abortion appointment that she had made.

Her eyes went to his. "Jerry, I—"

"Don't," he said, with disgust, "not if you're just going to keep telling me lies.

"But I—"

"Is this even my baby? Or is that why you never told me you were pregnant when you first found out? Were you trying to decide your course of action—leave me to raise this child with its real father, or stay with me and abort it so I would never know what you had done? He probably didn't want you either, am I right?"

226

"Jerry, you don't understand." Her voice was strangled. Her relief and joy had turned to raw fear and guilt.

"I'm waiting," he said evenly, controlled anger seething under the surface of his words.

"She's *ours*, Jerry. *Our* baby. Why would you ever think that I would—" She stopped, hopelessly. She had no words to defend herself.

"Because I could see no other reason why you would keep your pregnancy a secret from me." His voice cracked and weakened as he continued, "Because if what you say is true, then you're telling me that you were planning to abort *our* child."

"You don't understand," she sobbed. "I didn't think I could do this again—"

"What? You didn't think you could do *what* again?"

"*This*," she said, rubbing her stomach. "I didn't think that I could go through the pain of raising and loving and possibly losing *another* child."

"God, Lindsey, you selfish bitch!" he growled. "You stole months of my child's life from me *deciding* whether you could do this again. You sat there holding all the fucking cards and I was blind to the fact that *my* child's life hung in the balance!" He was enraged. To think that he had spent months trying to accept her grief, careful to ask no more of her than she was capable of giving. And this is what was going on inside of her all this time.

"Jerry, I wasn't trying to hurt you. I wasn't trying to hurt anybody. I was trying to heal."

"At the cost of what, Lindsey? Our daughter's life? Did you decide to keep this baby or did you *have* to come clean because you waited too long?" he spat.

"That's not fair—" she wailed.

"Screw fair, Lindsey. You've lost the right to judge what's fair."

-25 Weeks-

Finally, she was given a clean bill of health to get up and continue living normally again. She still had to take it easier than she had been up to this point, but at least she was able to get out of bed. Being holed up in her room all day and all night was too much of a reminder of who she had become after Max died, who she had been steadily trying to distance herself from ever since. The forced prison sentence had been overwhelming and was compounded by the fact that Jerry held her captive, attending her at her bedside after learning the truth that should have sent him flying to the other side of the universe to get away.

He spent the week raining judgment down upon her in the form of his constant presence and attentiveness. Every moment he spent nursing her was carefully measured to assure her that he was only concerned about the health of his daughter. In a thousand ways— gestures, tones, glances—he made his point that she had vaporized his trust. If she so much as got out of bed to go to the bathroom, he guarded her like she was on homicide watch, making sure she did nothing that would put his daughter at risk.

Lindsey was offended by his overt protectiveness about the baby. Even though she knew she deserved his anger and distrust, to have him act as though she was actually a threat to their child—she *wanted* this baby. And once she consciously made that decision, she realized that her heart had made it from the beginning. That was why she had never gone through with the abortion. That was why she had

228

always taken her prenatal vitamins. That was why she never drank alcohol or took any medication—not even when drowning her anguish and grief in a bottle of liquid or pills would have been sublime peace. That was why she had done everything to make sure their baby had the best chance. She was stronger than the part of herself that feared the future and made that appointment.

Her reality was grim, but Lindsey was not going to let hopelessness take over. She had been there before. That was how she had gotten to this point. She wasn't going to give up on living. Her marriage was probably already over, but she had time before Jerry was going to walk away entirely. Their baby was her saving grace from losing him immediately. His protectiveness would keep him close. She had months to fight and scratch and claw to regain her footing and tie the pieces of her life back together again. She would fight Jerry's impression of her. She was not going to roll over and make this easy on him. He wasn't the reason any of this had happened, but she wasn't going to let him get away with painting her with a broad brush. She wasn't finished with this family yet, and she wasn't going to let him be finished either. There was a welcome fire inside her that was refusing to be doused.

*****

"Mom, you're up today," Adam said, happily surprised to see the unexpected vision of his mother moving about the room, making her bed.

"Yes. I am. The doctor says I'm good to go," she said with a bright, real smile.

"Really?" He was relieved that she wouldn't have to stay in bed all the time anymore, although this hadn't been as bad as when she was just too sad to get up. At least this time his mom had still remained Mom. She'd even invited Dad and him to eat dinners in

229

bed with her and watch TV together. Unlike before, she still wanted to be a part of the family.

"Yup. So, what did you have planned for this wonderful Saturday morning?"

"I was hoping to get Dad to agree to pay me to rake the leaves."

"And why are you looking for a job?"

"Because there's a video game my friends have been talking about that sounds really cool," he said, momentarily lost in thoughts of video game glory. "Do you know where Dad went?"

"No, actually, I was going to ask you the same thing."

"I figured he would be in here."

"Nope."

His parents were acting strangely again. But it was a different kind of strange. He had watched his dad take care of his mom all week, but in all that time he had hardly heard them speak to each other. Something was definitely up, like they were having a silent argument. When he was around them, he felt like he was somehow caught in the middle of something. Where he had spent the weeks after Max died feeling like he was invisible in his own house and family, now he felt larger than life. It was almost like he was the rope in a tug-of-war between his parents.

"I guess I'll look for him downstairs," Adam said, wishing he had the guts to just ask what was going on this time. This was his house—his family too.

*****

Death left a lot of things unfinished. Max had left a Lego city, partially complete, on the family room floor. He had also left books closed around tissue bookmarks, showing his progress cut short. And he had left his Simple Plan CD in the car stereo that day. When Jerry had gone to the grocery store to pick up the car, he turned on the ignition and was blasted with the song, "I'm Just a Kid". It came out of the speakers and filled the car like a solid presence that froze him right there with his hands on the wheel. He sat there in the middle of the crowded lot, a grown man brought to tears by a song that signified the true extent of the tragedy that had just brought his whole world crashing in around him.

And now his marriage was dead. The unsaid had swollen and grown like a cancerous tumor between them, stifling them. To this day they'd never really had a discussion about what happened when Max died. They hadn't discussed the distance between them, or their thoughts and feelings. They never sorted through the pain. Eventually, they just got past it and started to live as a couple again. He wondered if the fact that they never actually cleared the air had polluted their relationship. It didn't excuse Lindsey's behavior. It didn't make up for anything, but it might help explain why love wasn't enough.

They had refused to go through the ugly truth to find the real, full-bodied closeness that used to bind them. Now nothing short of turning back the calendar to the day Lindsey learned she carried their child within her and instead made the choice to share their blessing with him, could ever make up for the pain she had brought him. She had shredded his heart, making him feel vulnerable and weak. Never had he been so certain of his futility in the face of life.

Unfinished mourning was terminal.

*****

"I see that Adam is outside raking leaves. How much is he taking you for?" she asked, trying to goad him into interacting with her.

"Ten bucks." His tone was cold.

"Not bad."

Jerry didn't respond, obviously choosing the conversation wasn't worth continuing.

"So, what are you up to?" she asked brightly.

"I'm not sure."

"Do you—"

"I don't really need a companion," he cut her off.

"I just thought that we could—"

"Could what? Turn back time to before you lied to me? Better yet, back to before Max died? How about all the way back to before we met so I could avoid all this pain to begin with?"

"You don't mean that," Lindsey said, her brave front demolished.

"Anything would be better than living like this," he growled.

"Even erasing Adam and Max entirely?"

"Don't even talk about erasing a child. *You* can't stand there and say anything to me about that."

"I love all of my children, Jerry. And even if having them might bring me pain, I am still glad I have them. I am still glad I have you," she said softly.

"Correction—you *had* me," he said forcefully. "You don't deserve any of us."

"I will fight for this family," she said, with all the conviction she could muster.

"You? Fight? You didn't even want to file a civil suit when your son died. You didn't want to fight then. You were adamant about it," he accused, even though he didn't give a damn about any suit. He just wanted to lash out and hurt her for taking his will out of the equation, forcing her opinion and making choices in her interest instead of for their marriage and family. She had ignored him entirely and made the decision. Just like she had done when she found out she was pregnant. That was what really pissed him off.

"You agreed with me!" Lindsey shrieked incredulously.

"I let it go. That doesn't mean I agreed," he snapped.

"If it was that important to you, you shouldn't have let it go."

"You insisted! You were hanging by a thread with everything else, but about that you were sure…. Like you didn't want to fight for your child in his death."

"That isn't fair, Jerry. You know how I felt."

"I don't know how you feel about anything, Lindsey. I don't even know who you are."

"Don't say that."

"Say what? That I find myself questioning everything that you ever said, everything about our relationship, wondering if I ever really knew you?"

"You can't erase the past just because you don't like the present," she said, her voice strong and steady.

"You should have *wanted* to fight for Max. You should have wanted someone to pay for it!" Jerry growled. He knew that he was hitting below the belt. He knew that she would have done anything for Max, and that made her disregard for their daughter even worse.

"You know you don't mean that, Jerry."

"Someone should—"

"I saw the man." she cut him off. "He didn't mean to do it. He didn't do anything wrong. He wasn't speeding through the lot like crazy. Max darted out in front. That man who was driving that car will go through enough. It will be with him the rest of his life. I know how he feels. I know the torture he will feel forever after. I could never—" She stopped because Jerry had already turned to leave in disgust. If he felt that way about the stranger who happened to be bound to them tragically, how did he feel about her part in Max's accident? If he wanted to find fault, he should be looking at her. *I should be the one to pay.*

-26 Weeks-

Jerry was moving through life in a daze. He worked late as much as humanly possible because being out of the house distanced him physically and to some degree emotionally from the reality of his marriage, which was over. He could hardly look at Lindsey, let alone consider trying to continue raising a family together. The only reason he hadn't already moved out was an effort to maintain a stable environment for Adam as long as possible and ensure the safety of his unborn child. He didn't really believe that she would try to harm the baby, but at this point he was angry enough to wish that a court would see it that way and award him full custody of both children. He just had to bide his time until it was prudent to put the paperwork through.

He wondered at how in five months' time he had lost so much. His family had been decimated. They had been *dreaming* of having another child, and now he had almost lost two—one, the victim of a horrible tragic accident; the other, collateral damage. Is that how she saw it? Did she really think that since she was so damaged by her loss it was okay to consider murdering their baby to avoid future pain?

For months before Max died they had been doing it like rabbits, hoping to add to their family. It didn't make sense that she could throw their dream come true away for anything. It was eating at him. He turned it over in his mind, struggling to reach back to their other life, before everything went to hell. There was a point when Lindsey

234

had shut down the pregnancy talk and stopped taking tests. *Had she known even then that she was already pregnant? Had she stopped wanting to have a baby? Had she ever wanted another child at all?.... No!* He shook his head to clear the offensive skepticism. *I know we were in this together back then. We were in this whole thing together.* He hated that his mind could even wander to this place, let alone follow a circuitous path to where Lindsey was a manipulative bitch who had lied to him all along. He didn't want to question everything he had ever believed about his wife. He didn't want to start rewriting their history together. He didn't want to start counting weeks to try to determine when she knew about the pregnancy. *This is about Max. I know that this is all about him. He changed her, in life, for the better... and, in death, he took her with him.*

It was just a cruel twist of fate that Max was killed soon after conceiving. He thought of those darkest minutes, hours, days and weeks after losing their young son and wondered at the light that could have shown upon them, a glow that could have led them through the worst, toward new hope. *If only we had shared in this pregnancy. If she had trusted in me and believed in us enough.*

As he drove home he had to fight to stay the course. He dreaded walking in the front door. When Lindsey was restricted to bed rest and his daughter's health lay in the balance, he had the upper hand to blame her for wishing this upon them. Now that she was up and around, she was stronger. And she was so close, challenging him to talk to her or confront her. *But there is nothing left to say.* There was a time when he thought he could forgive her anything, but this— there was no turning back from this.

He pulled in the driveway, only mildly surprised to see Shelley's Mustang parked in his spot. He parked behind Lindsey's car and got out just as Shelley was coming out of the house. He attempted to brush past her.

"Jerry," she said, grabbing him by the arm.

"What?" he snapped.

"You have a right to be mad at me. I did know about it."

"Like I couldn't figure that out on my own," he said bitingly.

Shelley ignored his jab. "I told her I wouldn't help her do it. I told her she couldn't do something like that and not tell you.... I told her to tell you about the baby, and she cut me out of her life."

"So you were my champion in all of this? Is that what you're trying to say? That I should be *thanking* you for all your help?" he demanded, angry and hurt.

She held his gaze, showing her strength. "I hoped that what I said would be enough. I prayed she wouldn't go through with it. She loves you too much. Even though she was feeling helpless, her love for you would guide her. I believed that."

"And *what if*, Shelley?"

"I couldn't tell on her. It's her body. Her decision. No one on earth could make her go through with this pregnancy. It was her choice to make."

"And as the father, where does that leave me?" he asked helplessly.

She stared at him, unwilling or unable to answer.

"It isn't fair. This baby is *our* baby. *Our* choice."

"But that isn't the way—"

"Bullshit! That's *pure* bullshit!"

"Jerry, there is no answer here. It's just a question of love," Shelley said softly.

"You're going to tell me about love? Love blinded me to what the hell was going on. Love almost lost me my daughter."

"That's not true—"

"Hell, you had an abortion, didn't you?" he challenged. "She told me you had one in high school."

"I did," she said, unflinching.

"What about the guy? What did he think?"

"He didn't think much of anything."

"Did you even tell him?" he demanded.

"No."

"So it's to hell with the father? It only matters what the mother thinks?" His frustration with the pure unfairness and diabolical coldness of reality was growing.

"I was young. I was protecting myself. I didn't want my decisions or problems spread around the school."

"So a baby is a problem?"

"At fifteen, yes, it was a problem."

"Is that what Lindsey thought about our daughter?" He felt his heart breaking under the weight of despair.

"Jerry, I still believe in my decision. But Lindsey isn't me. She can't sleep with someone without feeling. She can't conceive without love. She gave her heart to you and the boys. When it was broken, she didn't know that it could be fixed."

"But, Shelley—"

"I am not telling you what to feel or what to do. I just want you to know that it is still Lindsey. She is still there, living and breathing and hurting just like you are. Neither one of you is whole on your own, denying that will lead you to believing you don't need each other."

"What are you a psychologist now?" he mocked her.

"I just don't want to see you end it this way. Have a knock-down-drag-out fight. Scream at each other. *Feel* something, damn it! You two make me sick, throwing this away. I thought you guys were stronger than this. I thought you were better than the rest of us. And now I see that you're just a couple of cowards."

*****

Lindsey watched him from the living room window. He stood on the front walk, his back to her. She knew that Shelley had stopped him out there and put her two cents in, but she couldn't see her friend from the window. She had just gotten her own tongue-lashing and knew what Shelley was capable of dishing out, but the window and the neighbor's lawnmower muffled the conversation enough that she couldn't hear them.

When Jerry finally came to the door, she sifted quickly through her options. She could pretend to be busy working on something, or she could wait in the living room like she wanted to talk. She could be friendly and helpful, or she could give him the cold shoulder he had been giving her. She heard his key in the lock, even though she had never bothered locking the door after Shelley left. Before the door broke the seal, she hurried into the kitchen where she had left the mail on the island, a welcome diversion that would put her right in his way. She pulled her long cardigan sweater around her tight belly, against the chill in the room.

Most of the pile before her was junk mail, but she sorted through it with interest anyway, attempting to seem enthralled by a letter from their homeowner's insurance company imploring them to consider their other insurance needs. She put it off to the side in the maybe pile and plucked the catalogs out of the stack for later mindless perusing. She sifted through envelopes: a credit card offer, a warranty reminder and a deal on carpet cleaning. Then her heart almost stopped. Two postcards—one for Adam and one for Max. Checkup reminders. It was the last thing they had done at their last dentist appointment in April, set up their next visit and filled out their own postcards. She felt a fine fissure run through her as she looked at Max's unsteady hand, how he used all capitals in his first name like he just knew he was important. Each reminder of Max's life and death produced another invisible crack inside her that she feared would eventually compromise her to the point that she would simply fall apart.

Jerry fumbled around in the foyer, came down the hall and walked through the kitchen without a word. He disappeared into the family room with Sadie in hot pursuit, intent on being noticed. The front door swung open and Adam came trucking through in a rush, checking the time on the stove clock.

"I just made it!" he said triumphantly.

Lindsey looked at him, questioningly.

"Dinner? Five o'clock?" he prodded.

"Oh, dinner." Lindsey looked around the kitchen, helplessly. She'd had every intention of taking the stew out of the freezer for dinner, until Shelley came over.

"Hey, Sport, why don't you and I go to the park? We can toss the football around and then grab a hotdog at Dairy Queen," Jerry said, coming back through the room.

"Sounds great!" Adam sang out.

She watched Jerry's eyes skate around the cold kitchen, certain he was smug and satisfied with himself for abandoning her to an empty house and no dinner.

They were on their way out the door when Adam piped up, "What about Mom? Do you think she wants to come?"

"No, she doesn't want to sit around and watch us play," Jerry said with certainty.

Lindsey felt a flash of anger and a fire growing inside as she heard him dismissing her from their lives entirely. *I'm not going to let this happen. He will not do this.*

"Actually, I would love to come and watch my guys play ball," she said, forcing a smile over her fiery resolve.

Jerry noticed the resolution in her jaw and the gleam in her eye. He had seen it before. It had drawn him to her in the first place. She had the outward appearance of sugar and spice, but when she was challenged or cornered about something she believed in, this is what came out.

*****

They spent an hour at the park, under Lindsey's watchful eyes. Every time he stole a glance in her direction, expecting to see anger, he instead saw adoration. She looked like she was in love with the genuine act of spending time together.

He saw the strength of the woman he used to know—a woman who fought for what she wanted, enjoyed the things she loved and hungered for what the world could offer—and he was bewildered. Even as things had gotten better slowly after Max's death, he had not seen such stubborn certainty in Lindsey since before tragedy struck. So why was it coming out now? Why would she suddenly feel like life was worth something again? *Why is she putting up a fight when it's already over?*

At Dairy Queen, he watched her struggle with a foot long that was too loaded with condiments to eat safely. She ended up looking like a toddler who had just learned to feed herself. In another life he would have taken a napkin and helped clean her up. He would have cradled her face in his hands and gently wiped at the stray sauces. Now he simply handed Adam a napkin and said, "Give this to your mother; she's an absolute mess."

Adam didn't like being put in the middle. His parents used to keep their arguments to themselves, not that they had fought much. Now, their relationship seemed to be one long, quiet argument, and he had become the person they spoke through. He could tell that his dad was angry and being really short with his mom. She, on the other hand, seemed to be extra calm and nice. When he used to fight with his brother and hold a grudge, Max would be really nice to him until he finally gave in to being friends again. It usually happened because Max took something of his and destroyed it or lost it. He wondered what his mom had done.

He handed the napkin over and put his hand on her belly. "Do you think that the baby likes hotdogs?" he asked, partly out of interest but mostly just to divert attention from whatever was bothering his dad.

"I don't know," she said. "We have a while to wait before we can ask her."

"I think she just answered," Adam laughed. "She kicked at my hand!"

"She did! I think that's a yes!" Lindsey laughed along with him.

"You've gotta feel this, Dad! It's so cool!"

"I know, Adam. I know."

"Really, Dad, touch right here. That's where I felt it," he prodded. He wanted his dad to loosen up and enjoy their time together. He hoped that just touching that spot and feeling the baby kick would put an end to whatever was bothering him.

Jerry knew he had no option. Adam had called him out, putting him on the spot. He placed his hand on Lindsey's stomach tentatively, like it might be too hot to touch. "Well, I guess she went back to sleep," he said, after mere seconds.

Lindsey grabbed his hand before he could pull away, holding it firmly in place. When the swift kick bulged the skin beneath his hand, he felt it in his heart. She was alive and well in there. For a moment he locked eyes with his wife. Her gaze was a dazzling green determination; his was a wallowing, floundering sadness.

They drove home in the dark without a word, thankful for the sound of the radio taking up the space between them. Jerry waited through the interminable few hours until Adam was safely in bed for the night before he unleashed the words that were cutting through his insides.

"That was a dirty trick you played tonight, Lindsey."

"So you're finally going to talk *to* me instead of at or around me?" she countered, tired of the cold shoulder.

"I am not the one who started this."

"But you're going to finish it—is that what you want to say to me?"

"No," he said firmly.

"Then what?"

"I just—I can't be around you. I *hate* living here like this, but I am *not* going to walk out right now. Adam has been through too much," he said in frustrated resignation. "You know how I feel. Is this some kind of game to you? Do you get pleasure out of hulking over me?"

"I get pleasure out of spending time with Adam and letting him enjoy time with his parents," Lindsey said forcefully, enunciating her words like he was a small child.

He stared at her in utter disbelief. This was the same woman who had withdrawn to the point that she didn't interact with anyone, and now she was claiming it a necessity to spend time together as a family.

"Yeah, right. What a load of crap."

"You want the honest truth?"

"Yes, that's all I have ever asked for from you, and what I believed I always got, until—"

"Just shut up for a minute!" Her tone, a vicious whisper—part anguish and part righteous anger. "Punish me, damn it! Punish me all you want, Jerry! Rip me down for who I am and what I've done… but don't you try to squeeze me out of this family."

"You're the one who turned your back on the family—on me— on Adam—on our daughter. God, if you weren't pregnant, I would already be gone."

Lindsey's mouth gaped in shock. She had known it, but she had never expected to hear him say it. The words cut more than she would have imagined. She was on borrowed time. Fighting for control, she told herself that egging him on to follow through on his threats was not the answer, even though her knee-jerk reaction was to let him have it. She had to temper herself if she wanted to ensure that there would be more tomorrows and more time to keep what was left of her life together.

"I'm sorry you feel that way, Jerry."

She went upstairs and locked herself in their bathroom, more to keep herself contained than out of worry that he would follow her. She had to work against every fighting reflex she had, to leave the argument like that. She started the water in the bathtub, hoping to soak her frazzled nerves. Her whole body felt alive. It was not their first argument, but it was the first time since Max died that she felt her own strength. In the past months she had gone through numbness, into helplessness and frustration, then guilt and despair. She had felt so many things, but this was the first time she felt awakened to her power and desire to fight for her future.

*****

His eyes followed her as she left the room, shocked by the calm she left in her wake. It was like she had sucked all the anger out of the room with her, leaving him in awe.

At times, recently, he had seen her as something of a squatter in his life—unneeded and unwanted company. He had spent so much time wondering who she was to him, and how she could have even considered decisions about their children without him, that he hadn't bothered to notice the transformation in her that was suddenly before his eyes. Gone was the meek and mealy woman who had no answer for him when confronted about the baby. Gone was the spineless creature who had disregarded him and his feelings. This Lindsey would not back down. She stood her ground, and *he* ended up sounding unreasonable. It unnerved him. It aggravated him. It picked at the edges of old wounds.

The baby was coming sooner rather than later. Even though he had already made up his mind that their marriage was beyond saving, he hadn't made any plans on which to follow through. He didn't know where he would go when he left. Or how to handle their intertwined financial situation. How to go about getting custody of the kids. He hadn't actually put a single firm foot forward, and right now he felt like he was standing in quicksand. He didn't know what he wanted other than the fact that he wanted to *choose* his future. Complacency was something he couldn't live with. He couldn't allow himself to be lulled into living the status quo of a marriage without trust, one where love was hopelessly buried deep beneath grief and lies.

-29 Weeks-

A tomato.

She would have created a tomato suit, a big juicy ripe one. She could imagine him tottering around in it like a sumo wrestler. He would have loved being plump and round and running into things. He probably would have asked to have the suit filled with something gooey, so if it split open it would be like a real tomato, spewing seeds and juices. Tears ran down her face and she made no effort to stop them.

God, I hate Halloween!

She had dreaded it—feared something much worse than the ghosts and goblins. What wasn't there—what wouldn't be—haunted her. This would have been Max's seventh time trick or treating. It would have been his seventh... and best costume. His choice of a tomato would have been a huge leap, creatively speaking, from the standard superhero garb he had wanted in earlier years. At six and three-quarters, he probably would have made it all the way to the door of 1130 Sycamore Lane. Each year he had gotten a little closer before being frightened away by the owner, who dressed as a scarecrow and lay in wait on the porch chair with a bowl of candy. And there was Adam, always there next to his brother, to hold his hand or to collect his treats for him. Lindsey felt herself smiling through her tears at the bittersweet memories.

She wanted to remember everything about Max's short life. She wanted to keep every celebration and every average moment close to

245

her heart. She had reached the point where daily memories brought smiles more often than tears. But a time like this, that only snuck up once a year, was harder to accept. To know that she could no longer wrap her child in the excitement of tradition. She could no longer look at him the way parents looked at their living and breathing children. She couldn't imagine what the future would hold for him. She only had memories—wonderful memories—that would define who he was and never tell her who he would be.

She looked at Adam, standing in front of her, waiting impatiently for her to take a picture of him dressed as a punk rocker. *I'm trying. I am trying so hard to give you your childhood,* she thought, willing him to understand.

She felt the insistent shifting and bumping inside her stomach as if to tell her to snap out of it. She was never alone, and she had come to take comfort in that. It was strange that her mood didn't dictate her daughter's mood. It was more the other way around. The little girl she would meet someday had the power to overthrow her emotions. She responded to Lindsey's state and interjected her opinion as need be, like now.

*****

Adam dug through to the back of the linen closet, glad to have escaped anymore pictures. Every time his mom took the camera down from her face, he could see the puffiness around her eyes that told him she was fighting the tears. And then he would feel the same sadness wash over him. It was hard not to miss Max; this was his favorite holiday. He liked it even better than Christmas, at least until Halloween had passed and Christmas was actually approaching. Then he would start talking about Christmas being his favorite time of year. Max was such a goober, but it still hurt.

He upended towels and washcloths and sheets until he found what he needed—an old pillowcase he could fill with candy loot.

246

Technically, he was still going trick or treating, but tonight he would be out with his friends instead of alone with his parents. If it was going to have to be different this year, he wanted to be the one deciding how it would be.

He knew his mom wasn't keen on letting him go, but his dad had said yes immediately, cautioning him against any actual "tricking," like throwing eggs, spraying shaving cream and rolling toilet paper on trees and yards. Adam had the sneaking suspicion that his dad had probably done all of those things when he was his age, but to call him on it would be pointless. It was another of those times when grown-ups would answer, "do as I say, not as I do."

It was getting late, and the rest of the band was probably already at the party. There were five of them, and each was going with different colored Mohawks and ripped T-shirts and fake tattoos. Too bad they couldn't really play any instruments, but they had an awesome band name—Hanging Eyeballs. It was Justin's idea.

"Can we go now?" he asked with exasperation as he came downstairs and into the kitchen.

"Yes, Adam," Lindsey sniffled. "We can go now."

"Good. I don't want them to leave without me," he said anxiously.

"Let's go. Get in the car," Jerry said, keys already in hand. He didn't even look over at her, just gestured for Adam to follow him.

"But I was going to—"

"I'll take him, so you can hand out the candy," he said nicely, so Adam wouldn't understand that he was actually undercutting her and putting her in her place.

"Uh... well, okay." She was momentarily off-guard. Then she turned to Adam and kissed him lightly on the forehead. "Have fun, dude. Rock on!"

"Oh, Mom, you're so weird."

"Come on," Jerry prodded, not wanting to see her brave face or know that she was going to make the best of anything he dished out at her, including banishing her to handing out candy and the constant reminders of Halloweens' past that it would conjure up. "I have to stop by and talk to Rob. I'll hang there and wait to pick Adam up."

He didn't wait for her response. He wasn't going to allow her to question what he was doing or why. He was going to be his own person and handle this children's holiday—that was breaking him— the way he wanted to handle it. He actually didn't know what he was going to do between the time he dropped Adam off and when he picked him up. All he knew was that he needed to be out of the house because he was unnerved by the way that Lindsey had been trucking through the last few weeks with certainty and he, who had reason and right behind him, was unable to get steady.

*****

She drove at a snail's pace. There were little pixies and princesses, ninjas and cowboys, as well as plenty of ghoulish masks on the streets; the thrill of candy was in the air, making their movements erratic and dangerous. There hardly seemed to be enough parents about to keep watch on all the costumed madness. She saw light sticks swinging around and seeming to levitate in midair, the holders camouflaged by the night. She saw little reflective stripes and shapes bouncing along the pavement on joyful feet. Her heart constricted with the thought that last year her boys were two more happy children following the trail of treats from door to door.

She hoped the bowl of candy she had left on the porch would last until she got back, rather than getting swiped by the first person who happened upon it. If it did turn up empty, she hadn't left anything for the trick or treaters to take out their frustrations on. There were no jack-o'-lanterns outside to smash. She just didn't have the heart for it. A family of four pumpkins had always lived there, and only putting out three seemed a morbid way to share their new life with their neighbors. And a fourth, plain and untouched, seemed an even worse reminder that Max wasn't there to take part in his holiday. There was no way to pick pumpkins and not remember how Max would agonize over the shape of his jack-o'-lantern's head, or how he would draw and wipe off crayon eyes and teeth over and over again in preparation for carving. Last year he had picked the largest pumpkin of all, a tall skinny one, and given it a teeny, tiny scrunched up face with huge ears on the sides. No, there just didn't seem to be a right way to do things anymore… so she had avoided it altogether.

Once she reached the main road, the signs of Halloween dissipated to little and then nothing. She became lulled by the headlights of other cars as she made her way. Everyone's story was invisible to others when people were simplified to passing cars on the road in the dark of the night. She liked the anonymity. She was able to keep her story and her thoughts to herself alone. Reaching next to her, she grasped the paper lunchbag that sat on the passenger seat and put it in her lap. Its firm, solid weight against her legs was comforting.

As she pulled into the quiet drive that wound through the grounds, she wondered at the nature of what she was doing. High school kids dared each other to go to cemeteries on Halloween night. Scenes like that were favorites in hatchet movies. Mothers didn't visit their children at a time like this; yet here she was. She pulled to a stop where Jerry had parked when he brought them all here.

She held tight to the paper bag and walked through the grass to the beautiful spot where Max was buried. The earth seamlessly covered his grave, the truth highlighted by the moonlight that shined down upon him. The scars in the grass were entirely gone, as if the ground had never been opened at all. Was this nature's way of saying that it had been long enough? That healing should be complete? *God, it's so lonely here.*

"Happy Halloween," she said, her voice choked and quiet. It hurt to see his name carved in cold stone. "Remember what you wanted to be? I don't think I will ever forget. You said you wanted to be a tomato…. I never got to make you that costume, but I wanted to bring you something." She reached into the bag, the sound of the paper echoing in the solemn night. She placed the large ripe tomato on the barren soil in the pot at the head of his grave, wondering if it would end up nourishing the soil for the plant she knew was dormant underneath. She hadn't asked about the plant when they came here before, but she knew it was Jerry who had put it here. She knew that he came here to visit their son. She knew these things without needing to see for her own eyes. It was the man—the father he was.

"I am so sorry, Max. I wish I could take back that moment. I was right there. If only I had realized what was happening before—" She let out a heaving sob of anguish. This wasn't about her… or rethinking what happened. This was about her little boy. She steadied herself before continuing, "I think about you all the time. I want to see you every day. I miss your smile and your laughter. I want to hug you and hold you again…. I know you are too young to understand what you mean to the world around you. When you're a kid, you think that you don't matter because people are always either bossing you around or ignoring you. I want you to know—to understand—that you do matter. I don't even know how to be me without you." Her voice was tinged with the steady rain of tears. "We are all trying so hard, Max. But for such a little boy, you left a huge hole in our hearts."

Lindsey looked up at the stars in the sky and the slightly misshapen moon, as if searching for more strength and more words. Her hand on her stomach felt the life beneath her touch, just as her soul felt the emptiness beneath her body. This was a place to concentrate grief and thoughts and feelings away from the weight of collected earthly concerns that could be palpable at home. It was a serene place where lives could be immortalized for those who came later. It was a place of peace to talk to those who were passed. But

Max was not here. "Someday, we will all be together again. For now, just know that you are loved."

*****

"Hey guys! I hope you got a lot of loot!" Lindsey said, tapping Adam's stiff Mohawk on his way into the house.

Jerry saw the stiff set of her jaw that was intended to offset the puffiness in her face. He knew that she had been crying, and all he could think was that they should be in this together. They should be able to lean on each other through anything and everything. It was killing him to know that he had no partner in his life.

She sniffed lightly and asked, "Was it hard?"

He felt the ice inside of him melt the slightest bit. Without saying as much, those three words were her admission that it was a difficult night without Max. She was the only person in this world who felt the same pain for his lost son, and he longed to share it with her. Then he reminded himself that it was her fault that they were unable to bear this burden of loss together. She was the one who destroyed everything with her lies and omissions.

Long after Adam became a simple boy again and was tucked away in bed, Jerry found himself at the door of their bedroom. It was like the gateway to a foreign place now. Only a month ago they had shared it, before he started sleeping on the couch in the den, unable to handle being that close to her. He couldn't understand her, and he didn't even want to anymore. And now he had even more reason to wonder who this woman was—she had gone somewhere tonight. He came home after dropping Adam off, realizing that he had nowhere else to go. He felt lost and unable to escape from the mess that was his heart and his life, and he had come back here to confront that feeling—confront her. But her car was gone, and there was an empty bowl on the front porch. He hadn't even been able to trust her to stay home and handle Halloween for a few hours. She had escaped without a word or note. And then, when he got home with Adam, she had acted like she had been there all along.

This time he didn't knock; he walked right in, showing his power and ownership. When he came to her in the darkness of their bedroom, he did so with frustration and anger. He wanted to take something from her and lashing out with physical need and emotional disregard was the only weapon in his arsenal. He wanted to manipulate her feelings. He wanted to use her trust and then destroy it like she had done to him. He wanted to feel strong in this world, to stop letting her bat him around in her stiff and tortuous winds of grief and self-pity. He needed to get his rocks off and wanted to do it emptily and blindly. But he couldn't squelch his pain entirely. And somewhere in the middle he lost himself—lost the anger and felt the comfort of being one with her, sharing the intimacy of their common pain. And when it was over the darkness within him was suddenly gone, but the truth was left behind—their life together had ended.

*****

Lindsey woke to an image burned into her memory, the smoldering look of need and desire in Jerry's eyes. She had caught fire from that look. He had seemed raw and dangerous and driven by forces out of his control. He hadn't so much as touched her in weeks, and the passionate intensity of his need was all-encompassing. She didn't think to question it. She didn't want to stop it. She let herself fall completely.

Gazing upon him in the early morning light, she felt the beginnings of hope in her heart. When he stirred, she looked into his sleepy eyes, hoping to find a new start.

"Good morning," she said softly.

He looked at her like he didn't understand why she was there. She felt her heart speed up with trepidation.

252

"Hey," he said curtly, sitting up and getting his bearings.

It hardly seemed like the right kind of greeting after what had happened the night before.

"I'll go make some coffee," she offered, making a move to get out of the bed and feeling the awkwardness of all of her six months.

"Don't bother. I'll get my own."

"Is something wrong? Did you oversleep?"

"No."

"Then what—"

"Lindsey, don't make this any more strange than it already is."

"What do you mean?"

"Oh, come on. You don't think that this means anything." His tone was dismissive. "This—it's like the night after a drunken—"

"What are you talking about? We weren't drunk!"

"No, but you get my point. It's like a one-night stand. A last hurrah. Call it closure if you want…" he trailed off.

Lindsey fought the tears that started to form. She didn't want to give him the satisfaction. Controlling her voice the best she could, she said, "Don't pretend with me, Jerry. Don't make me feel—"

"Make *you* feel?" he asked incredulously. "Just what am I not supposed to make you feel like?"

"Some common slut you took home from a bar and used for a night."

"What's the difference between me treating you like trash and you treating me that way? You treated our whole marriage like it was trash! You obliterated the trust, Lindsey. There is nothing left!"

"The difference? You ask the difference between you screwing me over last night on purpose, making me feel things I'm afraid to feel for you… and… and—"

"And you planning to abort *my* child, who I didn't even know about? Go ahead. Let's see how you can compare a *grudge fuck* with a *life*!"

253

She winced, like his words struck a physical blow. "The difference is—I wasn't *trying* to hurt you. I wasn't—"

"Thinking about me at all? Is that what you were going to say?"

"No, I was thinking about you. But I was afraid, Jerry. I thought I needed to protect myself because I knew you were strong enough. I didn't think I was!"

-31 Weeks-

Her mother had been the last to hear the news. Even strangers on the street knew before her, the visual cues were a dead giveaway. Lindsey reasoned that the miles between them made it difficult to keep more than a tenuous connection between their daily lives, but it was a load of crap. This wasn't the days of the pony express. They both knew that if she had wanted to tell her about her granddaughter, she could have picked up the phone immediately. Perhaps it was guilt that prodded her into accepting the invitation to spend Thanksgiving with her family, rather than observing their normal tradition of staying at home and hosting Jerry's parents.

Since she had agreed to go, she had pushed it to the far recesses of her thoughts. She carefully avoided looking too far into the future at any potential stumbling blocks, like holidays and special events, that lay in the path of her continued healing process. Grief seemed best handled one day at a time, much like addicts and alcoholics in recovery. She had hoped that if she concentrated only on the moment at hand, one day she would wake up on the other side of her discomfort and pain. But now she found herself rushing headlong into difficult territory. Each passing day was another day closer to celebrating her daughter's birth and the legal death of her marriage. She couldn't help but look down the barrel at the future she had been avoiding. There was less than two weeks to go until Thanksgiving, and her relationship was in shambles. She had to fess up with herself that this bone she had decided to throw her mother, in an effort to make amends, was now going to be a tortuous, long weekend. She had to prepare.

Marie was shrewd. She could taste the truth and lies in your words and see it in your eyes. That was why she had avoided sharing the pregnancy as long as possible. It wasn't even safe to discuss the weather. The truth was hidden in everything she said, and her mother was a wonderful, strong and able person who could find it. Marie had a quiet and unshakeable faith in her Creator that gave her that strength. Lindsey knew that she had not faired the tumultuous storm of grief well. She knew that she had fallen short of who she had been raised to be. She had avoided her mother out of her feelings of inadequacy and embarrassment, and now she was going to stand before that woman and try to hide the truth and her growing shame.

As she stood at the island, making Adam's lunch for school, the weight of that realization suddenly hit her with its full force, making her back up to the kitchen table and sit down. She put her head down in front of her and closed her eyes to calm herself. *I can do this. She will be more disappointed if she knows the full truth about the abortion and my marriage,* she tried to tell herself. *I just have to keep it together long enough to look like a happy family.*

Lindsey heard Jerry's footfalls on the floor nearby and looked up to see him at the counter, fixing a cup of coffee and carefully ignoring her.

"Remember, we're going to my parents for Thanksgiving," she said blandly, by way of greeting. They had abandoned all niceties since that night when he had come to her in their room. Now they only spoke to convey factual information that absolutely had to be passed through their parental channels—family plans, field trips, school grades and assignments, repairs or finances.

"I know," he grumbled, his voice gravelly with sleep.

"We will have to—" She stopped to clear her throat. "—sleep together... in the same room when we're there, unless you want everyone to know...."

"I think you should be the one who is concerned about what people know. Not me," he said icily, looking at the upper kitchen cabinets—anywhere in the room other than at her.

His words bit deep and she bowed her head in an attempt to quell the frustration and tears she felt threatening. Collecting herself, she started again, "I just want to make sure that we are on the same page. In order to protect Adam, we need to put on some semblance of normalcy in our interactions and the sleeping arrangements."

"Fine," he said curtly, walking out of the room to put an end to the conversation.

She was filled with dread, wondering if Jerry's anger at her would overtake his ability and desire to avoid airing dirty family laundry. This would be the first time they would see a lot of the people who had come to Max's funeral. These people would undoubtedly, in ill-conceived attempts to sympathize with their incredibly difficult journey over the months, open up wounds that had hardly scabbed over. This was a lot to ask of a man who no longer trusted or loved her, and she only hoped that he would still be the rock she had always known him to be.

*****

Screw her, Jerry thought, marching back upstairs to get ready for work. *Who the hell does she think she is, trying to make sure that I'm going to behave properly at Thanksgiving? She's the one who doesn't know how to behave properly.*

A part of him, though, imagined how great it would feel to have her exposed in front of everyone for her treason against their union. People looked upon their entire family with pity for their loss and pain, but Lindsey didn't deserve pity.

God, how the hell did I end up in this position anyway? I don't want to go spend time with her family and old friends. How did my wishes not get figured into this? How did my parents get screwed in this process?

But he knew how it had happened. It happened when he was riding high on the news of their daughter-to-be. The plans had been made before life had gone to shit again. Before the roller coaster of their marriage over the past months had literally flown off the track entirely. So now, he would follow through with his side of the bargain.

He would not be manipulated by his wife, but he also wouldn't purposely hurt Lindsey's parents and family. It wasn't his place to tell them who she was or what she had done. That was between her and them. In a few more months, when their marriage was dissolved, she could choose to tell all of them what really happened, or her own version of the truth. It would no longer be his concern. For now, he would play his part for everyone, because no one else deserved to pay the price for her choices.

*****

"Dad?" Adam asked cautiously, poking his head around the bathroom door to spy his father shaving at the sink.

"Yeah, Sport?"

"Can you drive me to school today? I have to bring in the papier-mâché volcano we built."

"Whoa! That's not going to fit on the bus! Sure, I'll take you," he said, speaking to him through the mirror.

"Thanks," Adam said, standing there uncertainly.

"Is there something else?" he asked, stopping in mid-stroke to turn and look directly at him.

"I was just wondering…. Are you and Mom getting a divorce?" Adam asked seriously, almost choking on the words as he tried to force them up through his dry throat.

"Hey, why would you ask me that?"

"Because I know you've been sleeping in the den... and you guys just aren't you anymore," he said, unable to put into words what was so obviously different about them.

"Don't you ever worry yourself about your mom and me. We love you so much, and you have nothing to fear. Nothing at all," his dad said, chucking him in the shoulder and quickly turning back to the mirror to finish shaving.

And to avoid my eyes, Adam thought. He noticed immediately that his dad didn't deny it. He just skirted around the question. *If I ask Mom the same thing, I'll probably get the same answer. Even parents who don't agree about anything seem to agree about keeping kids in the dark and avoiding uncomfortable questions.*

I don't know who they think they're fooling. Just because I'm a kid, doesn't mean I don't understand that arguments and discussions that stop when I walk in the room are usually important, and they definitely affect me in some way. Or that utter silence is only normal in a library, and even there, at least there is some noise. Like I don't have tons of kids at school that can provide a play-by-play about life in a house with parents who go through a divorce. Like I'm not smart enough to know that everything has changed.

Too bad Max isn't here.... The thought of going between two houses and having two separate lives with two separate parents would be easier with him here. At least we would always be in the same place at the same time—heck, if he was here this probably wouldn't be happening at all. Maybe I'm just not enough kid to keep this family together. Obviously what I want doesn't count. And the baby, well, we don't even know her yet, so I guess her opinion doesn't count either.

*****

Jerry had left for work five minutes before, so when he came back through the front door like he had been shot through a cannon, he startled her. Lindsey dropped the laundry basket she had been carrying through the foyer on her way upstairs. The carefully folded shirts and towels jumped when the basket hit the floor, but only a few caught enough air to escape the confines of the plastic walls. She carefully squatted to put the things back in the basket and pick the load up again, wondering if Jerry would think to apologize for scaring her half to death and then realizing, as soon as he opened his mouth, that an apology was not on his mind.

"Adam wants to know if we're getting a divorce," he accused.

"Excuse me?" she asked, not understanding his anger.

"What have you been telling him?"

"Nothing." Her eyes were wide with shock.

"You must have said something because I certainly didn't."

"Jerry, he isn't stupid. I think he can put two and two together." She brushed past him to carry the laundry upstairs.

"I thought we were trying to protect him from the dissolution of our marriage," he pointed out, following her.

"We are. But unless you can change the whole vibe around here, he is going to pick up on things like the sleeping arrangements… and the fact that you can hardly look me in the eye." She busied herself with the clothes, thankful to have a reason to bustle in and out of rooms while they argued. She felt stronger when she didn't have to see the disappointment on his face.

"Well, not that I like lying to him, but maybe for now we can just tell him that you need space to sleep considering your new and… larger size."

Lindsey stopped what she was doing and turned to face him, catching the tail end of a smile he quickly squelched.

"In the interest of our son, I will accept the whale excuse," she said, bowing her head slightly in deference, and in an attempt to hide her own smile.

"Settled. I have to get to work." He was suddenly awkward, since most of their discussions and arguments ended with anger still smoldering. He turned and stumbled on his way out of the room.

"Have a good day," she called out after him, purposely breaking the unspoken rule of avoiding pleasantries.

-33 Weeks-

When her mom had said that everyone would be there for Thanksgiving dinner, she had hoped that she was embellishing. Looking around the rooms of her childhood home, though, Lindsey was hard-pressed to see the exaggeration. *Everyone is here*—old friends, relationships gone past, close relatives, relatives she had only met once or twice in her life. There was hardly a square inch of space to spare. She had forgotten what Thanksgiving was like with her parents. They had not come to the event since before Max was born, another reason she had said yes to the invitation this year. They had never shared Max with these people in this setting. Rather than trying to adapt their Thanksgiving to their new reality, she thought it would be easier on her heart to entirely change up the holiday.

There had been awkward moments. Several times she was cornered by some well-meaning person, trying to offer sympathies and gauge her well-being by looking deep in her eyes—just as she had feared and expected—but she made her rounds early, choked back the discomfort, and now everyone pretty much left her alone. She hid easily amidst the bustle of the crowd, backed deep into the corner of the living room, welcoming the small glimpses of Adam as he threaded through all the people at the heels of other young relatives. She had seen his trepidation about the weekend when they first arrived, but now he was entirely absorbed and it soothed her heart.

When she felt a tug on her arm, she turned, expecting to see Adam.

"Will!" she yelped in shock.

"Hey, little sis," he said coolly, sweeping her into a hug. "Wow! You're huge!"

She pulled away and popped him in the arm. "You don't tell a woman that. Not even a pregnant woman!"

"Oh, is that why I'm still single?"

"Yeah, that among many things," she chided.

His voice turned serious. "So, how are you?"

"I have my moments. Some things are hard to handle... like holidays. I guess that's obvious. I'm *here* for Thanksgiving, aren't I?" she said, motioning around her. "Trying to escape the ghosts at home."

"Well, I'm glad you're here no matter what the reason."

"Ain't you sweet? Actually, I'm surprised that *you're* here." She poked him in the chest.

"I'm broadening my horizons a little. Just because I'm clean now doesn't mean I can avoid family events. Plus, I heard you were coming."

"I am so happy to see you," she said heartily, her lips quivering with appreciation and eyes welling up.

"Haven't you cried enough yet?" he asked in mock annoyance.

She smiled through her tears. "Thanks a lot."

"So where's Jerry?"

"He's around here somewhere," she said, making a halfhearted attempt to pretend to look around.

"What's up?"

"What do you mean?"

"You and Jerry are like *this* at these things," he said, twisting his two fingers together and holding them in front of her face.

"Yeah, well—"

"Come here," he whispered, dragging her out of the room.

They retreated to the closet under the stairs, where he sat on a massive bag of dog food and let her have the upturned two-gallon bucket her mom used for all her cleaning chores around the house.

"Spill it," he demanded.

"What?"

"Don't play dumb with me. I can see it all over your face."

"Will, it's nothing. Really."

"Tell me or I'll resort to Indian burns and wet willies. I'm famous for the latter, you know."

She sat staring at him, challenging him to move, but as soon as he stuck his finger in his mouth, she caved.

"Things are kind of rough at home."

"What do you mean?"

"Well, you know how I told you about this," Lindsey said, rubbing her stomach with her hands.

"Yeah," he prodded.

"Jerry found out."

"Well, of course, you're as big as a house!"

"I mean, he found out about my plans to have an abortion… *after* I had already decided I couldn't and wouldn't do it."

"You told him?" he asked, shocked.

"He found out! He found the ultrasound and the appointment and everything!"

"I don't know what to say. Of course he would be angry, but—"

"He's going to leave me," she cried.

"What do you mean?"

"The only reason we're still together right now is to protect Adam from further trauma. Once the baby is born, and there is more distance from… Max—" She gulped. "—he wants a divorce."

"Lindsey, I am so sorry. That bastard!"

"He has every right to feel this way, Will. I mean, really think about what I did. It was awful."

"But you didn't *do* it!"

"I betrayed his trust. I ignored our union! I thought only about my own selfish fears, not about us and our family."

"You made a mistake, from the pit of despair," he said, bewildered.

*****

Jerry was a lost soul wading through madness. Sixteen years married to Lindsey, and he still hardly knew anyone here. It was strange to have the truth hit him square in the face—his wife's family was not his family at all.

He wasn't ignored. Many people had come over to chat briefly and say a few nice words of encouragement about dealing with grief and loss. They were people he had probably met at Max's funeral, but at the time he was so torn apart and bleary-eyed that he didn't recognize them now. While he knew they meant well and appreciated their kindness, he wished that others would stop rehashing his son's story and disturbing his wounds.

The day was terminal boredom for him, until ninety-year-old Uncle Gary mistook him for his good-for-nothing son-in-law. He got in Jerry's face the best he could, standing toe-to-toe and craning his neck almost a foot to look him in the eye. He shook his crooked finger at him and called him a lying, cheating bastard. Then his dentures flew out of his mouth and landed on Jerry's shoe when he attempted to call him a fucking asshole. That was when he took a swing at him with his palsied hand. And she had missed the entire show.

The old Lindsey would have found the whole thing hysterically funny, as were most of the things Uncle Gary did in his advanced age, with his considerably impaired vision. The new Lindsey had ducked out somewhere, though, and he didn't want to look for her or seem like he cared. But he did care—that was the problem. Usually, at parties, it was like they were sewn together at the hip. Neither cared as much for the company of others as they cared for each other, so they spent their time wrapped in themselves among the mingling people. It wasn't just that he was uncomfortable around her family; he was lost without her.

The only thing that made Thanksgiving remotely tolerable was the fact that Adam was having fun. He would occasionally catch sight of him laughing and running, in or out or through the house. His son was so absorbed that he seemed to have escaped the sadness of another holiday without Max. Jerry envied him for the attention span and spirit he was fortunate to be blessed with as a child, making all life experiences more malleable. Adults didn't grow or change naturally or willingly, becoming entirely dependent on routine to guide their lives, while kids were forced to constantly reassess their place in the world as their bodies and minds grew and changed. Children were resilient.

*****

It was like no other Thanksgiving he could remember. It had always been just him and Max and the adults having a big meal and watching football. He hadn't even known how many cousins— actually second cousins—he had who were around his age. There were several around Max's age too. He would have had so much fun here. He especially would have liked playing kick ball on the actual little league field at the school behind their grandparents' house.

A holiday that had entirely centered around the meal for his entire life so far was something totally different today. In fact, they hardly ate any food at all. And no adults forced them to—Max would have loved that since he hated turkey *and* all the fixings. Instead of a structured meal at the table, it was a free-for-all. You could grab a plate whenever you wanted and go through and serve yourself like a buffet. Then you could sit wherever you wanted—on the couch, on the floor, on the stairs. He had never experienced anything like it. It would have been Max's favorite dinner ever—buttered rolls and chocolate chip cookies and Jell-O if he wanted, and no one telling him he couldn't.

*****

Jerry stood in the room that had been his wife's long before she met him. He looked at the double bed, remembering the days when he would have welcomed the closeness it required. Tonight, he felt only discomfort. The bed assumed an intimacy that didn't exist between them now.

He stole a glance at Lindsey, who was walking across the room, rubbing lotion into her hands. She sat on the edge of the bed, as if testing its firmness. Then she looked over at him and held his eyes for a moment.

"Thank you for doing this," she said softly. "I know this wasn't how you would have chosen to spend Thanksgiving."

He scoffed at the understatement.

"It was just so nice to see Adam entirely caught up in something other than the drama of our lives. He was so happy today."

"Yeah," Jerry admitted, a small smile finding his lips at the thought of his son's carefree enjoyment of the day.

"Well… goodnight." She slipped underneath the sheets, facing her side of the bed.

Jerry stood, uncertain, wishing that she had tried to talk to him more. He wasn't ready for her to roll over. He wanted her to fight for his love, affection, attention. It hurt to think that she was giving in to the reality that he had put out there.

When he slipped into bed next to her, he jostled the mattress enough that if they were their earlier selves she would have protested his oafish behavior. But not a sound came from her side. He looked around the room in the glow of the small bedside lamp. It was a perfectly preserved picture of who Lindsey had been as a teenager.

267

The room was yellow with white curtains and a white bedspread. There were extra pillows and stuffed animals they had removed from the bed and piled in the corner. A white wicker bookshelf held more stuffed animals and tons of books that included classics she had probably been forced to read, as well as Ann Rice and Stephen King. There were some cross country medals and ribbons hanging on the walls, along with a poster of Christian Slater. It was a whimsical girl's room with a dark and tough edge, and he wondered what it would have been like to know her back then. By the time they met, she had been a couple years out of high school. A person was the sum of their experiences, and he wondered if things would be different with them today if he had met the girl who lived here instead of the Lindsey he did meet.

Eventually he heard her soft and even sleeping breath. The rhythm was comforting, and he could feel himself starting to tire. She rolled onto her back in her slumber, stealing much more than her fair share of the space. Rather than fueling annoyance, though, he found himself gazing at the height of the tower that was her belly.

Jerry had refrained from becoming part of this pregnancy with her. He would not give her the satisfaction. He avoided touching her, which made his point but also hurt him deeply. He missed the connection that he had had when Lindsey was pregnant with the boys. As he thought about all that was missing in their family right now, he saw her stomach bulge out where the fabric of her pajama top had slid up, exposing the tight skin underneath. The bulge disappeared and then popped in and out in quick succession. Her whole stomach seemed to quiver with small movements. *You're a feisty one, aren't you?* Warmth spread through him. His baby girl was alive and well.

It made him jealous to think that Lindsey got to cradle this life within her. She got to feel the rhythms of their daughter's movements and be comforted by the fact that she was never alone.

He had never felt so lonely.

*****

The day after Thanksgiving was always the beginning of Christmas as far as Lindsey's mother was concerned. Marie washed the autumn linens that had been used for the feast the day before and hid them away in the hutch until next year. Then she dressed the table in red and green and gold. She removed the harvest wreath and centerpieces, boxed them up and put them back in storage. Then she enlisted the men to pull out the Christmas decorations. In her parents' world, everything used to decorate was fake. The tree could go up as early as they wanted because there was no fear that it wouldn't last through Christmas twenty years from now. This was all normal to her, a quirky reminder of carefree life before marriage and kids and bills got in the way. Jerry and Adam, on the other hand, were shocked by the commotion. There had never been such an immediate and absolute transition between holidays before, except maybe at Macy's.

When they went home, they would still have a couple weeks before they would decorate for Christmas. They had adopted Jerry's family tradition of a real tree and real pine garlands, so the transformation into Christmas was slower for them. And even though she was contentedly watching her childhood ornaments go up on the tree at that moment, she still feared what it would feel like to decorate and celebrate at home, where every ornament had her own family's story. Each family member got a special ornament every year for their personal collection, to be hung on the tree by him or her alone. *Who will hang Max's ornaments on the tree this year? Or should his stay in the box—all six of them—left alone and untouched forever more? What about the big plastic Grinch head?* Max had gotten it out of a fast food kid's meal and insisted on hanging it in a prominent spot each year. She had always hated that ornament and threatened to "forget" to pack it away after Christmas so it would get lost and not be able to cheapen future trees. But it would be there in the box the next year, like always, awaiting Max's tender hands.... *And who will build the Lego ornaments?* The ones he insisted on breaking down into individual bricks after Christmas each year.

No, those concerns were not for her to deal with now. This was a safe place and time in which Max did not fit. She didn't look around this house and associate everything with the child she lost. She didn't associate anything with her life as it was now. It was simply like reliving a dream of her childhood. It was cathartic and welcome.

"Lindsey," her mom said, breaking her out of her reverie. "Why don't we make all these men some hot chocolate?"

"Yeah! I want some," Adam said, nodding his head so vigorously that it made the ornament bells hanging from his fingers clang together.

She watched him happily decorating the tree and felt peace within her that the decision to come, no matter what the reason, was the right one.

"Okay," she called to her mom, struggling up and out of the overstuffed chair in the living room where she used to curl up and read for hours on end.

Her mother was already grabbing mugs out of the cabinet when she entered the kitchen.

Marie whirled around. "What is going on with you and Jerry?"

"Nothing," she said quickly—too quickly.

"Nothing my ass, Lindsey. What is it?"

She was momentarily taken aback by her mom's words. This was a woman who had sworn only four times in her presence, and each time it had been something she bumbled over. This time her words were swift and bold.

"We just had a fight before we came, and with all the festivities and people around, we never got a chance to make up."

"Try again," her mother said, not allowing Lindsey to look away from her prying eyes.

"Really, it's nothing but a fight,"

"Oh, it's more than a simple fight."

Lindsey held her gaze as long as she could, but she felt her resolve weakening and her lip quivering.

"Tell me what happened between you two. I know that losing Max was hard on your whole family. I know that it was really bad at times. But things were better. I heard it in your voice last time we spoke."

"Mom—" she began, wondering if she could placate her and still avoid the truth.

"Don't try to pull one over on me," she warned. "Did Jerry do something?"

Tears started to spill from her eyes as she spoke the words she feared would change the way her mother looked at her forever. "Nothing. Jerry didn't do anything. It was me. It was all me...."

*****

Jerry looked in the rearview mirror and saw Adam, buckled up and sleeping soundly in the backseat. His earbuds were plugged into his ears; the volume probably up so loud that only a truly exhausted kid could possibly fall asleep. He wasn't surprised, with all the excitement of the weekend, that this would be Adam's contribution to the ride home.

He turned the car radio down so he could keep his voice low. "What did you tell your mother?"

"Does it matter?" she asked simply.

"She told me to take another look. That's what she said when she hugged me goodbye. Did you try to gain her sympathy?" He kept his tone steady, though frustration was building inside him.

"I didn't try to do anything except avoid discussing the matter."

271

"But you didn't."

"Didn't what?"

"Avoid discussing it," he pointed out.

"No, Jerry. I couldn't keep it a secret. I told her everything."

"Everything?"

"Yes… everything. I told her what I had done to you. I told her what I had considered doing," she said, caressing her stomach absently. "I told her that I betrayed everything our marriage stood for and planned to do the unthinkable in the name of 'saving' myself. I told her that I was selfish and that I didn't deserve you or your love. That I didn't deserve the great honor of this child, but I was taking it anyway because she is a vestige of what we used to be and who I used to be. My children are the best of me and if I can never live up to that again, at least I can know it lives on in them…. Those are the things I told my mother." She said all of this, staring straight ahead into the darkness at the unobstructed long road in front of them.

He didn't know how to respond or what to say. He had expected that she would have twisted the story to suit her purposes. It wasn't that Lindsey was that kind of person; even in these darkest hours of their marriage she had never tried to twist the story in her favor. She had taken everything he dished out. She had accepted her faults and practically begged him to judge her. The fact that he wanted to assume that she would turn people against him was his undoing, not hers. She was not the person he had been trying to paint her. It was so frustrating. He wanted her to be easy to hate—easy to leave behind.

-34 Weeks-

"She still needs a name, Jerry," Lindsey said evenly, trying not to instigate a fight, while at the same time forcing him to face the obvious and unrelenting future. "What do you think? Even if we aren't going to be together, we can still name her together. She is still part of both of us even if you don't want to—"

"Correction... *you* didn't want to," he said coldly.

"I didn't think I could. It was never a question of *want*."

Lindsey feared that all discussions about their daughter would end up here—when she turns four and wants to try to ride her bike without training wheels, or when she wants to get her ears pierced at nine, or wants to go out on her first date at fourteen, or wants to go to college on the other side of the country or globe.... All of their parenting decisions would boil down to the same argument—she had considered having an abortion. He would win on that.

"But how can you separate those things? How can you consider giving up something you want?" he asked.

"I didn't give her up... and deep down I know that I never could have." She had said it so many times already, and she didn't think it would ever get through to him.

"It just kills me to think that—"

"Jerry, I was sure I had already lost you before I even found out about the baby. I didn't know how you could ever look at me the same way again; how you would ever forgive me for losing Max.

And all I could think is that I would have to face this pregnancy alone—"

"What do you mean forgive you for losing Max? It was an *accident,* Lindsey. An awful, terrible, senseless—"

"One that I could have prevented if I had been just a bit more vigilant. Or one that I could have thwarted if I had left the store a minute earlier or later. Or one that never would have happened if I had let Max push the cart, or made him ride in the cart. Or if I had just gone to the store when I usually—" She was crying so hard that she couldn't continue. The words got choked off by her sobs.

"I've run through all of the scenarios. I've twisted the puzzle and looked at it from every angle, trying to understand it. But Lindsey, I never blamed you. There are so many variables, but you're the one variable I never would have changed."

"But how? How can you forgive me for being the last one to see Max, touch him, talk to him?"

Jerry could see the crestfallen expression on her face. She was probably lamenting her inability to regain footing with him. He heard everything she said; even believed it. But he couldn't understand. What hadn't ever registered with him before was the fact that she hadn't forgiven herself. She had been blaming herself since the moment Max ran out in front of that car. She had been blaming herself before he could blame her.

How could she believe that I would ever blame her for Max's death? How did her guilt over the death of one of our children translate into the intent to destroy another?

He was about to ask the question when Adam came into the room.

"Just looking for a game," he said awkwardly, holding up his hand in a gesture of surrender.

He had spent the last hour upstairs in his bedroom with his stereo on, so he was surprised to see both of his parents in the family room. They were usually only together when he was around, at

274

dinner or watching TV at night. Seeing them now, sitting on the couch, for one split second he thought that maybe they were themselves again. But then, as if his intrusion broke the spell, he saw them shrink away from each other.

The familiar sting of tears came to his eyes. He still cried at times when he knew he was safe and alone, but now it was not for the sadness of missing Max or for the fear that death could be just around the corner for anyone. Now he cried for his parents. He knew that they were hardly holding onto each other anymore. He couldn't explain what it was that his parents had between them before, but he could tell that it was gone—lost to their hurt. He was careful not to show them that he knew; always careful to hide his tears until he was alone. They didn't need to be worried about coddling him and pretending for him.

He was sure they must be headed for a divorce. He thought he was worldly enough to understand the issue, considering a lot of his school friends had parents who were divorced. The only thing that didn't fit was that his friends said the divorce came after all the fights. Adam hadn't heard much fighting. Silence seemed to have killed his parents' marriage. Their family was disintegrating in absolute silence.

Adam knew he could handle whatever happened. He had gone through much worse than a divorce. Besides, he had watched his friends and it didn't seem to be too hard on them. And then there was his sister. She was the lucky one. She would never know what their parents had been like before. Whatever she was born into was going to be normal to her. He was the one who had something to compare it to. Max would have understood how this new life fell short.

Lindsey saw the look in Adam's eyes. She knew what he was thinking. He had already asked Jerry about divorce, and he looked so uncertain in front of them that she was sure he was trying to piece together what he thought was going on in their family. All she could think was that he needed a distraction—all of them did.

"Hey, Adam, what do you say to a trip to the tree lot for our Christmas tree?" Lindsey asked, forcing joy and excitement into her voice that had so recently held desperation and sorrow.

He stopped rifling through a small pile of video games and asked, "Now?"

"Yes. Right now."

"Sure!" he said, looking to his father for cues.

Jerry quickly masked his surprise and said, "All right, I'll warm up the car. Everyone put on warm enough clothes that nobody is whining if it takes a while to find the perfect tree."

He got up off the couch and gave her a look that mingled a knowing smile with a tempered grimace. She knew that Jerry had seen Adam's reaction to them and that he, too, wanted to limit their son's pain. But she wasn't forgiven, and she wasn't out of the woods with him. She probably never would be.

Lindsey plopped herself in the car and did her best to turn and look at Adam in the back. "Are we going wide and fat, or tall and skinny this year?"

"This year was going to be Max's year to pick," Adam reminded her.

She had entirely forgotten that detail. She had seen so many of the stumbling blocks coming at them as Christmas approached, but this one had escaped her.

And then Jerry got in the car and saved her. "Well, I think that this year we should bring Sadie and let her choose."

"Seriously?" Adam asked.

"Sure, why not?"

"How's she gonna choose? Is she supposed to pee on the right one?"

"No way!" Lindsey burst out.

"Thankfully, she can't pee on it anyway," Jerry said. "But no, I was thinking more along the lines of her sniffing out the one she wants."

"Okay. Sounds good to me. Can't be any worse than what our family dork would have picked," Adam said lovingly.

By the time they walked the lot and sniffed out the right tree—Sadie relegating them to the sappiest one—it was past eight o'clock, and they were all exhausted. It was a physical and emotional drain. But when they got home, Adam was adamant about wanting to put the tree up and decorate it. Neither one of them had the heart to say no, seeing as how an empty tree outside was beautiful, but inside it was just sad looking.

They dragged the decorations down out of the attic and started putting ornaments all over the tree, saving the few that Max would have hung up until the end. They looked them over lovingly and told stories about each one, and then they each took turns hanging them up on the tree where they belonged.

After the decorating was complete, with the smiling Grinch face looking down from the top most branch of the tree—front and center—they sat and basked in the twinkling glow of hundreds of white lights. Adam quickly drifted off, which came as no surprise considering it was after eleven. Lindsey prodded him and sent him up to bed, promising to follow behind.

"That was a good idea, to get the tree tonight," Jerry said, as she got up to leave the living room and say goodnight to Adam.

"Thank you," she said softly. Her eyes were wet with appreciation.

"This one is hard, Lin," he said, realizing he hadn't called her that in a while. "This is harder than an average morning or summer vacation or Halloween... or all of it put together."

"I know. I keep hoping it is going to get easier, but this isn't even the end of it. What about his birthday or—" She stopped herself quickly.

But he knew she was going to say the anniversary of Max's death. He knew it because he feared that same moment too. They alone would understand the horrible significance of May 27th. Unless

Memorial Day landed on that date, it was a personal day reserved for birthdays or wedding anniversaries, or in their case, it was a day of death.

"Let's just get through this, and we will figure the rest out as we go," he said earnestly.

-35 Weeks-

It started with a tomato. At a time when he could only assume the worst of her, when it seemed that she was lost to him, he found understanding at Max's grave. He began to realize where Lindsey was whenever she was not with him in mind or body. She was with their son. Unable to let go, same as him. So he left a buffalo nickel on the "X" in Max's name—his son's favorite coin on top of his favorite letter—and when he returned, he found a red button in its place. Since that time there had been more things—a feather, a smooth and flat rock that was perfect for skipping (something he had been trying to teach Max how to do), a pine cone, a bottle cap, a seashell, an acorn hat, a paper clip, a pen cap, a wheel from a Matchbox car… because Max was a collector of things. The benign objects they exchanged were some of the millions of daily reminders of their son that showed up at unexpected times—on sidewalks, in drawers, between couch cushions and under car seats—triggering happy memories and sad realities for them. A button was no longer just a button, nor was a shiny candy wrapper just a piece of trash. These things were treasures. They shared the minutia of their grief this way, reminding each other that together they held the memory of their wonderful child, and neither one was going to allow that memory to be lost. He began looking forward to seeing what Lindsey had to say even more than the solitude he used to seek. It was there that he came to find his wife—the depth of her hurt and the power of her love.

These tenuous connections couldn't erase the things that had come between them. And they couldn't take the place of the volumes of things that had so far been left unsaid. But the intimacy of those small objects that meant something so much more than their physical form, served to temper his initial charges that Lindsey was not the person he had believed her to be. They reminded him of her passion for their life and family. They showed him glimpses of her fragile heart. And, over time, they made him want to listen. What had seemed like an impossibly convoluted labyrinth of secrets between them was really an overgrown path. They had lost each other in the death of their son and had been attempting to fight through despair alone. Now he wanted to know the woman who grieved as fiercely as he did. He wanted to know what she guarded so carefully. He wanted to know where they were going.

*****

She spent the day shopping, picking up the last of the gifts before Adam was out of school for Christmas break. She had gone crazy, as usual, making an effort to take note of every cool thing she had heard Adam talking about recently, and pricing and purchasing as much as she could. Now everything was safely stored out of sight of his excited eyes.

As she looked over her receipts, it struck her that she was well below their usual budget that they blew each year by showering the boys with all their wishes and more. It took her a moment to realize the difference. It wasn't that Max's absence wasn't with her at every moment, but more that she didn't realize just how many things it affected—the clothing budget, food budget, fun budget and gift budget. It seemed crass to think about their loss in monetary terms, but now that months had gone by and there was extra money in all of their accounts, she became truly aware of the difference between budgeting for a three versus a four person family. The whole idea of looking at the cost of raising their kids made her uncomfortable. They had never planned their family in that way.

"So, what did you do today?" Adam asked slyly.

"That's none of your business, mister," she said, thankful for the interruption into her morbid thoughts about their family finances.

"Aw, come on. Did you go anywhere?"

"Maybe," she said. "Maybe not."

"Give a guy a break," he groaned.

He was worried. He didn't know what kind of Christmas it was going to be after all that had gone on this year. Without Max here, he didn't know if his parents would be into buying presents and doing the whole holiday up like usual. They knew that he didn't believe in Santa, so without Max around, there was no need to pretend. That might mean that there would be no presents anymore. This Christmas might be a total bust.

It wasn't that he was only about the presents, but he did like getting them. What bothered him was he feared that without Max around he would get treated differently from usual simply because they didn't have the heart for it, or because they didn't care enough about him. When everything changed at home after he died, Adam wondered if maybe Max had been his parents' favorite. Maybe they did everything a certain way *because* of Max. Maybe he was just a sorry second. Maybe it wasn't just that sadness had gotten the best of his parents, but that they didn't have the same feelings for him as they had for his little brother.

"So you're really not going to tell me what you did all day?"

"Nope," she said mischievously.

Adam's worries eased a little. His mom seemed to be playing along, like she had something to hide from him. He just hoped that his parents knew that he still wanted to celebrate Christmas as usual, even if it was hard. He was still a kid, and he still got excited about it. He hoped that they wouldn't forget about him.

"We're not done here, Lindsey. I don't know how many times I can say it, and we still end up at the same place again. The same discussion about Max. How come you can't understand that I didn't blame—"

"Because I would have blamed you!" she snapped, finally releasing hold of the dreaded words that kept bubbling just below the surface all these days and weeks and months.

"What?"

"I would have blamed you if something happened to the kids on your watch."

"Do you hear what you're saying?"

"Of course I hear what I'm saying. I'm not proud of it, Jerry. I'm just being honest."

"Well, that's shitty honesty," he said, wounded.

"Listen to me," she begged.

"I don't think I need to hear any more." He made a move to get up.

"Yes, you do," she said, pulling him back to her. "You need to hear this. *I* would have blamed you, so I was sure that *you* had to blame me. Not because I purposely didn't care enough or love them enough, but because there was a moment—a millisecond—that I let my guard down. In that moment, maybe you would have been vigilant. Maybe if they were with you this wouldn't have happened. That was why I blamed myself *for* you. I thought that if only I hadn't been the one in charge then it wouldn't have happened."

"But—"

"Remember when Adam broke his arm falling out of a tree?"

"Of course."

"I was out with Shelley, shopping, and I came home to find you bandaging him up with a sling in preparation for a trip to the emergency room. God, I was so pissed off. He was supposed to be in a school play that next week, and he would have to have a cast on."

"Yeah," Jerry snorted, remembering Adam's rendition of Benjamin Franklin with a neon green cast.

"I knew you hadn't put him up in that tree. I knew that it was Adam's doing. And it was something he had done countless times when I was the one at home. But I was still angry. Like you could and should have stopped him *that* time," she said, searching his face for understanding. "I know it isn't right, Jerry, but that is the way I felt. So can't you understand that I might believe that you would think the same way?"

"But, Lindsey, I know you. I know how fiercely protective you are."

"All the more reason to figure I had fallen down on my job!"

"You don't think very highly of me, do you?"

"I think the world of you, Jerry."

He looked away, quickly, not wanting to see that she was telling the truth. He took a deep breath and forced himself to look back at her again.

"We keep rehashing the same thing, over and over," he said. "How many different ways can we say it? There has to be a point where we stop this madness. Face it, sometimes even when we teach our kids everything they need to know, and we do everything within our power to keep them safe, bad stuff still happens. I know you would never have intentionally disregarded Max's safety."

Lindsey looked deep into his eyes. "Then why would you for a moment think that I could really do something to her?" she asked, placing his hands on her stomach and covering them with her own.

It was such an intimate gesture that he wanted to run from it. He could feel the fight leaving him though. If he ran now, it would be him running from fear, not anger. At this point he had a choice to make; he could keep freezing her out of his life and upset the possibility of what they could build as a family again, or he could let go of the pain of the last months and choose to be a survivor.

He felt the chill of her skin and the slight tremor in her body. He looked into her deep green eyes, past the smooth glass surface, knowing every fleck and variation within them. He knew her. This was the woman he had loved from day one. She was flawed, and her will and spirit had been tested, but he saw the depth of her character. He saw determination and strength.

"Are you cold?" he asked, seeing her shiver.

"A little," she admitted.

"You shouldn't come outside on an autumn night like this with a holey sweater on," he said, poking a finger through the wide knit design.

"No, I shouldn't." She bowed her head in defeat.

When he stood up off the bench that sat nestled deep in their backyard, Lindsey felt her throat constrict with the certainty that he was about to walk out of her life. She had never wanted to put her feelings into words. She had never wanted to give such thoughts voice. And when she finally spoke the awful truth, the words hung between them as if they had immediately frozen in the cold air as soon as her breath escaped her lips.

Her eyes were closed and her head was down when she heard his voice.

"Let's get you inside," he said softly.

She opened her eyes to see his hands before her, offering her a lift. She looked up and saw the change in his expression. His face was clear of everything but kindness. She placed her hands in his and allowed him to heave her off the bench.

"I think this is a night that is made for hot chocolate," Jerry said.

As they walked, he wrapped his arm around her shoulders protectively and kissed the part on top of her head. The house before them glowed with warm light, looking inviting and comforting in a way that it hadn't for a long time now. As they reached the deck steps, their footfalls summoned Adam to the door.

"There you are!" he called out, breaking the silence with childhood exuberance.

"Hey, Sport, I was just telling Mom that we need some hot chocolate tonight."

"Really?" he asked hopefully. It wasn't just the hot chocolate he was excited about. He liked seeing his parents *together*, not just in the same place at the same time.

"See if you can dig up some marshmallows in the pantry," Jerry said, in answer.

"Hot dog!" Adam said, scrambling back inside.

"Where did he get that expression from?" she asked, chuckling. "It sounds like something you'd hear in some old movie."

"He's a strange kid."

"He's a *great* kid."

"Yup. That he is," Jerry agreed, leaning in to kiss her head again. This time she was looking up at him and captured the kiss with her lips.

Lindsey felt his lips linger close to her face and felt his breath warm on her cheek.

"Is everything okay?" she whispered, afraid to break the spell.

"Did you feel that?"

"What?"

"That moment…. It was like a first kiss."

-37 Weeks-

Things had definitely changed. Adam couldn't put his finger on exactly what had happened or when it had happened, but things around the house had become normal again. It was a new kind of normal—nothing could make it like it was when Max was still alive—but it was still a good kind. He no longer felt like he had to check his feelings and thoughts around his parents, or worry about every word that he might use or how he might act. It was easy to breathe again. It was okay to be happy now. He could race through the house with good news, or just have good news in the first place. He no longer worried that his happiness meant that he didn't care that his little brother had died. It was okay to laugh now, but it was also still okay to cry. If he wanted to talk about Max, he could. If he wanted to talk about going bowling, he could. Nothing was off limits—not the fear he still felt about what had happened to his brother, or his hopes that he would get a new skateboard for Christmas. It was okay to look at the future and feel excited about things like his first school dance and the sixth grade class field trip and tryouts for the middle school soccer team. It was okay to forget to miss Max, if only for a little while.

As he lay in bed, his eyes refusing to close and give in to sleep, he looked around at the room that he used to share with Max. Adam looked over at the empty space where last Christmas Eve Max had been lying awake staring back at him, and he felt the familiar sadness in his heart. They had always spent this night nervously talking about what they hoped to find under the tree in the morning. But tonight his room seemed way too big and empty. His mind wandered uncomfortably, realizing Max would never get to experience the joy of opening a gift again, while he was hopeful and itching to open presents in the morning. But before guilt could overtake him, he remembered Max's smile and his exclamations of pure joy and excitement over all of Adam's gifts. He had always been thrilled to see what his big brother got and then usually added that same thing to his list for the next year. Max had always found joy in other people's happiness. He would never begrudge him for enjoying Christmas.

*****

Lindsey woke up with a start and looked at the time. It was after eight o'clock. She couldn't believe that it was Christmas morning and they had slept in. Usually Max was bouncing up and down on their bed by six. But Adam hadn't woken them up.

Sitting up slowly, she felt the extreme tightness that had come over her belly recently. Her skin was already stretched to the limit, and she worried that she might just spontaneously burst open with any kick from within. She let out a long tired sigh and pushed on Jerry's shoulder several times until he spoke groggily and swore he was awake. Then she heaved herself out of bed and shuffled into the bathroom to brush her teeth. Shivering at the chill in the air, she pulled on her robe, which was generously sized but getting tight on her pregnant body just the same. *Can I get any bigger?*

Down the hall, she found Adam reading in his bed.

"Hey there, why didn't you come wake us up?" she asked.

"I just got up a little while ago," he mumbled.

"But it's Christmas morning! I thought you couldn't wait to get downstairs!"

"I'm excited," he said flatly.

"Could have fooled me."

"No, I am. It's just…. I'm eleven now, and *we* know how to be patient."

"Well, I'm in my thirties and I'm not patient," she said incredulously. "I'd race you downstairs but for this extra person I'm carrying around with me."

"Oh, all right," he said begrudgingly, but his quick movements to close his book and bound out of bed told her differently. He threw on his robe and slippers that he really only used on Christmas and snow days—both were too small for him, so it was good that replacements waited under the tree. When he finished, he stood anxiously at the door.

"You go. I'm going to check on Dad and make sure he got up," she said, wanting to give Adam space to drink in the experience without watchful eyes on him. This was a bittersweet moment, and he needed to find his peace with it, without worrying about how he thought his parents wanted him to react.

*****

Adam was almost afraid to look. Usually, he would have snuck a peek at the tree the moment he woke up. He had still woken up way too early, worried about what he might or might not find waiting for him, but he couldn't bring himself to check. And his plan to distract himself by reading had been a bomb. In almost three hours he had read only about thirty pages and couldn't remember any of it.

When his eyes panned the living room, he took in the stockings on the mantle. There were four up there; he had insisted that Max's should be hung up. Adam's was the only one that was bulging with gifts. It was a sad sight. Then he turned to the tree, expecting worse. But what he saw was a normal Christmas morning. There were plenty of gifts, just like always. Everything looked *right*.

His heart lightened as he realized that his worst fears were only imagined. He didn't have to worry about anything. His parents still saw him. They knew he was there and that he needed both of them. Not everything had changed since Max died.

*****

They went down the stairs hand in hand. They could hear Adam spinning the wheels on the new skateboard they had left unwrapped and leaning up against the wall next to the tree. Jerry stood at the threshold of the living room and for a moment his mind took him back to the last Christmas before Max was born. Adam was only four when they had last been a threesome. Back then, Lindsey had been pregnant too. Their family at that time was so different, unrecognizable from the people they were now. Just like their family with Max was different from both then and now. It wasn't just tragedy that brought change. Triumph changed people too. The conditions of life were constantly shifting and requiring you to adjust if you wanted to succeed, or allowing you to fight and stagnate destructively like they had attempted to do. Now, as he looked around the room at his family, he realized that they had finally decided to grow and change and become who they needed to become in order to prevail.

"Dad, this is awesome!" Adam said, holding up the skateboard.

"Cool!" Jerry said, smiling at his son's unabashed happiness.

He held Lindsey tight to his side as he took in the rest of the room. "What did you do?" he whispered.

"Who me?" she asked, with her hand at her chest demurely.

"Where did all of this stuff come from?"

"Santa, I guess," she said simply, walking past him to sit on the couch.

When they had put the presents under the tree late the night before, Jerry felt his heart sink at the paltry mound. The tree looked lonely without Max's gifts. Now, though, the tree was bursting with presents. The pile had doubled overnight, and he wondered if Santa had gotten the memo that only one boy lived here now. His worried gaze followed Lindsey.

"Can we start?" Adam asked, excitement dripping from his words.

"Sure," Lindsey said, trying to wrap her robe tighter around her stomach as she sat on the couch.

Adam reached for a gift and started to tear into it like an addict needing a fix, then stopped and looked up like he feared he had done something wrong.

"Go ahead," Jerry prodded.

"It's weird that I'm the only one opening something."

"Then find something for someone else. Those can't all be for you. You weren't *that* good this year," she laughed.

"Very funny." Adam looked through the gifts. "Who opens these?" he asked, holding a gift out toward his dad.

Jerry took the gift and read the tag: To, Baby Strane; From, Santa.

He looked at his wife, realizing what she had done. She must have stayed up most of the night, wrapping the new baby clothes and toys and supplies and putting them under the tree as gifts to their daughter. She hadn't wanted Adam to feel the same weight of grief, looking at the sad tree with so few gifts compared to last year. And maybe she wanted to commemorate their daughter's first Christmas, for she was definitely there in body and spirit. Her presence had already transformed their grief and sadness back into love.

-39 Weeks-

He couldn't believe where they had been in the last seven months. It didn't seem possible, looking at it from where he was now, here, in the hospital again. The same hospital that had held the body of his young son in tragedy would now hold the body of his baby daughter in triumph.

Jerry felt cagey and nervous. It was only January 6th, almost a week early. Lindsey's labor had come on strong in the early hours of the morning, but she had insisted that they wait until her doctor's office was open to get checked out. He understood her reason for being stubborn. She didn't want to try to bring a life into the world through the same emergency room doors through which they had wheeled her dead son. He felt the same way. Thankfully, her obstetrician's practice was in a building that attached to the hospital, so they were able to immediately transfer her over to the third floor for delivery after her examination showed she was effaced and dilating.

Now he stood in the waiting room, anxious for Shelley to get here and sit with Adam so he could be by Lindsey's side for the delivery.

"You okay, Dad? You look worried."

"Just excited. How about you?"

"I'm okay. I don't mind it up here so much. I'm just glad we're not in the emergency room." Adam shuddered faintly.

"Me too," Jerry agreed.

291

Maybe this building would cease to bother him so much after today. Maybe the birth of his daughter would heal more than his family. Maybe it would heal his faith in life.

*****

She held her daughter's precious little body in her arms, cradling her tiny hands and unfurling her fists to see ten perfect blushing red fingers complete with tiny thin translucent fingernails that someday would be hidden under so many different shades of color. The drops they had put in her eyes looked like big wet tears that magnified the dark gray-brown of her irises. She stared contentedly through the slits of her swollen eyelids, her skin trying to make sense of its new environment.

Lindsey had unwrapped her to reassure herself that everything about her daughter was as she prayed it would be. Unlike Adam, she was content, even loose in her blanket. Adam had required a crash course in swaddling in order to keep him calm and comfortable those first few days after birth. She was also unlike Max, who seemed intent on motion from the moment he breathed his first breath. He had embraced the world without hesitation. She, on the other hand, seemed reflective—content to lie in the circle of Lindsey's embrace and take stock of her surroundings, feeling the sensations of this world outside the womb and knowing that she was safe right there.

Jerry knocked lightly and poked his head through the crack between the jamb and the door.

"Are you decent?"

"I wondered where you went off to... come here," she said, her voice strained from the exertion of labor.

"I didn't know if you might be trying to feed her."

"And even if I was?"

He shifted uncomfortably on his feet.

"I want you here," she said, speaking softly and looking at her daughter but saying it to both of them.

"I just…. I don't really know what to do with myself."

"The same thing you've always done," she said simply, looking up at him.

"So much has happened and so much has been said, Lin. I—"

"I want this moment to be the start of it all, Jerry. Right now. Our life starts again right now," she said earnestly, tears welling in her eyes.

"But what about—"

"I can't think of anything else but the beautiful daughter we created—the three beautiful children we created. We are *good* at this, Jerry. We are too good at this to let it all go. I'm not saying that I didn't do things I'm ashamed of, or that you should just suddenly stop feeling hurt. I am saying that I have seen the future and it's great as long as you're in it. It is going to be bright, Jerry. You might want to get a good pair of sunglasses."

He looked at his wife, lying there so naturally. He saw absolute serenity in her form. All of the angst and frustration was gone. She was at total peace, and he realized that their journey through the wasteland of grief was over. He couldn't say that it was the Lindsey he had once known, but rather the woman before him was even more than that.

He looked down at the loose bundle she offered him, a little pink knit hat hiding all but the smallest soft blonde curls at her temples and on the nape of her neck—Max's hair. Taking her in his arms, he held her close and basked her in unabashed adoration. She was stunning, and soon enough she would be running him ragged. He knew that she would never cease to amaze him. This little girl had the strength to move mountains. She had pulled them together. She had brought her mother with her through the haze of grief and uncertainty that had almost claimed their family.

"What are we going to name her?" he asked softly.

"That's what I've been asking you."

"Well?"

"Well?" she challenged.

"I am not leaving the hospital with an unnamed baby. I'm not going to be one of those," Jerry said firmly.

"Me neither," she agreed.

"Tina? Rebecca? Stacy?" He rattled them off in quick succession.

"No. No. And no," she answered in kind.

"What's wrong with any of those?"

"Nothing really. They're just not right."

"Yeah? What have you got?"

"What about Celia? Like in that song…."

"What song?"

"You know… the one by those guys…."

"That narrows it down."

"It's an old song by…." She snapped her fingers in frustration, and then spit it out in triumph, "… Simon and Garfunkel!"

Jerry smirked.

"What?" she asked defensively.

"You're cute."

"You're cute," she mocked him, pouting. She outstretched her arms and wiggled her fingers to ask for the baby back.

"You know what? I do like Celia." He looked down at their daughter. "I like it a lot."

"Oh, don't patronize me."

"No, really, I do."

"Really?"

"Yes. Just promise me you won't tell people you got it from that song," Jerry pleaded.

"Why? You think it's dorky?"

"No. Because it's not actually the name in the song."

"Yes it is," she insisted.

"No," he said, handing her their daughter. "The song is actually, 'Cecilia'."

"No—oh my God, you're right!" she grimaced, turning pink with embarrassment. "Well *that* name sucks."

Jerry laughed.

*****

Adam walked into the room, tentatively.

"Come here. Meet your sister, Celia," she prodded.

He reached the edge of the bed, looking at both of his parents uncertainly. This could be the end of everything for them. He might still be a kid in their eyes, but he knew that this baby was the center of a lot of strife even while at the same time she was the glue that was holding together what was left of their home. This was another moment that would change his life forever. He had experienced a lot over the past months, and this was a blow he had been preparing himself to face.

"Do you want to hold her?" his mother asked.

He looked unsure, but he held his arms out like a practiced veteran at holding babies. It had been a long time, but he had held Max when he was an infant. Back then, he had always had to be seated though, and now he was big enough to stand there and take his baby sister in his arms. She was so light. He never remembered Max being this little, but he guessed it was because he was a lot smaller then.

"Celia, I love you… no matter what happens," he whispered to her, under the guise of kissing her cheek.

"Well, Sport, what do you think? A little sister to protect and defend from all the boys who try to pull her pigtails."

"They won't have a chance." Adam physically puffed up his stature to show his size.

"No, I don't think they will," Jerry said in wonder. "Well, we need to let our girls get some rest."

"Okay," Adam said, offering his sister back to his mom.

He watched his dad lean over the bed and kiss Celia lightly on the forehead, and then let the kiss on his mother's forehead linger. He saw a look pass between them of words unspoken. He saw his dad brush a tear from his mom's cheek. He saw a smile on his mom's lips. He heard love in their whispered voices. He felt peace sweep through him.

Even in his brief respite on earth,
he touched people with his smiles and laughter,
his questions and his tears.
We will never know what he was capable of becoming,
but we can be heartened by who he was.
Max, knowing you was worth every moment.

~Lindsey Strane

2 'Til Series by Heather Muzik

2 Days 'Til Sundae
2 Months 'Til Mrs.

Other Novels by Heather Muzik

Apathetic

Visit http://www.heathermuzik.com for more information about Heather Muzik and her work, including book club interviews and the latest information about upcoming releases.

Contact: heathermuzik@bellsouth.net